W9-ALK-843

---------------- ★ ----------------

"That's the coach driver in there!" Rosa said.

"He's in an almighty hurry," Ben said as he watched the car roar out onto the main road. "It's madness pulling out at speeds like that in these country lanes."

"That's not what's bothering me," said Rosa. "Didn't you see who was in the back?"

"The old man?"

Rosa stared at her husband anxiously. "No doubt about it. But he looked like he was fast asleep!"

"You reckon he's been got at?" Ben hurried to the road and peered in the direction that the car had taken. "He'd have to be! You don't go from visiting the 'Gents' to being fast asleep in less than five minutes, that's downright impossible."

"Where have they gone, though?" Rosa said. "And who can we ask? About the grey Jaguar and the driver, I mean?"

"How the hell would I know?" Ben said bleakly. "And who'll believe us anyway? There was only us two that saw it."

---------------- ★ ----------------

MISS McGUIRE IS MISSING

EILEEN ROBERTSON

TORONTO • NEW YORK • LONDON
AMSTERDAM • PARIS • SYDNEY • HAMBURG
STOCKHOLM • ATHENS • TOKYO • MILAN
MADRID • WARSAW • BUDAPEST • AUCKLAND

If you purchased this book without a cover you should be aware that this book is stolen property. It was reported as "unsold and destroyed" to the publisher, and neither the author nor the publisher has received any payment for this "stripped book."

Recycling programs
for this product may
not exist in your area.

MISS McGUIRE IS MISSING

A Worldwide Mystery/January 2012

First published by Robert Hale Ltd.

ISBN-13: 978-0-373-26784-2

Copyright © 2010 by Eileen Robertson

All rights reserved. No part of this book may be reproduced or transmitted in any form or by any means, electronic or mechanical, including photocopying, recording or by any information storage and retrieval system, without permission in writing from the publisher. For information, contact: Robert Hale Limited, Clerkenwell House, Clerkenwell Green, London EC1R 0HT, Great Britain.

This is a work of fiction. Names, characters, places and incidents are either the product of the author's imagination or are used fictitiously, and any resemblance to actual persons, living or dead, business establishments, events or locales is entirely coincidental.

® and ™ are trademarks of Harlequin Enterprises Limited. Trademarks indicated with ® are registered in the United States Patent and Trademark Office, the Canadian Trade Marks Office and in other countries.

Printed in U.S.A.

PROLOGUE

THE DOCTOR LOOKED UP when the coroner entered. 'Just finishing off. Didn't expect you to be so early.' He signed the document.

The coroner smiled as he opened his briefcase and got out the forms. 'Morning's the best part of the day,' he gazed down at the sheeted corpse, 'though not always for some.' He returned to his notes. 'Time of death?'

'4.33 a.m.'

'Cause?'

The doctor sighed. 'His heart gave out. He'd been a patient here for just a few weeks. He had a severe leg injury, an old war wound that gave him constant pain. I'd prescribed morphine.' He looked across at the coroner. 'He was, after all, eighty-seven.'

The coroner nodded. 'Indeed.' He continued to read through the document. 'I assume that the next of kin have been informed?'

'Oh, yes,' the doctor replied. He watched closely whilst the coroner signed the death certificate. 'His great-nephew has already made plans for his cremation.'

ONE

'BEN HAMMOND, will you get a move on?'

'Stop shoving, woman. There's no rush.'

'There's a queue a mile long behind us. Budge over, so at least they can get past.'

'The coach won't go without its passengers, Rosa. There's no need to get aireated.' Nevertheless Ben squeezed against the driver's seat and allowed the other pensioner's to ease past him.

Rosa glared at him.

'I was only trying to get a look at his gearbox.'

A passenger giggled. Rosa grabbed Ben's sleeve and towed him along the aisle of the bus.

'Leave it out, Rosa.'

'We've to look for seats G1 and G2. Oh, and keep an eye out for H1 for our Anna. Oh, here they are. And don't forget to put your seatbelt on. Would you like the window seat or not?'

'Er, I'll take the aisle seat, I think. You always like to look out of the windows.' With ponderous slowness Ben took off his coat, folded it, pushed it into the luggage rack and looked around. 'Here, we're a hell of a long way from the driver, aren't we?'

'Are you going to grumble all the time?' Rosa drew a deep breath and then spoke calmly. 'Best seats I could manage at such short notice. Now you sit tidy and have a look at the nice view.'

After allowing Rosa to settle into her seat Ben leaned

forward and, remembering his 'orders', looked out of the window and contemplated the contours of a dirty hawthorn hedge. In the foreground an overflowing rubbish bin displayed its contents. He sighed. 'Nice view' indeed. Why the hell had he gone and allowed himself to be conned into going on this trip with the women. On the Richter scale of things he liked least, going on a pensioners' outing on a Sunday must qualify as a definite seven point five. He should have stood firm. He should have held his ground and come up with a good excuse when Rosa started to persuade him. He might have had a chance had not his dreaded sister-in-law butted in and joined forces with her. For a while he listened to the high-pitched chatter around him, then he got out his iPod and put it on. Leaning back, he allowed the music of Glenn Miller to seep through him. That was better. He could escape into his own tunnel of sound.

He thought about his lovely vintage car, stuck at home in the garage. If only those brake shoes had arrived as the suppliers had promised, then they could have all gone for a proper spin, instead of being stuck here on a coach trip.

A pincer-like nip on his right arm made him wince. Rosa was staring up at him, her lips moving. With reluctance, he removed his earpiece.

She sighed. 'It's easier getting through to Voyager One. Do you have to put that thing on the minute you sit down?'

'You told me to look at the view and all I could see was a rubbish bin. What do you want then?'

His sister-in-law leaned over his shoulder and rattled a paper bag under his nose. 'I thought you might want a sweetie. They're those nice sherbet lemons. I eat them all the time, such a fresh acidy taste….'

'That figures,' Ben muttered.

'What's that supposed to mean?'

'Sour taste, sour face.'

'Don't be so rotten.'

'You are what you eat, so they say, and some might say that you're the living proof of it.'

With an agitated crackle, the paper bag was snatched away and Anna's face loomed over him. 'You're just being bad tempered 'cause you can't get your silly old car to go. Should have bought British like sensible people do, then you wouldn't have problems with spares and such.' She paused then smirked. 'If it had been me, I would never buy foreign.'

Ben stifled his irritation. Anna was, after all, family. 'I keep telling you, my car is not foreign; it is vintage American. Built in the days when cars were cars.'

'Still not British. Not only that, it's a left-hand drive.' Anna tossed her head indignantly and her bifocals flashed. 'If it was up to me, well, I could never drive a left-hand drive.'

'Don't be so bloody daft, woman!' He felt a sharp pain in his ribs and glared at his wife. 'And will you stop digging your elbow into me.'

Rosa pursed her lips. 'We'll change the subject, shall we?' The sound of the coach engine increased and she looked about her. 'Oh, I think we're off.'

Ben was not to be deterred. He hissed. 'No good changing the subject. Your sister is forever getting these daft ideas. And I don't give a hoot how long she worked on the police force. As far as cars are concerned, she's do-lally.' He raised his voice. 'And it might interest her to know that one of the reasons why I bought a left-hand drive is so that she won't start "borrowing" it.'

There came a gasp from Anna and Rosa intervened. 'Stop harping on. She's my sister; she's all I've got.'

'So that makes her a saint, does it? Well, I'll tell you this. When I wed you, you never said *The Force* was part of the deal.'

'Will you shush? People are looking.'

Ben slumped back in his seat, jammed his earpiece into his ear and lapsed into injured silence.

ROSA STARED OUT OF the window. Trees, meadows, villages and towns flashed past her, but she looked at them with indifference. Both Anna and Ben wanted her sympathy, yet neither of them considered how she felt. Between the pair of them, she was near the end of her tether. She felt sorry for them both, but at times they made her feel like a bone that was being gnawed between two mongrels. It was true that since Anna's divorce they'd seen a lot of her, too much even for Rosa's taste. As for Ben, he had troubles of his own. Time and again he'd told her that he was not looking forward to retirement and, as he put it, 'being tossed on the scrap heap at sixty.' Now that it had happened, what would he do? Would he turn into a couch potato, or drive her mad as he had done yesterday by knocking hell out of his car in the garage and trailing into her kitchen in smelly overalls with his hands all covered in grease. She drew a deep breath; be patient, she told herself, he will be all right, but he needs to find something that interests him. Meanwhile, all that she could do was to sympathize and try to keep the peace.

Resolutely she forced herself to think of other things; she wondered if they would visit the same place as last time. The food there had been excellent. A good day out, except for that odd business with the lame man. She frowned; weird that, an old man going missing on a

day trip. He'd probably wandered off somewhere. Rosa
smiled in reminiscence; she'd stopped and chatted with
him during the lunch break on that day and he'd told her
about his 'Dunkirk war wound'. 'Got it in the knee,' he'd
claimed proudly, 'been lame ever since.' He'd seemed
such a nice old boy. Pity that he'd missed the coach. What
had happened to him? Had he spent the night at the hostelry, or had he managed to get a lift? Either way he'd
have had to make his own way home. Rosa sighed, it was
no good starting to worry about things like that; she had
enough on her mind already; she closed her eyes and
began to doze.

BEN'S BACK ACHED. As he wriggled in his seat trying to
find a more comfortable position he became aware of a
rasping sound near his ear. He froze and squinted down
to his right. Rosa, with her mouth agape, was snoring
gently. He smiled down at her. He had intended to ask
her to get him a packet of biscuits down from the rack,
but he was reluctant to disturb her. He risked a glance
over his shoulder at *The Force,* but she too had her eyes
closed and appeared to be in the land of Nod. He shuffled
again, eased his back into a more comfortable position
and tried to doze. Yet sleep wouldn't come; the more he
tried the more restless he became.

A movement in the aisle of the coach caught his
eye. He watched a slight female figure walk towards
the driver. He wondered what she wanted. Perhaps the
lady wasn't feeling well. He peered along the aisle of the
coach. He felt a sense of something familiar. He knew
that walk from somewhere. There was something author-
itarian in the way that she stood with her back towards
him, talking to the driver. He searched his memory. If

she would just turn round. He needed to see her face. He rested his arms on the seat in front of him and waited.

The woman turned and made her way back down the bus. Ben stared at her. Age at least eighty; face narrow, almost fleshless, except for the jawline where gravity had taken its toll. Steel-rimmed spectacles, with dark eyes glinting behind them. Grey hair scraped back from the face, leaving a harshness in the expression.

The correct 'file' clicked into place, and with it came recognition.

'Miss McGuire!' Ben said.

Rosa stirred in her sleep.

'It's Miss McGuire!' Eagerly he nudged his wife.

The woman walked past his seat. For a split second it seemed to Ben that she looked straight at him and then through him. He tried to think of a suitable greeting but she was gone before he could speak.

Rosa yawned and pulled herself upright. 'What's the matter? Are we there?'

'I've just seen Miss McGuire!'

Rosa's eyes narrowed and she stared at him with suspicion. 'You've not been at the cheese again?'

'It wasn't a nightmare. I'm serious, Rosa. My old maths teacher is right here. She must be at the back of this coach.'

Rosa stifled a yawn. 'Ben, it is well over forty-odd years since you were at school. How could you recognize her after all this time? She'll look a different person now.'

'It *is* her…at least I'm ninety per cent sure it is. I would have to talk with her to make that one hundred per cent. They say the voice hardly changes. Besides, it's got nothing to do with the way she looks now; it's the way she holds herself. The way she moves.'

Rosa squeezed his hand. 'Well, don't look so worried,

love. We'll be stopping for lunch soon. Then maybe you'll get the chance to have a word. And if you're right, all's well and good and if you're wrong—'

'I'll get hand bagged! I shall look a right fool then, shan't I?' He slumped back against his seat, folded his arms across his chest and glowered at his wife. Does she think I've gone gaga already, he thought indignantly. I should know what my old school teacher looked like, not her. I know I'm right and I'm going to prove it.

Rosa nudged his arm and smiled at him, 'Now Ben, it's no good glaring at me like that. Come on, cheer up. We might stop at the same place as last week; they do a lovely roast beef lunch there.' She looked thoughtful, 'although with these mystery tours you can never be certain where you'll end up and you have to watch out that you get back on the coach on time as well or—'

'You mean like what happened last month to that lame man?' chipped in Anna from behind them.

Ben turned to her. 'Don't tell me some bloke had one too many and decided not to come back?'

The two women looked at each other and Rosa said, 'We don't rightly know what happened, but I don't think the driver would have bothered to check if I hadn't told him that an old man was missing.'

'Then we had to wait for another twenty minutes whilst the driver went looking for him,' Anna added.

'But he found him, though?'

'No, he did not,' Anna said. 'That Terry, the driver, just set off without him. You know, that sort of thing happened all the time when I was on the Force. People went out of the house to buy a newspaper, or a loaf of bread, and that's the last anyone saw of them. You should have seen our Missing Persons File.'

Ben was still puzzled. 'But on a coach trip? Surely this bloke must have turned up again? At home perhaps?'

Rosa shrugged. 'We don't know. Let's hope so. I suppose Terry would have checked. This driver checked our IDs before we got on this coach; said it was to stop gate-crashers.'

'Gatecrashers!' Ben burst out laughing. 'Who the hell would want to gatecrash a pensioners' mystery tour? The ultimate in excitement.'

'Ben, will you stop shouting.' Rosa hissed.

'I wasn't shouting, I was laughing.'

'You were making a lot of noise. Heads are turning.' She peered out of the window. 'Oh, thank goodness, looks like we're here.'

The coach came to a halt outside the restaurant. At once there came the raised chatter of voices from the passengers as they prepared to get off. Ben stood up and dropped his iPod. He bent down to retrieve it. When he got up again he looked closely at the departing pensioners, but he could see no sign of Miss McGuire.

TWO

SOME TIME LATER Ben pushed back his plate and smiled in satisfaction.

'Roast beef all right was it, dear?' Rosa asked.

'Very nice, thank you. No complaints at all.' Ben drank the remainder of his beer then leaned back and gazed around the dining room. It was large and busy; clearly the place was popular for Sunday outings. He looked over his shoulder and saw that there were more diners seated behind him and, amongst them, many old ladies.

Waiters carrying large coffee pots glided everywhere, and it was difficult to see what was happening at the far end of the room. Ben thought again about his former teacher and his gaze sharpened. There! For an instant he caught a glimpse of her near the French windows.

'Back in a minute,' he called as he got up from the table and hurried across the room. He felt nervous as he rehearsed what he would say to Miss McGuire, just as he used to do when he was a schoolboy and he was approaching her with a maths problem.

He reached the French windows and looked around. She was nowhere to be seen. Yet she *had* been there, he knew that he'd seen her. He walked out into the grounds and looked about him. Not a soul in sight. What was he to do. The woman must be somewhere. How could he go back and tell Rosa that Miss McGuire was not there after all. Should he tell her he'd been mistaken? But he had seen her, he hadn't imagined it. His optimism vanished and frustration built up within him. All that he'd wanted was to say a few words, perhaps reminisce for a minute or so about the old days.

Feeling a deep sense of disappointment, he went back inside and made his way to his table.

Rosa looked up at him. 'Well then, did you catch up with her?'

'No, when I got there she'd gone.' Ben sat down and poured himself some coffee.

'Perhaps she's a look-alike,' Anna said. 'When I was on the Force, it was uncanny how many people could look like one another, especially on identification parade.'

'Maybe she's a doppelgänger,' Rosa said. 'They say everyone has one.'

Ben stirred his coffee. 'We won't find that out or anything else either. Not unless I get a chance to speak to her.'

Rosa watched him for a moment and then said carefully, 'Do you think she might *not* want to speak to you?'

'Why shouldn't she?'

'Listen, love, it's not every woman that wants to be greeted heartily by some former pupil of long ago. I mean, looking at it from her point of view, it isn't as if you made top of her class, or head boy, or even turned out to be someone famous, is it?'

'I didn't do that badly. I never got quite to the top, but I've always had a good head for figures. Both of the adding ups and the "goes-intos".' Ben winked at her. 'And of course, the female variety.'

Rosa laughed and patted his hand. 'Yes, dear, I've noticed that. But the point is, if she's recognized you, and for reasons of her own is avoiding you, then it won't do you any good being pushy.'

'Pushy! I'm not pushy.'

'He's just bloody stubborn.' Anna smiled.

'It doesn't matter what you are,' Rosa said. 'It just may seem that way to a frail old lady.'

'Frail?' Ben stifled a laugh. 'You don't know the woman.' He leaned back on the chair and grinned. 'Rosa, in my class any lad demented enough to describe "Ratbag McGuire" as *frail* would have been sent straight to Nurse and told to lie down in a cool, dark room.'

Rosa frowned. 'As bad as that?'

'Now don't get me wrong. These days, people might describe her as a bit of a bully, but credit where it's due, without Miss McGuire's help and sheer bloody-mindedness, I for one, would never have got through my maths exams. She made me work until my brain was steaming.'

'Sounds more like dedication than bullying to me,' Anna said.

Rosa looked at him. 'Just don't you get so fixated about talking to her. You know very well how pigheaded you can get about this sort of thing.'

'All I know is that thanks to her I've a lot to be grateful for. And I'm going to tell her so.' His eyes searched the dining room in frustration. 'If only she'd give me the chance.'

FOR BEN, THE REST of the day passed pleasantly. The coach took them through many North Yorkshire villages and they had a happy time buying trinkets and gadgets from the craft fair and Sunday market.

He pushed all thoughts of Miss McGuire to the back of his mind and began to feel more cheerful. He strolled around, breathed in the crisp October air and watched with amusement the women's futile attempts at bartering with the local traders.

Towards evening, they returned to their coach and, after a short journey, they stopped at a large hostelry where sandwiches and drinks were set out for them. They ate with gusto, for after all the outdoor exercise they were hungry and it was with a feeling of contentment that they made their way back to the coach for the return journey.

'Those were good sandwiches,' Rosa said as she sat down beside her husband in the coach and unfolded her Sunday newspaper.

'Yep, they'd plenty of ham in them,' Ben said and a gleam came into his eyes. 'Couldn't complain about the barmaid either. Cassie her name was. She was tasty, all right.'

Rosa nudged him fiercely. 'Don't think I didn't spy you trying to chat her up. At your age? You silly old fool.'

'I was just making conversation. It's not often that a pretty young blonde smiles at me.'

'It's her job keeping the customers happy; it's your money she's after.'

Ben chuckled; he couldn't resist the chance to wind Rosa up. 'She could charm the birds off the trees could that one. With a body like that she could have anything she likes.'

'Oh yes.' Rosa laughed, 'Well, you dream on then, and think on: *you* can't have anything *you* like, least not whilst I'm still breathing.'

Ben grinned at her, patted her hand and watched her fondly as she turned the pages to the women's supplement of the newspaper. His gaze moved on to the front of the bus where a few late travellers were scrambling aboard.

They would soon be on the move; most of the seats

were full. He looked around again at the rear of the bus; nearly full back there too.

Ben counted the empty seats. Four. He relaxed; they'd all be here soon. If he remembered rightly there had been three vacant seats when they set off this morning, so there was only one passenger missing.

Rosa giggled quietly at some item in the newspaper. He glanced at her and knew that some Sunday scandal was keeping her entertained. As he watched her he recalled the doubt he'd seen in her face at lunchtime when he'd returned and told her that he couldn't find Miss McGuire. Had she been humouring him then? Or did she really think that he was hallucinating, or maybe starting to live on past memories? Well, he wasn't and he would show her, yes both her and her know-all of a sister. He had seen Miss McGuire and come what may he was going to prove it.

A thought came into his mind and once again he looked over his shoulder at the empty seats. Ben scowled and tried to think back. Rosa had mentioned earlier that she thought she'd seen someone fitting his description of Miss McGuire just now at the hostelry but then… The engine roared and the bus pulled away. Ben looked back again at the four empty places. There should only be three. The missing passenger couldn't be at the front of the bus; there'd been no spare places there. Unease gnawed at him. He looked at Rosa, who was trying to complete a crossword. For a moment he hesitated, then he gave her a nudge.

She looked at him in surprise. 'Now what's up? You're not hungry again already?'

'Miss McGuire. She's not on the bus.'

Rosa put down her paper. 'Now, Ben…'

'I'm not joking, love. There's four empty seats back there.'

'There were empty seats when we first got on this coach.'

'Three. I counted.'

'Maybe you missed her. Maybe she's up front with a friend.'

'She's not.'

Ben stood up in the aisle, looked around the coach and felt a growing anxiety. 'We can't leave a little old lady stranded,' he said. 'I'd best have a word with that driver.'

ROSA WATCHED HER HUSBAND make his way down the coach. Where had the woman got to? She looked out of the window and saw street lamps flash past at an alarming rate. Each mile was taking them further away from a poor soul who might be in trouble. The woman could be anywhere; she could even be on the wrong bus.

A few minutes later Ben returned to their seats.

'What did the driver say?'

Ben beamed at her. 'No panic. He says the passenger's not taking the journey home. She has to visit her sick sister. Seems like she lives near that hostelry we just stopped at.'

'Whew,' Rosa let out a deep sigh of relief. 'At least that's sorted.'

He grinned at her. 'I'll bet that brought out all your old nursing instincts. Go on, admit it. You were already organising a search party.'

She smiled in embarrassment.

'Well, at least the driver's put my mind at rest. I was getting worried.'

Rosa was sympathetic, 'I know you were, love, but

now you know that everything's okay and, if you've no further objections, I'll get back to my paper.'

For a while Ben watched Rosa working on her crossword. As usual, she'd been right; there was nothing to worry about. Yet something niggled at the back of his mind. He stared blankly at the seat in front of him as he tried to figure out what it was. They'd had a good day out on a mystery trip. The food had been great. Everything had been taken care of.

So why, then, had he got this gut feeling that something somewhere was wrong?

THREE

JACK PAUSED IN HIS WRITING, looked at the caravan door, switched off his radio and listened. Just for a minute he'd thought he heard the sound of an approaching coach. Terry should be arriving any minute. He shook his head, picked up his pen and checked his watch. Almost half ten.

He returned to his task of copying certain entries from the local evening paper. After a while he counted the entries that he had circled and checked that they tallied with the copies he had made. Every detail must be correct. Eight entries in all, not a bad haul for a Saturday night edition. The boss would be well pleased.

He drew a pack of cigarettes from his pocket, lit one and felt a sense of well-being flood through him. He knew that Terry and the coach would be here any time now, unless... He glanced at his mobile, leaned across the desk and made sure that it was still switched on. Having reassured himself he relaxed once more. His work was almost done for today and only the tips and ticket stubs had yet to be collected.

Jack looked at his watch again. If Terry got a move on he might just make it to the Red Lion for a pint. A thought occurred to him and he looked down at his half-smoked cigarette. With a sense of urgency he checked the remaining contents of his packet. Three. What if Terry was late? He pinched out his cigarette, blew on it, and placed it behind his ear. If he didn't get to the pub before closing time, three ciggies were barely enough to see him through until morning.

He heard the sound of a coach approaching and got to his feet. No mistaking it this time. He walked to the caravan door, opened it and looked outside.

Out of the darkness, headlights glared at him and from the driver's seat a pale hand waved. He waved back and stood to watch the coach edge its way past him and park in the garage. The engine was switched off and Jack heard the sound of the coach door slamming. He stood waiting in the doorway until he heard footsteps echoing hollowly over the cobblestones and Terry greeted him.

'Now then, Jack, what you been up to?' Terry grinned as he reached the caravan.

Jack smiled, 'I've been working away like a good 'un, waiting for you to bring home the bacon.'

With a laugh Terry climbed up into the caravan then walked past him to the desk and looked down at his paperwork. 'My, you have been busy!'

Jack followed, picked up the papers and placed them neatly in the Out file. 'Yep, everything's in order now. How about you?'

Terry crossed to the kettle, shook it to check that there was enough water in it to make a drink and lit the gas. 'Not a bad trip.'

'Any bother with the old guys and dolls?'

'Just the usual fussing. All they ever worry about is loos and grub.' Terry fished in his pocket, got out an envelope and a plastic bag, and tossed them on the desk.

Jack looked at the plastic bag. 'Good tipping day, was it?'

'Nineteen quid, I makes it.' He turned and poured hot water onto the instant coffee in his mug.

'Here, that's not much for nigh on sixty pensioners. I take it they did all turn up?'

'Yep, very nearly full, we were. What you has to remember though is that the oldies knows how to hang on to their pennies.'

'You did check down the sides of the seats and such?' Jack said as he began to divide the contents of the plastic bag into two small stacks of coins. 'You often finds plenty of cash down there.'

'Not tonight, mate. Not so much as a ten pence piece. In fact, they was real quiet this trip. No sing songs, no hokey-cokey. No nothing.'

Jack looked up from his counting. 'Not even one complaint or query?'

For a split second Terry hesitated and stared down at his drink. He took a last gulp from the mug, wiped his mouth, and went to rinse the mug under the tap. 'Nope, nothing at all.' He gave a sardonic laugh. 'You could say that for once all was quiet on the North Yorkshire front.' Walking over to the desk he stood and watched Jack remove the ticket stubs from the envelope and start to count them. 'Haven't you got a home to go to? You knows I'll take care of that. Just you pick up your share of the tips, and let's see the back of you.'

Jack grinned, put the money in his pocket and tossed the caravan keys onto the desk. 'Well, if it's all right with you.' And he walked towards the door.

Terry laughed. 'Go on; get off, the Red Lion's still open.' He stood motionless until the caravan door slammed shut behind Jack then his jovial expression changed. He hurried over to the desk, ignored the small stack of coins, and started to check the ticket stubs urgently. There was no room for error. The boss hated mistakes.

FOUR

LATER THAT EVENING Ben squatted in front of the television set, flicked down the flap of the colour control and clicked his tongue in exasperation. He was not one to whinge but someone had been fiddling with his television set.

Rosa was not the culprit; there was no doubt in his mind who the guilty person was. This sort of thing had been happening frequently ever since *The Force* had started to use his house like it was her second home. It's not good enough, he thought, I've got to have a word with her. It might mean yet another row but... He paused, listened to the rattle of crockery coming from the kitchen and sniffed the air in appreciation as he identified the aroma. Minestrone. Best wait a bit, no sense in spoiling a good supper.

He returned to his armchair and flicked the remote control until the screen showed the sports channel. Here Ben stopped, saw that a replay of this summer's Wimbledon was about to take place and leaned back in his chair.

Rosa called from the kitchen. 'Two bread rolls all right?'

'Make it three please, love,' he said. Then he glanced down at his paunch. It wasn't getting any smaller. 'But no butter on them.' Having calmed his conscience, he looked again at the screen and watched as the tennis ball bounced to and fro. He stretched out his legs. This was bliss, the sheer joy of watching the ball hit the racquet, backwards and forwards, forwards and backwards. His eyelids drooped. Tap, tap. Rap, tap. Rap, tap. Yes, that was how Miss McGuire always got their attention. Rap tap. The rhythmic sound of her ruler beating down on her desk. And when the silence grew they heard the sound of her thin precise voice. He could hear her now. Her instructions biting sharply into his brain....

'So, boys! You are about to sit the first mock exam of this term. Before you begin, I would remind you of the following points. One. Remember to number your answers. Those who fail to do so I will deal with later. Two. Remember to read both sides of the paper. Three. When dealing with fractions what must you always *remember, remember, remember?* Benjamin Hammond! Answer please!'

'Look for the common denominator, Miss!' Ben yelled, and sat bolt upright in his chair.

Rosa rushed into the room. 'Are you all right? What the heck are you shouting at?'

Ben looked at his wife dazedly. 'I must have been dozing. Just thinking back.'

'That blessed teacher again, eh?'

'I must be losing me marbles—'

'Of course you're not. Only it's a shock when you haven't seen someone for ages.' Rosa glanced at the TV. 'I'll just switch channels for a sec; I want to see what the weather...'

She bent over the remote, inadvertently pressed the wrong button, and the voice of the tennis commentator blared out. 'Jenny has played tennis since she was five. She comes from a large family. Three brothers and four sisters.'

Quickly Rosa pressed another switch and the voice was silenced.

'What did he say?' Ben shouted.

'She comes from a big family, or something.' Rosa stared at him. 'What are you getting all excited for?'

'But *she* didn't! Don't you see?'

Rosa sat down. 'Who do you mean, love?'

Ben clicked his tongue. Why was Rosa always so slow off the mark? 'Miss McGuire. Who else? Don't you see? Years ago, she told me. She had an invalid mother and she was an only child.'

'Happen you misheard what that Terry said.'

'No. I should have remembered, even then.' Ben sighed and looked at his wife.

'It's all coming back to me now. You see, love, when I was in her class, we both shared a common denominator.'

'Meaning?'

'We both had problems with our mums.'

'But your mum was not an invalid, Ben.'

'No, she was an acute depressive. Well, that's the label the medics call the illness these days. When I was a lad they just called it "being bone idle". Anyway I had to do most of the shopping and cleaning 'cause mum was always too tired. So it was easier for me to bunk off and not go to school and my schoolwork suffered. Not that I was bothered, but Miss McGuire spotted it and came to see mum one night.' Ben frowned. 'I never did find out what she said to mum, but from that day on she sat with me after school and went over my maths…' He broke off, looked at Rosa and tried to smile.

Rosa stroked his hand, 'Oh Ben—'

He continued, 'It was only years later, when I'd left school and landed a good job, that I realized that even though Miss McGuire had an invalid mother and other worries, she'd given of her own time to tutor me… and, as I've said before, I'd never…' He hesitated and looked embarrassed, 'You do see, don't you, love, just how much I owe her?'

Rosa got up, leaned over Ben and kissed him gently on his forehead. 'Why didn't you say before?' she scolded softly.

He looked up at her, 'You'd have thought I was being soft.' With an effort Ben sat up straight, patted his wife gently on the rump, then frowned. 'But back to what happened today. There's no doubt about it, love. That driver was lying.'

Rosa nodded and went into the kitchen. She returned with a tray, placed it on the small table in front of him, sat down and studied him thoughtfully.

'What's that look in aid of?'

'Ben, I've been thinking—'

'That's good, Rosa; it helps the brain keep ticking over, does thinking.'

'Benjamin Hammond, will you let me finish what I was going to say, instead of trying to be sarcastic?'

Ben picked up his spoon and took a bite from his roll. 'Get on with it then. Me soup's getting cold.'

'About that Terry, the bus driver. You know, he told you Miss McGuire got off the bus to visit her sister?'

Ben put down his spoon. 'Rosa, we've already discussed this. All of two minutes ago.'

'Will you stop interrupting? You're missing the point. The thing is we were on a mystery tour. And mystery tours rarely stop at the same place twice.'

'But we did, 'cause you knew about the roast beef lunches at the hostelry.'

'Yes, I did notice that. I'm not stupid. But that was unusual. What puzzles me, though, is how did your Miss McGuire know the bus was going to stop there? I didn't mention it, but I thought I saw her at that hostelry earlier on, yet I know for a fact that she wasn't on any of the trips that Anna and I'd been on.' She stared at her husband thoughtfully, 'And if, as you say, she hadn't any sisters or relatives, why on earth didn't she get back on the bus to return home?'

Ben looked at her. 'How would I know, Rosa? Just what was that driver up to? What's his game?'

'Whatever it is, it bothers me,' said Rosa. 'If your schoolmarm's gone missing, I can't help but wonder what happened to the old man that vanished the other week?'

Ben dunked his bread roll and then put it down again untasted. He stared at the soup in silence, then with a sigh he lifted both tray and table and put them to one side.

'First things first, love, let's get this straight. You say you thought you saw Miss McGuire?'

'I didn't tell you, I thought it might upset you, but I thought I caught a glimpse of her at that big hostelry. The Full Moon Inn, I think its name was.'

'And you say a few weeks before, on the same tour, another man went missing?'

'That's right. Anna was with me. We told you about it. Don't you remember?'

'So you did. So, the coincidence is this—'

'Don't like coincidences,' Rosa shivered, 'they brings me out in goose pimples.'

Ben sighed again. 'Okay, I'll be scientific then. The common denominator is this: two people go missing, same tour, same place, and on a trip run by the same excursion company. The only difference is that when they vanished, they were several weeks apart.'

'And that Terry, the driver, told a whopper.'

Ben looked irritated. 'Yes, yes. I do remember that. You don't have to keep going on.' He stood up, looked down at the now luke-warm soup in dismay and paced the floor. 'Have you got the name of the coach company?'

Rosa hurried into the kitchen. 'I've got the phone number,' she called, 'I put it in the drawer for safe keeping.' She returned with the leaflet and gave it to him.

He looked at it, checked both sides and scowled. 'This is just an advertisement. It only gives information about the tour.' He waved the leaflet at her in exasperation. 'There's no address. No trading name. The only information it gives is the phone number, an email address and the special price of a pensioner's ticket!'

Rosa looked defensive. 'That's why we went on those outings. I thought that the price was very reasonable. You saw how full the coach was today. We were lucky to get seats.'

He waved the paper at her again. 'That's not the point, Rosa. Look, love, have you still got the letter that came with this offer?'

Rosa folded her arms and her jaw tightened. 'As I recall there was no letter. I just found it shoved into our letterbox one day.' She looked at him in defiance. 'It seemed like a very good offer to me. How was I to know that some passengers would go missing?'

'Didn't you think to check the firm out? For all we know the driver could have been a madman, the coach might not have been roadworthy, and we've no idea who the owner of the company is.'

Rosa frowned. 'I did ring them. They always told me to "pay the driver and bring your IDs and he'll give you a ticket". Which we did. And, as you well know, everything went tickety boo. Except—'

'Some poor bugger went missing. And now we've only a phone number to complain to.' Ben stopped and looked

at his wife's troubled face. Her lips trembled as she fought
back the tears. He went and put his arms around her.

Rosa gave a defiant sniff and rested her head on his
shoulder.

Ben stroked her hair. 'Never fear, love.' He glanced
again at the crumpled leaflet and pushed it into his trou-
ser pocket. 'Just you see. First thing tomorrow, we'll sort
this lot out.'

FIVE

ALTHOUGH IT WAS OCTOBER, the next morning was as soft and as mellow as summer and Rosa was not anxious to get home.

Anna strolled along beside her as they returned from the village shops and informed her with relish of the work that she intended to do in the garden that afternoon. Rosa tried to pay attention to her sister's words but her mind was elsewhere. It darted like a demented wasp from thoughts of yesterday's trip, to Ben's intended complaint to the coach company, and to the control of his blood pressure. But, more than anything else, her thoughts kept returning to the disappearance of that little old school-marm.

She stopped for a moment, put down her shopping bags and loosened the scarf that was around her neck. There, that was a bit better. Perhaps a few deep breaths of good clean air might ease her sense of anxiety and guilt. She thought again about Ben and knew that if he didn't get a satisfactory response to his complaint, he'd cause trouble.

Ben was right. She should have been sensible. Buying tickets on impulse from a firm she didn't know was stupid. She'd behaved like some scatter-brained twenty-year-old and she was, after all, a mature woman. And now, because of her thoughtlessness, all hell might break loose.

'Are you listening to me, Rosa? What have you stopped for? I'll carry a bag if you're that whacked.'

'I can manage!' Rosa snapped. She stooped, picked up the shopping bags and strode on at a brisk pace.

Anna hurried after her. 'Now what's the rush? You've not gone and left the cooker on again, have you? Even if you have, your Ben's there.'

Rosa stopped in her tracks and scowled at her sister. 'Could I just have a few minutes silence from you, please? You've talked non-stop for the last hour, and I need time to think.'

Anna watched as her sister strode on ahead. She called, 'I know what it is. It's about that trip. And you're still worrying about what your Ben might do to the coach company.'

Rosa looked over her shoulder. 'That, amongst other things.'

Her sister caught up with her. 'Come on then, let's get on home and see what Ben's found out. As they say in the Force, there's nothing worse than not knowing.'

They reached the garden gate and stopped. From the garage came the sound of ferocious hammering. Rosa relaxed a little; so far all seemed normal. She walked towards the garage. 'Shall we go see Ben?'

Anna shook her head and grabbed her sister's arm. 'Let's go in and make a drink first. He's bound to want one anyway.'

They went into the kitchen and put the groceries down.

Anna pulled out a chair and flopped down at the table. She loosened her coat. 'Do you think he's phoned them, Rosa? She looked around the kitchen and her eyes narrowed when she saw the wall phone. 'Don't bother to answer that, I can see the black grease from here. He's had a go at them already.'

Rosa tutted, got a cloth from a cupboard and hurried over to the phone.

'You've still not managed to house-train him then?' Anna smiled. 'You know, I never had that problem with my Harry.'

'Maybe that's why he's not your Harry anymore,' Ben said as he came into the kitchen. He grinned. 'Well, not since he hopped it with that redhead from the Bingo.'

'That's none of your business, Ben.'

'Nor is our marriage any of yours.'

Rosa sighed. 'Will you two stop bickering? Ben, you can wash your hands and sit down for a minute, whilst I make the tea.'

Ben went to the sink and began to lather his hands. 'Don't you want to know what they said?'

'Have they found the old lady?' asked Rosa.

He rinsed his hands, dried them and gave a bitter laugh. 'In order to find a person, you first have to admit that you've lost them.' He sat down and gestured at the phone. 'And, according to that lot there, no *incident* occurred on yesterday's tour. No one left the coach tour at the pub. And, so they tell me, no person by the name of Miss McGuire ever went on their blasted mystery tour—'

'But she did; we saw her.'

''Course she did,' said Anna.

Ben's face flushed. 'Will the pair of you let me finish? Not content with making these statements, do you know what those idiots had the cheek to say?'

The women shook their heads.

'They said they thought I'd contacted the wrong coach company, and that it was easy for people of my *age* to become *confused*.' He slammed his hands down on the table. 'So? What do you make of that then?'

Rosa watched him with concern and pushed his mug across the table. 'Drink your tea and calm yourself. You look as if you're going to burst a blood vessel. You did take your tablets?'

''Course I did.' He scowled at her. 'But don't you see what they meant? They tried to tell me that *I'm* confused. Or, in other words, that *I* am senile!'

Rosa tried to reassure him. ''Course you're not senile. We know what we saw.'

Anna got up and went to the phone. 'Can you give me that number, Ben?'

'What are you going to do?' Rosa asked.

'Have a go at the coach company, of course.' Anna squared her shoulders and drew herself up to her full five feet eight inches. 'As a former police officer I still have some clout. If they should dare to call me senile, I'll bend their ears for them.'

Ben stared at his sister-in-law's ferocious expression. 'Just hold on a mo, Anna. I've got a better idea.'

Anna slammed the receiver back on its hook. 'Well, you would of course!' She folded her arms and leaned against the wall. 'Go on. Out with it then.'

He fished the paper from his pocket and tossed it across the table to her. 'There's the leaflet. They do three trips a week. Do you reckon one of your old mates might give us some help tracing that number?'

Anna picked it up. 'Looks like a mobile number to me and that's odd but not unknown for a business line.' She studied it. 'Always hard to get the address though. I'll try phoning an old pal later.'

'Then I think we ought to go to the police and report Miss McGuire as a missing person,' Ben said.

Anna looked superior. 'We'd need a few more details first. Her address would be useful. She might not live round here anymore and, then again, she's only been gone twenty-four hours and the police—'

'All right, all right, clever clogs, we know you're a know-all, you don't have to prove it.'

'I was just trying to say—'

'Er hem,' Rosa cleared her throat, got up and reached into the shelf by the phone. 'About Miss McGuire's address. Shouldn't we try this first?' She handed the phone book over to Anna who immediately began to flick through the pages.

'What's your teacher's first name, Ben? I've got eight McGuires listed here.'

Ben thought for a moment. 'Elizabeth. Yes, that was it. I remember she used to sign our report cards as E McGuire, and one day I asked her what the E stood for. Seems hard to have to think of her as Elizabeth, or even Lizzie. To us lads she was either "McGuire", "old Ratbag" or "Hitler".'

'There's an E McGuire here on Devonshire Avenue. It's the only one listed. Shall I try ringing her?'

Ben nodded. 'Go on then, and let's pray that she answers.'

Anna keyed in the number, listened for a while then frowned. Irritably she pressed the disconnect button and keyed in another number. 'Yes, operator, I'm trying to get Halifax 7586. Anna paused for a while and listened, then said, 'Thank you.' She put the phone back on its hook.

'Now what's wrong?'

'Curiouser and curiouser. That number is now an empty line!'

Ben got to his feet. 'Then there's nothing else for it. We've got to go to the police.'

'But Ben, you see—'

'When you two have finished arguing, might I have a word?' Rosa said loudly.

Anna and Ben stared at her.

'That's better. I was beginning to think that I was the invisible woman around here.' Rosa picked up the phone book. 'Now it says here E McGuire and the address given is on Devonshire Avenue. Don't you think it might be a good idea to check this out first?'

Anna scowled at her. 'That's what I was going to say if Ben had let me get a word in.'

'Oh yes, everything's my fault; what else is new?'

'But it's true.'

'Will you stop it, the pair of you, and let's get on!' Rosa looked at her sister. 'Now, I don't know where Devonshire Avenue is. I don't recall seeing it in this part of town.'

'I've got a street map at home. I can soon find it.' Anna looked across at Ben and a wry smile creased her lips, 'And I suppose you'll need the use of my car?'

'That would be good, only—'

'On one condition. I'm driving.' Anna said.

'Well, of course,' said Rosa.

Anna nodded and walked towards the door. 'Okay then, give me five minutes and I'll bring the car round. She turned to Ben and smiled smugly. 'It's only a battered old Ford Escort but, unlike your car, Ben, it still goes.'

SIX

Monday afternoon

THE FORD ESCORT PULLED UP at 83 Devonshire Avenue and three pairs of eyes gazed at the Yorkshire stone terrace house in silence. The house was neat; the net curtains that adorned the windows were clean and fresh. The dark-blue paintwork on the door and window frames looked glossy and in good order. Even the small forecourt in front of the house was tidy and well swept. Yet for some reason the dwelling looked austere; no friendly vase of flowers or ornaments gazed out from its windows. No milk bottles, full or empty, stood sentinel on the doorstep. A small metal plaque beside the letterbox testified to the character of the house's inhabitant.

Anna turned to Ben. 'Aren't you going to get out and see if she's in?'

'You sure this is it?'

'It's the only Devonshire Avenue listed, at least in this town.'

Ben got out of the car, walked towards the gate and stared at the house. 'Then it must have been her mother's, it certainly looks old enough.'

Both Rosa and Anna joined him. 'Well, go on then,' Rosa gave him a nudge. 'Knock on the door and see if she's there.'

'And if she is?'

Anna snorted in exasperation. 'All of our problems

will be solved then, won't they? And you'll have dragged us here on a wild goose chase!'

'But if she does answer, what the hell do I say to her?'

Anna clicked her tongue. 'Just say that you were concerned about her disappearance last night.'

'What's it say on that plaque, Ben?' Rosa interrupted hastily in an attempt to stave off any further dispute.

Ben peered at it. 'No circulars or hawkers.'

'For heaven's sake,' said Anna, 'will you knock on that door. If that old woman is in there and can see us she'll be wondering what on earth we're up to.'

Ben grunted then rapped loudly on the door and waited. The three of them stared silently at each other whilst Ben resisted the urge to peer through the letterbox. After a while he looked at Rosa and raised his eyebrows.

'Try again,' she mouthed.

Once more he knocked on the door but no one answered.

'She can't be here,' said Rosa. 'Of course she might just be out shopping.' She walked back to the gate and looked along the road.

Three doors down a middle-aged woman was standing in the forecourt cleaning her windows. She worked at a leisurely pace and every now and then she paused to regard the trio with interest.

Rosa strolled towards her. From many years of experience, she had learned to deal with this type of neighbour. Such people had the eyes of hawks, they missed nothing, and such a person could prove to be very useful.

'Good afternoon,' Rosa smiled as she stopped outside the woman's gate.

The woman nodded politely and began to polish her windows with increased vigour.

'Wish my windows looked as good as yours; you're certainly making an excellent job of them.'

The woman paused in her task, turned to smile at Rosa then stood back for a moment to admire her handiwork. 'Gotta keep ahead of the muck round here,' she said proudly. She gestured at the road, 'There's always them cars flying past and the minute you blink the muck's back again. It's never ending you know.'

Rosa nodded and leaned against the gate. She began cautiously. 'I wonder if you could help us? We're looking for a Miss McGuire. We believe that she lives a few doors down from here.'

'Aye' the woman said, 'I did happen to see you all knocking at her door. Not that it'll do you much good like.'

'She's gone shopping then, has she?'

'Naw! That one's hardly ever here, and even when she is she can barely manage to bid the time of day. Keeps herself to herself does that one.' She lowered her voice. 'A bit toffee nosed, if you ask me.'

'You don't happen to remember when you last saw her?'

The woman looked thoughtful, 'Now there's a question. Come to think of it, it must be all of two months since I last saw her trotting down the road. 'Course I've not lived here all that long, and they do say, the neighbours I mean, that the house belonged to her mother. Between you and me I reckon that she must have another house somewhere else.'

'Then she doesn't really live here?'

'I didn't say that. As I said before, I do catch sight of her now and again. And sometimes when I go past the house I see a light on.'

'When did you last see a light there?' Rosa asked with barely concealed eagerness.

'Let's see now, today's Monday, windows day, when it's dry that is.'

Rosa repressed a sigh.

'So, it would be the Saturday night before this Monday, and yes, that's it. I was just coming home from the bingo and it had started to rain. Just when I'd washed out me forecourt as well that morning. So anyway, I was hurrying past her house and I'm sure I saw her living room light on.' The woman hesitated and looked at Rosa cautiously, ''Course, I couldn't swear on a Bible, or give a statement like.'

'It's all right; we're not from the police.'
'And it might have been the lights from passing cars reflecting on the windows.'

'But it was Saturday night? You're sure of that?'

'That I'm certain of. It isn't as if I can afford to go to bingo every night, and yes, I saw a light, but whether it was—'

'It's quite all right. Thank you ever so much. We must have missed her by a few days.' Rosa turned and walked back towards the car where Ben and Anna were waiting.

'Perhaps if you was to write to her?' The woman called after her. Rosa looked over her shoulder, 'We'll try,' she smiled and waved goodbye.

'What did you find out?' Anna asked as they drove off.

Rosa told them what the woman had said and Ben's expression darkened. 'It gets more and more confusing. If she really was here on Saturday night why would she go on a day trip from here on the Sunday morning and not return home on the Sunday night? And why all the lies from that so-called Mystery Tour Coach Company?'

He shook his head. 'Something's not right, I can feel it in me water.'

Anna said irritably. 'Look, Ben, I think that you're worrying too much. Just because you're newly retired it doesn't mean that you have to go dashing off like some Don Quixote trying to find an old schoolteacher. I'm sure that Rosa and I can find you lots of other more pleasant things to do.'

Ben groaned inwardly; that was all he needed, his sister-in-law trying to take over his and Rosa's life. Well, it was not going to happen. No way, not if she was the last person on the planet. He'd do what he wanted. His jaw set stubbornly. He leaned forward and tapped Anna firmly on her shoulder. 'Now you look here, I don't want you to think that I'm being ungrateful to you for driving us here, but I'm still not happy about this Miss McGuire business, and I'll have you know that I'll not rest until I've got it sorted.'

'But Ben, that is ridiculous! We've done all that we can.'

'Wrong! *You've* done all you can by giving me a lift. But as for me, I need to find out more. Now if Rosa wants to tag along with me, that's fine, but if, as you say, you two can find much more pleasant things to do?'

Rosa turned in her seat and looked back at him. 'Don't be so daft. 'Course I'm coming with you, you silly old thing.'

He grinned at her gratefully, 'We'll have to think this through properly, love. Go right back to where it started.'

''Course we will, and we'll need to be thorough,' she glared at her sister. 'I, for one could not bear the thought of a little old lady vanishing, and no one in the world caring.'

'You're both crackers!' Anna snorted. 'We've done

enough. Folk disappear all the time. You have to look after number one in this life, never mind anyone else. If you two go swanning off trying to do the "rescue" bit, it'll lead to nothing but trouble. You mark my words.'

They stopped outside Ben's house and Anna jerked the hand-brake on fiercely. For a few seconds the trio sat in stubborn silence then Rosa opened the car door and got out. She stood on the pavement, looked down at her sister and said stiffly, 'Thanks for the lift. You coming in for a drink?'

Anna shook her head, watched as Ben clambered out of the back seat and joined his wife, then said, 'You two really are going to carry on with this, aren't you?'

'We'll be all right.' Ben said. 'You've done your bit. No one's asking you to come along.'

Rosa saw the hurt in her sister's eyes and blurted. 'But you can if you want, it's all right…' She stopped in mid sentence when she saw Ben's angry look. 'We could always do with a bit of police expertise,' she added hastily.

'You're both mad,' said Anna, 'or at least well on the way to going mad, but I'll think about it.'

They watched as Anna's car drove off down the road then they went into the house.

Ben closed the door and looked at his wife, 'What did you have to go and say that for?'

Rosa didn't answer, she walked into the kitchen, filled the kettle and plugged it in. Stifling a sigh she muttered, 'Please Lord, grant me patience.' She turned to look at Ben. 'She is my sister, you know, and I don't want her to feel left out.' She saw his bewildered expression then added realistically. 'Besides, at the moment she is the only one with a car that's roadworthy and we might well need the use of it.'

SEVEN

ANNA MARCHED INTO THE HOUSE, slammed the door, and tossed her jacket over the hallstand. She was about to walk through to the kitchen when she remembered Ben's bit of paper. She fished in her jacket pocket and brought it out.

Looking at it, she felt tempted to toss it into the dustbin, but then Ben might ask whether she had checked that number and she couldn't be bothered to lie to him. Besides, it was a matter of principle; if she had said she would do a thing she would do it. She did not want people to think of her as being scatterbrained.

She went into the kitchen, opened the fridge and brought out a bottle of diet Coke. For a second her eyes strayed longingly towards the cake tin in the corner but she tightened her lips, unscrewed the cap of the bottle and took a deep swig from it. She needed to calm down.

She walked into the living room and sat down, picked up the phone and keyed in a number. Whilst she sat there listening to the ringing tone her gaze drifted around the room and she smiled contentedly. This was her favourite room. It had taken her months to get it colour coordinated in tones of cream through to mahogany through to the deepest of reds. Even the arrangements of silk flowers, (real ones being too messy) had been selected in exactly the same shades as the furnishings. Visitors, on seeing this room for the first time, always complimented her on her imagination and good taste.

As Anna thought about that her smile deepened; she knew that an artistic mind was not the prime requirement of a policewoman, but that a realistic one was. She had seen a picture of a room in a home and county magazine and loved it. She had then done the logical thing and copied it from the picture, item by item. Well, as close as she could. Now she glanced at the glass-topped coffee table where three magazines, also all beautifully colour matched, lay. Automatically she leaned forward and straightened one; it had seemed a little askew.

The ringing tone stopped and a voice answered.

'That you, Mitch?' Anna said. 'Hi, how are you? Yeah, me? I'm fine.' She looked down at Ben's bit of paper and the number scrawled across it. 'Look, can you do me a favour?'

Anna replaced the receiver, got up, went over to the window and looked out at her neatly trimmed lawn. She thought about the call she'd just made. She'd done what Ben had asked of her, not that it would do any good. Her former colleague, Mitch, had said she would check out the number and get back to her as soon as possible. Now all she could do was wait. She looked again at her lawn and thought about the rose bushes that she intended to plant out there this afternoon. They would make a lovely show next summer. When she'd been on the Force she'd had so little time for gardening, so they'd had to make do with a large lawn. They? What was she thinking? Her ex, Harry, had never done any work in the garden. He was always too tired, he claimed. Anna scowled. He was always too busy chasing redheads and anything else that was female; that could have tired him out, she supposed. She gave an angry sniff; she was well rid of him. She tried to push all thoughts of her ex-husband out of her mind. She didn't need him. She was glad it was over… yet for some reason the pain still lingered.

Think about the rose bushes, she told herself firmly. She was going to plant a display of yellow through to orange and then to the deepest of reds. She knew exactly where she would place them. She'd already put the magazine picture from *Gardener's World* beside the tools in the garage.

She went back to the armchair, looked down at the half-empty bottle of Coke, picked it up and went into the kitchen. It was no use: she was hungry. She opened the tin, took out a piece of cake, hesitated, then took out a second slice. She hadn't had any lunch and it would give her something to do whilst she waited.

Her mind went back to today's events and her mouth tightened in annoyance as she thought about her brother-in-law. Why was that man so stubborn? And why did he always seem so determined to have everything his way and do whatever he wanted to do without the slightest consideration of Rosa's plans? Anna sniffed indignantly and with her finger she blotted up the few remaining cake crumbs from her plate, ate them, then went to sit by the phone in the living room.

Why was Ben always so pigheaded and emotional? He behaved like an overgrown schoolboy most of the time. Yes, that was it. He was still a schoolboy at heart, and now he had gone and got himself a problem with his old schoolmarm. A problem entirely of his own making. Anyone else would let things be, but no, as usual Ben was like a dog with a bone and there would be no stopping him until he thought he had the solution.

The trouble was that Rosa felt she ought to get involved. Anna sighed. That had always been Rosa's problem. She just did what Ben… The phone rang, startling her. She picked up the receiver. 'Hello? Oh, hi, Mitch. You have? My, that was quick.' She listened carefully for a while then picked up the bit of paper and reread the mobile phone number to the caller. She listened again then said thoughtfully. 'Thanks, Mitch. Yeah, you've done all that you can.'

She replaced the receiver, and with a sense of puzzlement digested the information that she had been given. Mitch's words filled her mind. 'This number has been disconnected.' But how could that be? She hadn't expected this result. Although her brother-in-law was irritating, she knew that he wasn't exaggerating when he'd said that he'd spoken to the coach company on that number only this morning. The only conclusion was that someone somewhere had acted very quickly. She got up, and still holding the scrap of paper went back into the kitchen. She needed to think this through.

Firstly, on Sunday there was that business of the schoolmarm, who, when Ben went to try and speak to her, repeatedly evaded him, and who, according to Ben and Rosa, vanished mysteriously on the return journey home.

Secondly, there was the visit this afternoon to the teacher's house, but she was not there.

Thirdly, now there was this mobile number that did not work; yet this morning it had. She stood silently thinking over the events of the last two days and frowned; none of it made any sense. Automatically she opened the biscuit tin, grabbed a handful of biscuits and began to munch on them. At least three parts of this puzzle did not fit. Grudgingly she realized that Ben could be right. Maybe there was cause for concern. She came to a decision, replaced the biscuit tin lid firmly, brushed down her top and went into the hall to get her jacket.

Of course, this would mean having to delay making a start on the rose bushes. It would also mean having to bite her tongue as far as Ben was concerned, but one thing was certain, her curiosity was aroused and she needed to find out if something odd was going on. She chewed on her lip as she thought about her sister and Ben and wondered what can of worms they were about to open. With an impatient sigh she strode to the door. It was no use; she would have to go along and keep an eye on what they got up to.

'I KEEP TELLING YOU, ROSA,' Ben said as he spread the road map across the kitchen table, 'if we go straight up the A1, we'll get there in no time.'

'But that hostelry wasn't on the A1,' Rosa insisted in a tight-lipped sort of way. Her finger jabbed at a small red line on the map, 'I reckon that it was somewhere near here...just after that crossroads. You remember? Where we saw the sheep with blue plastic Macs on their backs.'

Ben looked irritated, 'Nearly all North Yorkshire sheep have them things on their backs come winter. As for the crossroads, that could be anywhere.'

'Perhaps we had better get the coach again then? They just might *not* recognize us.'

'No way! We'd end up doing a disappearing act as well.' Ben thought for a while. 'The best thing would be to hire a car, seeing as mine's still off the road.'

'Have you any idea what renting a car costs these days?' Rosa asked. She hesitated then said, 'I had thought our Anna might be persuaded.'

'We both know what your Anna thinks about this.'

Rosa looked thoughtful. 'I could try talking to—'

Ben started to protest when they heard a knock on the door.

'It's only me,' Anna said as she came into the kitchen.

'See!' hissed Ben, 'if you talk of the devil she's bound to appear.'

Anna stared at him stonily, ignoring his comment. She glanced down at the map and with a superior smile looked from Rosa to Ben. 'About that phone call you asked me to make,' she handed the leaflet back to Ben, 'my friend says the number's been disconnected.'

'What?' Ben said. He looked at the paper, 'That's incredible, how can that be?'

Anna shook her head. 'I don't know, Ben…but for once I think your suspicions could be right. Something's wrong here…so I've decided that if you're going to look for the old woman, I'd better come with you.'

'By heck,' Ben looked at her in awe, 'wonders will never cease.'

'Don't you two start off arguing again,' Rosa said hastily. She smiled brightly at her sister. 'Er, Anna, Ben and I *are* going to look for the old lady, and we *do* want you to come with us, but you know that we've got a problem with transport and I did wonder? What with you having a little car? We'd pay for the petrol, of course.'

Rosa watched as Anna's lips curved into a knowing smile and she said slowly, 'Well, I had intended to make a start on planting my rose bushes today, but,' her gaze drifted to Ben and her smile grew wider, 'as a special favour, of course I'll drive you.'

EIGHT

The Full Moon Inn: Tuesday morning

DAVE HODGSON PUT the last of the slimline tonic bottles on the shelf, picked up the empty case and consulted his list again. 'Two more cases of pineapple, three ginger ale, and four soda waters.' He rubbed his aching back then returned once more to the cellar.

As he opened the door to the beer cellar he hesitated and listened to the scurrying of the mice; or something worse. He pushed down the light switch, waited until his eyes adjusted to the dimness and peered down into the dusty room. To his left at the foot of the stairs were the cases of soft drinks and mixers. To his right were the beer barrels and just below the loading doors were crates and boxes full of empties, waiting to be returned. One thing about this place, no one could ever complain about the lack of space. A smile tugged at the corners of his mouth; you could lodge an army in here, either that or a boatload of illegal immigrants. Dave grinned at the thought. That, at least, would be far more profitable than his present situation.

He winced as he stacked the cases onto the stairs; his gut ache was back again. He should never have eaten that pepperoni last night. The doctors had warned him about spicy food, but he hadn't wanted to behave like an old fusspot in front of Cassie, and today he was paying the price.

He looked around him; he was getting too old for this kind of heavy lifting. Why on earth had he let Cassie talk him into taking over this great barn of a pub? He must have been insane. The heating costs alone were staggering and it was in the middle of nowhere. But Cassie had insisted and Cassie had persuaded. Dave thought about his new wife with her blonde curls and her 'persuasive' ways and his expression softened. The truth was, of course, that she'd always fancied herself as a kind of 'Lady of the Manor.' At least that's what she'd told him. He knew that she'd wanted to leave London after ending an abusive relationship. He dwelt on that dark thought for a moment then dismissed it. She was his wife now, whatever her past life might have been, and he was going to do everything he could to keep her happy.

Having checked his list he eyed the stack of cases and for the hundredth time wished that he'd had sufficient clout with the owners to persuade them to install a lift down here. Or, failing that, the budget to employ even a part-time cellar man.

'Ah! Got yer! So this is where you are.'

Dave looked up, saw his wife in the doorway and laughed, 'You didn't think I'd run off with another woman, did yer? Not when I've got you.'

Cassie giggled and peered down at him. 'I should hope not. If some young tart tried to pull you, I'd scratch her flaming eyes out.'

'No worries there, my love.' Dave lifted up three cases and climbed the stairs.

''Ere, let me give you a hand with them.'

'Just you stay right where you are, my darling. I don't want you spraining your ankles. Besides, these are too heavy for a little thing like you,' Dave said breathlessly.

Cassie leaned against the cellar door. 'Don't be so daft, I'm not made of cotton wool.' She picked up a case, 'Now, what was it I was going to tell you?'

Dave paused, as he was about to pass her, 'Was it that you were missing me?' he asked hopefully.

''Course I was, but, ah, I've got it. The Brewery rang. Something about a delayed delivery, I couldn't find you so I said you'd get back to them. I'll have you know I've been racing around upstairs looking for you, and I couldn't find a soul.' She looked down at her black strappy sandals, 'and I almost broke these bloody heels coming down them stairs.'

'If you will wear them heels, sweetheart.' Dave carried the cases into the bar and edged them onto the counter. 'Anything else?'

Cassie followed him, 'No. Well yes, there were some messages on the note pad. Chef must have taken them. Some query about the crisps order, oh, and a message to ring the nursing home.'

Dave paused in the act of opening a case, looked at his wife and tried to keep his voice calm, 'Nothing else?'

She shook her head. 'That's about it, lover.'

He turned away from her and struggled with the cardboard lid of the case. With a sense of relief he heard the sound of an engine as a coach parked up outside. Dave looked at his watch, two minutes to opening time; he'd have to get a move on. 'If you'd just do the doors, darling; don't want to keep the customers waiting.'

Dave watched as Cassie hurried to open the pub doors. She was a joy to him and for the umpteenth time he wondered what he, a man well into middle age, had done to deserve someone like her. Whatever it was, he would do his best to keep her happy, even if it meant... His gaze drifted towards the main doors, focused on the coach outside, and his expression darkened. He tried not to think about how weird it seemed that he was being paid 'bonuses' from these coach tour operators, when, as every publican knew, it was usually the landlord that had to bribe them.

He lifted the bottles of ginger ale out of the case and put them on the shelf. He was worrying too much. The perks that he got from the nursing home and the coach tour company were a life-saver to him. All that they asked of him was to see nothing.

'The punters are coming, Hoorah, hoorah!' Cassie sang as she trotted back round the counter. She gave him a quick squeeze as she edged past him, 'Here, let me help you with those. It'll take that lot a minute or two to settle down and decide what they want.' She bent down and pushed the bottles onto the shelves.

'I'll not say no to that.' Dave leaned against the bar and eyed Cassie's rear appreciatively.

'Tell you what though, Dave. Wouldn't it be nice if we could have walkie-talkie radios like what they do in all them big hotels. Then we wouldn't be forever playing hide and seek in this place looking for people.' Cassie straightened up and looked at him. 'I can never find young Claire when I want her.'

'She's usually in the kitchen talking to chef. And if you can't find her there, try looking where the new guests are. She's a great little cleaner, but as for gossiping, she could talk for Britain could that one.'

'Tell me about it. As far as I'm concerned she can chatter as much as she likes.' Cassie grinned at Dave, 'She's the best that we can afford, so fingers crossed, lover. Let's hope she never asks for a pay rise.'

Tuesday morning

BEN SAT IN THE FRONT SEAT next to Anna and tried hard
not to wince as she crunched though the gears. He peered
down at the map on his lap. 'We're on the A64 now.
What we have to look for is the turn off to Pickering on
the A169...should be coming up in about five minutes.'

'You sure we're on the right road, Ben?' Rosa asked
uneasily. 'It doesn't look like the same road that the coach
took, to me.'

Ben turned to his wife, 'That's because I've worked
out a short cut for us.'

'You mean you think you have,' Anna muttered tes-
tily. 'Time alone will tell on this one.'

'If you two women think you can navigate better?'

'No, no, leave it as it is,' said Rosa, 'I'm sure we're
going to get there, sooner or later.'

'Is that the A165 or the A169 coming up? I can't see it
properly, there's a branch in the way.'

'Hold on a mo, I can't find me glasses, I had 'em here
somewhere.' Ben fished inside his overcoat pocket, found
his spectacles and peered again at the map.

'It's no good looking at that now,' Anna gave a cynical laugh. 'We've passed the turn off. I don't drive at five
miles an hour.'

'No need to get stroppy,' Ben said, 'and anyway, I
don't think that was it. It's a bit too early yet; might take
another minute or so, and all of us should keep our eyes
peeled.'

'It didn't seem this far before,' Rosa said doubtfully.
'We've been travelling for two hours, you know, and as
I remember, that hostelry was just past the crossroads.'

'Aye! But which bloody crossroads? You daft twit.'

'Now, Ben, there's no need to bully your wife like that.'

'I'm not bullying anybody! You can't drive around Yorkshire just thinking "crossroads". I mean, there's millions of 'em.'

'But I'd know this one again,' Rosa insisted.

Ben opened his mouth to argue the case but before he could speak Anna said, 'There's a sign coming up now. Yes, I think this is it.'

'Hooray for that then,' muttered Ben.

'Yes,' Anna said. 'If I remember rightly we stay on this route until we are about a few miles on the other side of Pickering then we turn onto a "B" road.'

'And that's quite a bumpy road as well. I can remember that. That's when everybody's shopping bags kept sliding off the luggage rack.' Rosa tapped Ben on the shoulder and said firmly, 'And once we come off it, that's when we'll see the crossroads!'

Tuesday lunchtime

JACK LEANED AGAINST the front of the coach, watched his passengers make their way towards the pub then lit up a much needed cigarette. So far, so good. He for one was glad of the rest. The traffic had been a nightmare this morning but then it was always bad round these parts on a market day.

He turned and looked through the window of the bus; the old boy was still sitting there as per his instructions. Jack grinned up at him encouragingly, then repressing a sigh got out his mobile. Now it was back to work.

He keyed in a number, waited for the answering voice then said, 'Jack here. We've reached the Full Moon Inn and our "client" is on board the bus.' He paused, listened to the orders and said. 'Give me an hour? Yeah, see you later.'

He put away the phone, took another thoughtful drag on his cigarette and tried to shake off the persistent sense of anxiety that had come to live with him since he had taken on this job. There was no doubt that the money was good. No, that was an understatement. The money was fantastic. He could never have earned this kind of pay working as a truckie, even on the overseas hauls. 'Money makes the world go round.' At least that's what his partner, Irene, always said, and boy, she should know. She couldn't half spend it. He broke off, his thoughts distracted by the sound of tapping on the coach window and looked up to see his elderly passenger waving at him through the glass. Our client is getting impatient, he thought; better get on with it.

Jack smiled and walked round to the door of the bus to assist the passenger as he negotiated the coach steps. As he watched the old gent struggle down the coach steps, Jack tried to push back the doubts that plagued him. 'Just do what you're told, that's what you're paid for,' he told himself. It was best not to think about what was going on up at the nursing home.

THE FORD ESCORT came to a stop on the forecourt of the Full Moon Inn and a few yards away from the mystery tour coach that was parked there. Three pairs of eyes watched as the passengers from the coach disembarked and hurried towards the welcoming doors of the hostelry.

Ben started to open the car door but Anna pulled at his sleeve. 'Hang on a minute.' She nodded in the direction of the coach and the trio watched silently as the driver helped a white-haired old man towards the entrance of the pub. The driver seemed friendly and patient, but the man, who walked with the aid of a stick, looked very frail and unsteady.

'What I want to know is,' said Rosa, breaking the silence, 'what is that blooming mystery tour coach doing here, when by all accounts that business is not supposed to exist? I've a good mind to go and have a word with that driver, give him a piece of my mind, I would.'

Ben turned to her, 'Then you'd be wasting your breath. He'll not tell us anything.'

'No' said Anna thoughtfully, 'but the passengers just might, especially if they've been on these mystery trips before.'

'We'd have to be crafty about asking questions, sort of carefully casual like,' said Rosa.

Anna nodded, 'We'd have to split up as well. There's more than fifty-five people on that coach.'

'Then somebody somewhere must have noticed something,' Ben said. A gleam came into his eyes as he looked at the glass entrance doors, 'I think I'll make a start on questioning that blonde barmaid.'

Rosa snorted loudly and Anna raised an eyebrow. 'True to form as ever, Ben?' Her face softened into a smile, 'But you're right, if anyone knows anything, it's likely to be the staff. So you take the barmaid. And I'll have a go at the landlord. Agreed?'

'Who do I interrogate then?' Asked Rosa.

'You don't *interrogate* anyone,' Ben said. 'We're not the Spanish Inquisition. You have to be nice and chatty, and try to pick on someone who's sitting alone.'

'They've all gone in now,' said Anna.

Ben got out of the car. 'Then we'd best see what we can find out, but first things first, let's get ourselves a drink.'

NINE

Cassie smiled up at her customer, 'One pint best bitter, one half shandy, one bitter lemon. Would that be all, sir?'

'Yes, love. For the minute.'

She rang up the total on the till. 'And your thirty pence change, sir.' She watched as the man turned to the two women and gave them their drinks. To her surprise, the ladies, having taken their drinks, turned and walked away from him. The tall, well-built, dark-haired woman made her way along the bar to where Dave was working, whilst the other trim little lady wandered over to a table at the far side of the room. What the hell are they up to, Cassie thought. Have they been having a bit of a barney?

'Er…hem,' said the man who had remained standing at the bar.

Cassie turned to look up at him; tall, well upholstered, with rugged features, quite handsome in an old sort of way. He grinned back at her, seemingly unconcerned by her inspection, or by the fact that the two women had deserted him. 'Can I help you, sir?' she asked.

'You do lunches, don't you?'

'We sure do.' She handed him a menu. 'Waiting time between twenty-five and thirty-five minutes.' She smiled as she thought about her last remark. Of course, they could serve up the grub far sooner than that. Most of the dishes had been prepared earlier. All that they needed was a quick zap from the microwave. But business was business and in thirty-five minutes the punters could down one hell of a lot of ale. That's where the real profit was. Besides, she and Dave didn't half need the money.

'Well, let's have a look-see then.' After reading the menu he looked up. 'I'm not right sure what to choose. What would you recommend?'

Cassie's mind automatically shot to the dish with the highest mark-up. 'Our chef does a very tasty lasagne.'

'Then that's what I'll have,' said the man. He paid for the lasagne and she gave him a receipt. 'I'll have to have a word with the ladies to see what they want.' He gave Cassie a sheepish grin. 'Don't want to get myself into hot water by ordering for them.' He drank from his beer and looked around, 'Seems quite a busy place for a country pub.' He nodded in the direction of the coach outside. 'Do you always get a lot of coaches stopping here?'

'Mainstay of our business, coaches is, 'specially at weekends.'

'That must keep a bonny lass like you busy. Is it always the same firms that come here, like the same coach tour operators, I mean?'

Cassie continued to smile up at her customer but a warning light went on in her mind. She hesitated. 'Oh, there are various ones,' she said airily. After all, she thought, this bloke could well be from the Inland Revenue, or worse. 'It's hard to say which firms come here most often. I never takes that much notice.'

'They'll be mostly pensioners on these outings, then?'

Why on earth does he want to know about that? She wondered. This guy was getting a bit too nosy for her liking. She beamed up at him brightly. 'Do you know, I haven't got a clue about things like that. I only works here, darlin'.' She fluttered her eyelashes at him, 'Although I do try to serve the customers as best I can.'

'And a very good job you make of it too, my dear.'

The man grinned. With that he tucked the menu under his arm and ambled off to towards the tables where the other customers were seated.

Cassie's gaze followed him. Was she getting nervy? She turned to look to the far side of the room to where the coach tour driver and a white-haired old man were sitting talking. The driver was speaking in an animated fashion to the old man. And the man appeared to be listening carefully. As Cassie watched them a chill ran through her and she rubbed her arms fiercely. Not another one! She thought.

ROSA LOOKED TENTATIVELY at the middle-aged woman seated at the table. She was plumpish, nicely dressed and her sandy-coloured hair had a well-groomed look about it, but was she the talkative type? There was only one way to find out. 'Excuse me, is this seat taken?'

The woman looked up at her and smiled. 'Feel free, love, I'm here all by myself.'

Rosa placed her shandy on the table and eased herself into a seat. 'You've come on the mystery coach tour, have you?'

'Yeah, I likes a nice day out now and then. You gets to meet lots of new people, 'specially if you travel alone.'

'Meet lots of new people,' Rosa thought. By that does she mean men? She said aloud, 'There seems to be lots of married couples in here, though, not all that many lone tourists.'

'Aye,' the woman agreed, 'and trouble is, most of the loners are women.'

I was right, thought Rosa. She does mean men.

The woman's face took on a glum expression, 'There aren't that many fellers on their own these days. Men haven't got our stamina, see. Not once they get into their sixties. One minute they're here, next thing you know, they've popped their clogs!' The gloomy look deepened, 'Shame, really.' She picked up her glass and drank deeply from her gin and tonic.

Rosa's eyes focused on the woman's ring finger. She said hesitantly, 'I take it that you're a widow then?'

'Too true. He passed on three and a half years since. Mind you, I've got used to it by now.' She looked around the crowded room, leaned forward and whispered, 'But at times a woman has *needs,* if you know what I mean. Not that I would ever marry again. I did very well out of the Co-op insurance. Besides, if you wed them they only want you to wash their sweaty socks.' She wrinkled her nose. 'No, that's not for me. I much prefer a bit of romance. Like going away together for a mini-break, or them bringing me boxes of chocolates and flowers and things.'

'Do you ever meet anyone on these outings?'

'Sure do! Quite a few in fact, 'cause I'm the friendly type. Trouble is, I find out later that they've either got wives or girlfriends sitting at home, or they turns out to be pigeon fanciers or something daft like that.' She looked thoughtful, 'Though there was this lame feller a few weeks back.'

Rosa leaned forward and tried not to sound too eager. 'A lame feller? You met him on one of these outings?'

The woman nodded. 'He were a bit old for my taste. I likes 'em to be strong and sturdy with a bit of "go" in them, if you know what I mean. But he was nice. A gentleman in a shy sort of way. He had quite a bad limp, though. I'd just sat with him and got him chatting and he was telling me all about his stocks and shares and his other investments. Right here at this very table it was.' The woman scowled, sat back and folded her arms across her chest. 'Then that bloody driver came swanning up and whispered something in his ear, and before I knew what was what, they'd hopped it.'

Rosa tried to curb her impatience. 'Did you catch what the driver said to him?'

'All I heard was something about a nursing home and some mutterings about trifles.' The woman looked indignant. 'I could have told him I could make him an excellent sherry trifle, there were no need to go dashing off like that.'

'But you saw him again later?'

'No! That's just it! That night when we was all on the coach ready to go home, that feller wasn't there. And the driver didn't seem at all bothered. He went to look for him for a few minutes and then came back and said it were no use. He'd have to set off; he'd got to stick to his timetable, or so he said.'

'My sister and I were on that trip,' Rosa said eagerly, 'I can remember a man going missing.'

The woman stared at her. 'I can't say as I remember you, but then I don't bother looking at other women, not unless they happen to be wives and sweethearts on the warpath.' She shuddered and looked around her. 'Jealous women can't half get nasty, y'know.'

Probably with good reason, Rosa thought, but she said, 'Did you ever see that man again?'

'No. Though I still keep on looking for him. All I can think is that they must have given him a good deal more than a bloody trifle up at that nursing home. They must have given him a damned good banquet as well!'

WITH A SHRUG of her shoulders Anna picked up her bitter lemon and turned to survey the people seated in the bar area. It had been a waste of time trying to question the manager of the pub. It had taken her all of three minutes to realize that this man was an old pro in the questions and answers game, the type that would never give anything away. What she needed to find was a more amiable, more gullible target.

Her eyes came to rest on a cheerful-looking elderly man seated alone by the window. With a determined smile, she surged towards him. She felt nervous but it was all in a very good cause. Besides, it had been a long time since she'd had to chat up a bloke, so she really could do with the practice.

She decided upon the confident approach. 'Don't mind if I sit here, do you?' she said cheerfully as she sat down opposite him.

'Not at all, love.' The man's gaze flickered from her to his near-empty beer glass then on to Anna's drink, 'What's that you got there?'

'Just a soft drink, I'm driving, y'see.'

A look of alarm crossed over the old man's face, 'Ere! You're not taking over from our coach driver are you? 'Cause I don't rightly hold with lady drivers.' He picked up his pint and drained it anxiously.

Anna concealed her annoyance, 'No fear of that. I've come here by car.' She forced a smile. 'Are you on the coach trip then?'

'You could say that. I'm what they call a "regular", I goes everywhere on coach trips.' He leaned across the table and stroked Anna's hand. 'It's the wanderlust you know, it keeps getting to me.' His eyes strayed to Anna's ample breasts and he began to stroke her fingers urgently. 'Along with other little lusts,' he whispered.

Anna tried discreetly to pull her hand away, but it was no use. The man had a grip of iron. Her smile became frosty but she remained polite. 'Then you'll probably know all of these people on this outing?'

'Most of 'em. Of course, there's some that come, and some that go, just like that,' he snapped his fingers, 'and you never gets to see them again.'

This was getting interesting, Anna thought. She looked puzzled. 'What do you mean?'

The man picked up his empty pint glass and held it up to the light. 'All gone,' he said. He looked at Anna hopefully, 'It isn't half hot in here, me throat's getting ever so dry.'

'I'll get you a drink,' Anna said hastily, glad of the excuse to pull her hand away. 'What would you like?'

The man's grin broadened, 'A pint of Tetley's would do nicely.' Anna was about to get up when a woman's voice screeched, 'Stanley! What are you doing?'

Anna turned to see a tall, rake-thin woman storming towards them. The woman's face was contorted with rage, even worse she was carrying a large handbag, and she was staring straight at Anna.

Trouble! thought Anna. She stood up and pushed her chair out of the way. She wasn't scared; she had been well trained in the art of self defence, but the last thing that she wanted was to draw attention to herself. Diplomacy, as ever, came to the fore.

Anna smiled ingratiatingly. 'Oh, hello,' she said 'I guess you must be this good gentlemen's wife. My name is Anna and your husband is helping me with a survey on pub outings.'

'I'll bet he is!' The woman glared at Anna. 'I can't even go to the ladies now without some young hussy trying to get off with him.'

'But I wasn't—'

'I saw you! You Jezebel! Holding hands with him, bold as brass. What kind of survey is that then?'

'She were going to buy me a pint,' growled Stanley, 'before you stuck your nose in.'

'Look,' Anna said hastily as she became aware of heads turning in their direction, 'I'll buy you both a drink. Just sit yourself down, Mrs...er?'

'Her name's Rachel,' said Stanley. He glared at his wife, 'Sit down and shurrup for a minute, afore I die of thirst.'

Anna smiled through gritted teeth and wondered if she could claim the drink's money from Ben later. 'What will you have, Rachel?'

'A sweet sherry then,' the woman replied. She looked Anna up and down, then added waspishly, 'Make that a large one, if you please.'

ANNA SEATED HERSELF at a table near the back wall of the dining area and automatically checked out the other diners seated nearby. Old police habits die hard, she thought; after all, you never knew what villains you might spot, even in pubs that were in the middle of no-where. She picked up the menu card then stared again at her luncheon receipt. She was hungry, but then stress always did have this effect upon her, and after spending the last twenty minutes with the Romeo and Juliet from hell, she was in need of refuelling. She sniffed the air and glanced hopefully in the direction of the kitchen but, as yet, there was no sign of any food. She thought back over the last half hour. All in all, the 'odd couple' had been quite informative once the woman had calmed down. They claimed that at times some passengers were not on the coach for the return journey, but they'd always supposed that they'd made their own way home.

Anna looked about her and smiled when she saw that Ben was ambling towards her and that Rosa was a few yards behind him. She wondered what information they had managed to glean from the coach passengers, and whether they'd had any luck in finding out the whereabouts of Ben's missing schoolmarm.

Ben sat down opposite her, 'Rosa not here yet?'

'I'm right behind you,' said Rosa as she seated herself beside him. 'I tried calling out but you were concentrating on not spilling your beer.'

Ben grinned. 'Got to get my priorities right.'

Anna leaned forward, 'Well then, you two, what news have you got? Come on, what did you…?' She looked up, saw the barmaid approaching with the food and said, 'But let's have our lunch first, we can talk whilst we eat, okay?'

'THERE'S NO DOUBT about it,' Rosa said as she finished off the last bit of chicken. 'People are definitely going missing.'

'But there's no word about Miss McGuire, not even a whisper.' Ben said. 'So were we three all gaga on that mystery tour, or what?'

'Remind me again what this McGuire woman looked like,' Anna said. She scowled and looked around the pub, 'I'm sure there's something odd going on around here.'

'Small, a bit scrawny, wore glasses, had grey hair pulled back into some sort of bun,' Ben looked thoughtful, 'and a thin face with eyes like lasers.'

'Age?' asked Anna.

Ben shrugged. 'She must be close to eighty.'

'But it's not just your old schoolmarm,' Rosa added. 'We now know of at least several persons who have gone missing over these last few weeks and that's from questioning just a few people in here.'

'So what can we do? It's Miss McGuire we're looking for,' Ben said. 'It isn't as if we work for the missing person's bureau.'

'Still,' said Rosa thoughtfully, 'when you hear about folk vanishing you can't just ignore it. I mean, it's not decent.'

'Shush a minute!' Anna hissed. She grabbed Rosa's arm. 'Don't make any sudden moves; just look over your shoulder casually.'

'What's happening?' whispered Ben.

'See for yourself.'

With a nonchalant air, all three glanced in the direction of the bar area and watched as the coach driver helped the old man walk towards the doors marked 'Cloakrooms.'

'Happen he needs the loo,' said Rosa.

Anna stared cynically at her sister and wondered how she had managed to stay so naive all of her life. She watched as the coach driver pushed open the 'Cloakrooms' door and her mouth tightened. 'I'm not too sure about that.'

Ben got to his feet. 'Nor me. Best be safe. Come on, Rosa, let's toddle along behind them, just to make sure all's well.'

'I'll keep an eye on things out here,' Anna said. She watched as Ben and Rosa made their way towards the cloakrooms and wondered whether both she and they were overreacting. Or was it her police training that was making her so suspicious? Once more her gaze flicked around the room and her doubts grew. She was sure she was right. In the past her gut feeling had never let her down. As far as she was concerned, in this pub there were far too many coincidences.

TEN

'RIGHT,' SAID BEN AS the cloakroom door closed behind them and they found themselves in a long passageway. 'Where did they go?'

Rosa looked down the corridor and eyed the threadbare carpet with disapproval, 'We could try the loos first.' She walked towards the door marked 'Ladies'.

Ben stared after her. 'They're not likely to be in there.'

She looked over her shoulder at him. 'You never can tell. Hadn't you better check the Gents?'

Ben grinned at her, 'If you hear me scream will you come to me rescue?'

'Not on your life. You're big enough to take care of yourself.' Two minutes later both of them met up again. 'Any sign of anyone?' asked Rosa.

'Not a soul.'

'They've got to be somewhere,' Rosa said worriedly, 'what with people disappearing all over the place. You read about stuff like this in magazines. You know...sort of time warps and parallel universes.'

'You reckon there's a black hole in the beer cellar then?' asked Ben.

'Look, if you're going to start sending me up I'm going back to sit with our Anna.'

Ben squeezed her arm. 'Oh, for goodness sake, don't start throwing wobblies on me. Now come on, love, let's have a look down here.'

'You go first then,' said Rosa, ever the cautious one.

'Certainly. Which door is it to be?'

'Try the lot. You never know what we might find.'

'That's what's worries me.' Ben stopped at a door, 'I think this one's—' the door opened inwards and Ben disappeared, followed by a succession of thuds.

Rosa ran to the entrance and leaned in through the doorway. 'Ben! Are you all right? What are you doing?'

In the gloom Ben picked himself up and looked up at Rosa in annoyance. 'Well, I'm not playing hopscotch, am I? I fell down the bloody stairs! That door wasn't locked properly.'

'Are you hurt?' asked Rosa.

'Don't think so. I can't see a rotten thing down here, though. Try and find the light switch, will you?'

There came a click as Rosa located the switch near the door and a light went on. At the bottom of the stairs Ben brushed himself down then surveyed the beer barrels and cases of whisky and spirits. He whistled softly and looked up at her with a cheeky smile. 'Well, what do you know? Fancy nearly meeting my maker surrounded by all this. I'm in a boozer's paradise.'

'Never you mind about that, Ben Hammond,' Rosa said sharply. 'And don't you dare touch anything. We'd only have to pay for it.' From the top of the stairs she peered round the cellar. 'No sign of the driver and the old man?'

'Nope, there's only me.' Ben rubbed his knees and winced, then walked around, examining the stored cases, and looking up at the ceiling, 'but the loading doors are here, so we must be somewhere near the back entrance.' He hobbled up the steps towards Rosa. 'So I reckon we'd better find the back door.'

They hurried along the corridor until they reached the

rear exit. As they emerged into the concrete area they stood for a while and looked about them.

'Can you hear something?' said Ben.

'Like what?' whispered Rosa.

'Like the sound of an engine running.'

'Ben! We're near a main road, there's traffic coming and going all the—'

'No! It's much nearer than that and before you start, it's not a coach either.' As Ben spoke a grey Jaguar came round the corner and sped past them.

'That's the coach driver in there!' Rosa said.

'He's in an almighty hurry,' Ben said as he watched the car roar out onto the main road. 'It's madness pulling out at speeds like that in these country lanes.'

'That's not what's bothering me,' said Rosa, 'didn't you see who was in the back?'

'The old man?'

Rosa stared up at her husband anxiously. 'No doubt about it. But he looked like he was fast asleep!'

'You reckon he's been got at?' Ben hurried to the road and peered in the direction that the car had taken. 'He'd have to be! You don't go from visiting the "Gents" to being fast asleep in less than five minutes, that's downright impossible.'

'Where have they gone, though?' Rosa said. 'And who can we ask? About the grey Jaguar and the driver, I mean?'

'How the hell would I know?' Ben said bleakly. 'And who'll believe us anyway? There was only us two that saw it.'

FROM BEHIND THE WINDOW of the dry goods store Dave Hodgson, the pub manager, frowned at what he had just witnessed. Deep in thought, he picked up the two cartons of cheese and onion crisps and made his way back to the door.

As he walked he could feel the knot in his stomach tightening and the pain increasing. 'Avoid too much stress,' Doctor White had told him, otherwise that peptic ulcer will be back.

How did you avoid stress, he thought as he went back into the bar. 'By concentrating on the job in hand,' he said out loud and he slid the cartons of crisps onto the shelves underneath the bar. He turned and looked across the room at the customers. The bar was nearly full. People had come here and had their lunches and drinks, which had made it a profitable day for him. He tried to look on the bright side. He shouldn't grumble; how many other country pubs could boast this kind of trade on a weekday lunchtime, yet still the doubts in his mind tormented him.

Through the pub window he could see where the coach was parked. He knew that most of his trade was due to these coaches and the passengers that they brought here. Where would he be without them? He shuddered as he thought about that possibility, but...? The questions crept back into his mind and he tried to shrug them off...he was a businessman, for God's sake! He should worry about his profits and not about people. There was always a price to pay.

'That driver's gone again,' Cassie's voice whispered in his ear.

Dave started and looked down at his wife's anxious face. 'What?'

'And he's taken that old gent with him.'

Dave sighed, 'He'll be back in a bit.'

'Like what happened before? With no old gent?'

'Cassie, lover, it's none of our business. There's no

need for us to worry about stuff like that,' he smiled
down at her and teased, 'it'll only give you wrinkles.'

'Sod the bloody wrinkles. What I want to know is
what's happening up at that nursing home to those oldies?
That's four of them that's gone walkabout these last few
months, and that's only the ones that I've noticed. Dave,
I know you know more than you're telling me, but there
comes a time. Why won't you tell me what's going on
around here?'

He winced and clutched his stomach.

'Dave?' Cassie stared at him. 'What's wrong? You've
gone drip white. You all right, lover?'

''Course I am. It's just… Cassie!' Dave said urgently,
'Will you lower your voice? Customers might hear. We
can talk later once the tourists have gone.'

Cassie stared up at him and for an instant Dave saw
the anxiety in her eyes. 'Dave, you are not all right; you
look ill. And if you ask me it's all this worry that's causing it. You've got to tell me, lover,' she clutched his arm.
'Sooner or later you'll have to tell me what you know.'

'It's not what I know, darling. It's more, what I suspect. But we can't— Yes, sir?' He broke off to attend to
a customer.

After serving his customer, Dave watched Cassie as
she returned to her duties. His wife smiled and chatted
with the customers in her usual professional manner, but
every so often he saw that her face took on a thoughtful
expression, and that her gaze drifted towards the doors
of the cloakroom.

ANNA SAT AT THE TABLE and pretended to read the desserts
menu but her eyes darted frequently in the direction of
the cloakroom doors. Still no sign of Rosa and Ben. She
thought about ordering another bitter lemon but then her

stomach was already awash with the stuff. Besides, there would be no comfort stops on the two-hour drive back to her home. She looked up and with a sense of relief saw her sister and Ben coming through the main doors at the entrance of the pub. As they reached the table she said, 'Any news?'

Ben slumped down onto a chair whilst Rosa bent over her and whispered, 'He's taken him off in a car, and we couldn't stop him!'

Anna raised her eyebrows then looked from her sister to Ben. 'The coach driver has cleared off with the old man in the back of a car,' Ben translated wearily.

'He looked to be asleep,' Rosa added.

Anna controlled her impatience. 'I take it by that remark you mean the old man and not the coach driver?'

'Now don't you start getting clever with your sister, Anna,' Ben warned, 'I've had one hell of a day so far.'

'He fell down the beer cellar stairs,' Rosa explained. 'Lucky he didn't break any bottles, else we'd have had a massive bill.'

Ben looked at Rosa, 'That's what I like to hear, lots of tender loving care. Never mind about me bruised knees. Never mind that I could have been killed. I could have been permanently disabled.'

'Which brings us back to the old man again,' Anna prompted impatiently. 'Tell me exactly what happened from the minute you two went through those cloakroom doors.'

'Well, at first we—'

'Here!' Ben said, 'Look who's just come in!'

'The coach driver,' Anna said, 'he's making straight for the bar.'

Rosa looked at her watch, 'He's back quick. They can't have gone far.'

Ben got to his feet. 'What's he done with the old boy, then?'

'Hold your horses, Ben, don't do anything rash,' Anna said. 'Just to be sure, Rosa and I will have a look in the coach outside, in case he's put the old man on it.'

'Yeah, you're right for once, Anna,' Ben said grudgingly. 'Best not jump to any conclusions. Off you go then, I'll stay here and keep an eye on laddo.'

Ben waited until the two women had left the pub then walked up to the bar, ordered a pint, paid for it, and perched on a nearby stool. He watched whilst the coach driver ordered a drink.

'One Pepsi coming up, Jack,' said the landlord.

'Soon be getting back to the grindstone,' Ben said to the driver. He nodded in the direction of the tourists.

'Too true,' Jack replied, turning around to gaze at his flock. 'Still, they'll all be quiet now, seeing as their bellies are full. They'll be nodding off once we get going.'

'This seems quite a nice place, and the beer's good. Do you bring the trippers here a lot?'

Jack nodded, 'Our coaches come several times a week, but not always for lunch. 'Course it's not always me that drives this route. It varies, it just depends.'

'Bet it has its perks?' Ben winked broadly, 'plenty of tips I mean.' Too late, he realized that he'd said the wrong thing.

Jack's expression changed. He stared at Ben and the tone of his voice became guarded. He said coldly, 'Looking for a job, are you?'

'No, no,' Ben said, 'I've given up working, but I've often been on these outings and the passengers always have a whip round. Maybe I've got it wrong but I've always thought the driver's must do quite well if it's all tax-free?'

Jack frowned, 'We earn every penny we get. We've got other things to do as well as driving.'

'Yes. I saw you helping that old man earlier,' Ben said, 'You know which one I mean?' His face took on an innocent expression as he gazed around the bar then he looked at Jack in surprise. 'That's odd, I can't see him now, but he must be here somewhere?'

Jack seemed not to hear. He drained his glass then rubbed his hands briskly. 'Well, best get my lot together again; we've got a long afternoon ahead and I've gotta keep to my timetable, else we'd not get home before midnight.' He turned and addressed the crowded bar. 'Come on folks, let's be on our way rejoicing,' and with a curt nod in Ben's direction, he headed for the main doors.

Ben remained seated on the barstool and watched the driver and his passengers make their way towards the coach. Stonewalled again, he thought. Although the women were checking out the coach, Ben thought it unlikely that the old man had been returned to it, and if that was the case, where the hell was he? Ben studied his reflection in the mirror-backed wall of the bar and pondered; had poor old Miss McGuire been whisked off in much the same manner?

His gaze drifted from his reflection to the notices at the back of the bar. He peered at the bed and breakfast price list and nodded in approval. That was fair enough. He caught the landlord's eye and beckoned to him, 'I'd like to book a room, please.'

Dave nodded and got out his book. 'Would that be a single or double, sir?'

Ben looked over his shoulder and saw Rosa come in through the main door, 'Just a single, please. The missus has got to get back home tonight,' He looked at the price list, 'I take it that this includes a full English breakfast?'

'Of course.'

'It isn't half getting cold out there,' said Rosa's voice in his ear. She stood beside him, trying to warm her hands by rubbing them together.

Ben looked around, 'Where's the other one?'

'Anna? She'll be along in a minute,' Rosa whispered. 'She's gone to check out the back.'

'Happen she'll disappear too,' Ben said with a tinge of hope in his voice. He glanced warily at the landlord who was standing close by. 'If you're cold, perhaps we'd better move over near the fire. There's a table over there.'

Rosa looked at the rows of bottles facing her and said, 'Yes. All right, but I think I'd like a brandy first, just to warm the cockles.'

Ben raised an eyebrow.

'It's purely medicinal! You know I don't normally drink shorts.'

Whilst Ben paid for the drink, Anna came up to them. She looked longingly at the brandy that was placed in front of Rosa and sighed. 'I suppose I'll have to have a coffee?'

'One of the penalties of being the driver,' Ben grinned. He waited until Anna got her coffee then said, 'Come on, let's go over there.' They carried their drinks to the table and sat down. 'Well, you two?' Ben said, 'Did you find out anything?'

'We couldn't find any trace of the old boy. He's not on that coach, that's for sure,' Rosa said.

Ben looked at Anna. 'How about you?'

Anna took a cautious sip from her coffee. 'There's a grey Jaguar parked round the back,' she said quietly.

'Must be the one we saw.'

'That's what I thought,' Anna said. 'Anyway, it's now locked and empty, I checked it out. The bonnet's still warm, though. I even listened at the car's boot, just in case.'

'You don't think?' Rosa began.

'I deal in facts,' said Anna flatly. She looked at her sister. 'And the facts are that the old man has been taken somewhere that, judging by the time factor, can't be far from here.' She looked down at her cup, 'And he's not returned.'

'That woman I interviewed earlier mentioned something about a nursing home,' Rosa said. 'Mind you, she really had it in for that coach driver because of the way that he'd hijacked that lame man.' Rosa finished off her brandy. 'The thing is, I forgot to ask her just where this nursing home was.'

'Leave that to me, Rosa, I'll have a good scout round,' Ben said.

'I'll come with you,' Rosa said eagerly, then, on seeing Ben's scowl, 'or, we could all look in different directions, one of us is bound to find something.'

'Or, some of us are bound to get lost,' Ben replied. 'No, I'll deal with it. I've already booked a bed for to-night. I reckon you two had best go on home before it gets dark.'

'I see,' Anna gave Ben a suspicious look, 'doing the solo bit, are we? Or is this a good excuse for a night out on the booze?' She nudged Rosa. 'Told you, you should never have let him near that blonde barmaid.'

'Oh, do stop trying to stir things, Anna,' Rosa replied. 'You know as well as I do that when my Ben gets his mind set on something, he'll never let go.'

'Bulldogs have much the same problem,' Anna muttered.

'Listen you two, don't start arguing. We don't want to draw attention to ourselves. I've had enough funny looks from the landlord already. See, I'll stay here and try and find out what I can and I'll call you tomorrow. It's no good all three of us asking questions now that the tourists have gone. The staff will get suspicious.'

Rosa thought this through. 'You will phone us, though, if you find out anything?'

"Course I will, just as soon as I can.'

Anna buttoned up her coat and stood up. 'And if you don't find anything?'

'I'll phone Rosa either way, though you might have to come and pick me up. That is, if you don't mind?'

Anna nodded at Rosa. 'She'd nag me to death if I didn't.'

A few minutes later Ben stood at the pub door and watched the two women drive off down the road, he waved, then went back inside. Perching on a barstool, he picked up the dinner menu and scanned through it without reading it. He felt a mixture of confusion and sheer bloody obstinacy. What had started out as an enquiry about his missing schoolmarm seemed now to have taken a much more sinister turn. Ben gazed round the now near-deserted bar. Something here was not right. Someone here was doing wrong. The anger grew within him. Whoever it was, he would find them. He would see this through to the end.

ELEVEN

AFTER CLOSING THE PUB Cassie bustled in from the bar to the kitchen and frowned when she saw what Dave was eating, 'Dry toast, darlin'? You on a diet or somethin'?'

'Nope, just a bit of gut ache.'

Cassie put the cash box and pub keys on the table and peered at him, 'Look, I can soon rustle you up a decent sandwich.' She wrinkled her nose. 'Don't like to see you eating that stuff. We ain't that poor.'

'It's the only thing that helps when I've got this.'

For a while Cassie watched him eating then she said gently, 'Well, you know best I suppose, though maybe a drop of brandy might do some good?'

Dave groaned, 'About the last thing I need, sweetheart.' He tried to smile and said, 'I could fancy a mug of cocoa, though.'

'Cocoa!' Cassie gaped at him. 'As you wish, lover.' She got out the milk, went over to the stove and poured it into a pan to heat. As she set about making the drink she watched Dave out of the corner of her eye; he did look deadly pale. She tried to mask her anxiety by making her voice light. 'You sure you wouldn't like me to run and fetch you some slippers as well?' She said as she placed the mug of cocoa in front of him.

Dave patted the chair next to him, 'Come and sit with me instead.' He gave a tight smile, 'A kiss and a cuddle might help.'

Cassie sat close to him, kissed him gently and hugged him to her. She looked into his eyes. 'Now, tell the truth, darlin',' she said sternly. 'No more porky pies. This gut ache that you've got, it's not appendicitis, or something serious like that is it?'

'Nah, I had that out years ago. This is something that flares up now and then. There's nothing at—'

She pulled away from him and said angrily, 'Dave! I want the truth. Don't you dare to keep hiding things from me.'

He sighed. 'If you must know, I think it's a peptic ulcer. A new one starting up, I mean. I had one a while back, before I met you.'

Cassie felt hurt. 'Why didn't you say?'

'Didn't want you to think that you were marrying a sick old man.'

'A bit less of the old; it ain't as if you're doddering,' she said with a frown. 'I just don't understand why you hide this stuff from me.'

'Not so much hide. It's more of a "don't talk about" thing.'

'You mean, what I don't know can't worry me? You think?'

'I'm sorry, sweetheart, I didn't want to offload on you. We got enough worries what with the money, the pub, the staff shortage and you having to work like a scivvy.'

'I ain't complaining, am I?'

'If it wasn't for them blasted coach tour operators and the nursing home we'd be right up the creek. I thought we were onto a good thing with that firm, what with their offers of cash-back bonuses. It all sounded brilliant on paper. Them giving us dividends for "Our care of their elderly and disabled passengers, and our courtesy and patience towards them".'

'We always do our best. That goes with the job, don't it?'

Dave looked doubtful. 'Yeah, but think about it, Cass. Why the hell should the tour operators give us bonuses? There isn't a landlord within miles round here that wouldn't snatch their hands off for such midweek trade, especially in the winter. I should have had more sense. I should have spotted it. There had to be a catch, and there is. Now they're telling me what *not to see and hear* in my own pub.'

Cassie felt a shiver go down her spine as she remembered her earlier suspicions. She said cautiously, 'What is it that you're *not seeing* Dave? Is it the same as me, them poor old geezers disappearing every odd week or so,' she gulped, 'and they never comes back.'

'I'm not blind,' Dave said tightly. 'Every man has his price, so they say. I know that what I'm doing is…not right.'

'Then don't do it!'

'Easy to say, Cassie, but if I split on them, we'd be out of a job and homeless, and if what I suspect is right, that won't be the worst of it.'

Cassie was silent for a moment, then she whispered, 'What do you suspect, Dave?'

Dave shook his head and didn't answer.

After a while Cassie whispered, 'As bad as that?'

He looked at her, 'I hope I'm wrong, lover. I just don't know.' He winced and hunched over the table.

'Dave, you have got to see a doctor. We'll deal with what you said later. You're in agony now.' She jumped to her feet. 'I'm gonna phone him.'

'Leave it.' He grabbed her wrist. 'It's going off now, honest it is.'

'But you should see—'

'All right. I'll see Dr White from the nursing home first thing tomorrow. I promise.'

Cassie looked doubtful. 'Doctor White? I dunno. I cringe when I think of him.'

'He's been helpful to me in the past.'

'How so?'

'Never you mind.'

Cassie frowned at him. Did he really think she was an airhead? Her lips tightened. 'Look Dave, if you won't tell me, then I'll ask him myself.'

Dave sighed. 'He did my insurance medical, didn't he? Remember? The one that the brewers asked for before their lawyers would let me take over this place.'

'That's his job, ain't it? Any doctor would do the same.'

'Not every doctor would have passed me, not with my history of peptic ulcers. If the truth were known, I'm lucky to have a job as a manager at all! 'Cause it's all stress related, you know.'

'Aw Dave! Now you tell me. Why didn't you say?'

Dave smiled tenderly at his wife's pretty face. 'And risk losing you? You wanted this place, and now we've got it. Perhaps if we work hard and mind our own business, things might turn out all right?'

'No, Dave, they won't. Look what it's doing to you already.' Dave gave a deep sigh, picked up his cocoa and made for the door. 'I'm off to my bed, sweetheart.' He tried to smile. 'Are you coming? We can talk more about this in the morning. I'll call the doc first thing, I promise.'

Cassie got up and walked towards the sink so that

Dave wouldn't see her face. 'Be up in two ticks, love. Just got to write a note for chef first.' She heard the door close behind her. She reached for the notepad and for a while stared blankly at the paper. What to do? Any fool could see that this situation was making Dave ill. As for those oldies disappearing? Stiff with anger, she picked up a pencil and wrote down her instructions to the cook, yet all the while one thought burned itself into in her mind: there had to be a way out of this. If Dave couldn't find it, she damn well would.

Wednesday

BEN AWOKE the next morning to the sound of a muffled vacuum cleaner. He frowned, Rosa must have got up early and gone on a cleaning spree. He became aware of the pattern of the flocked wallpaper and wondered why it was so unfamiliar. Memory returned and he smiled in relief. For one dreadful moment he'd thought he'd gone off into one of his nightmares again, though even in his nightmares he'd never seen wallpaper like this.

He snuggled back into the pillows then groaned as he felt the dull ache in his back. He must be covered in bruises from that fall. He lay for a while collecting his thoughts then noticed that the sound of the vacuum cleaner was getting louder. Glancing at the clock radio, he saw that it was well after nine and he got out of bed. He'd need to shower and dress quickly or else he'd miss his breakfast.

When he left the room and walked along the hall-way, he saw a young dark-haired girl busy vacuuming the carpet. He remembered Anna's remarks about the staff in the pub being the ones who really knew what was going on and he slowed his pace. This young woman might well be able to give him some information; at least it was worth a try.

As he reached her she looked up and switched off the machine. 'Whoops! Sorry sir, I thought you'd already gone down. Hope the noise didn't disturb you?'

'Not at all, love, you're fine, I was up anyway.' He watched as she pulled the vacuum cleaner to her and spoke quickly before she could switch it on again. 'Er, miss, I hope you don't mind me asking, but do you live round here?'

The girl nodded. 'About a mile down the road with me mum.'

'Then you know these parts?'

She laughed. 'Should hope so. I was born here.'

'Must be nice to live out here in the country.'

'It's all right in summer, but come winter,' the girl shuddered and rubbed her arms. 'Getting in to work is murder. Having to ride a bike in all that slush and ice... still,' she smiled at him, 'a job's a job and I have to hang on to it.'

'Isn't there any other work round here then?'

She pulled a face, 'Nothing, except for up at the nursing home, and I can't say as I fancy that.'

Ben's ears pricked up, 'Oh, so there's a nursing home nearby, you say?'

'Yeah, just up the road. You turn sharp left as you come out of the forecourt. Lots of old folk stay there.' She looked at him then blushed. 'No offence like.'

Ben shook his head, 'None taken.'

'Well, they go there to rest and it's a good job too, 'cause that's where most of our passing trade is.'

'Ah, I see. You mean visitors?'

'Those? Yes, and of course there's all the coaches as well,' she looked at her watch then frowned. 'I'll have to get a move on now, sir, if you don't mind. I've loads to do.'

'Right, love, I won't keep you any longer.' Deep in thought, Ben made his way down the stairs. His curiosity was aroused; several people had mentioned a nursing home. Could there be some connection. Once he'd had breakfast he'd take a little walk and see what he could find out.

CASSIE CAME INTO the bar, picked up the reservations book and flicked through the pages. 'Dave, this Mr Hammond? Do you know if he's checking out today, or is he staying on another night?'

Dave paused in his work and looked at her. 'Don't know; he never said.'

'Only Claire wanted to know if she needs to do his room.' She smiled at him. 'Not to worry darlin', I'll ask him soon as I see him.'

Dave stacked the last of the clean glasses on the shelf and walked over to her. 'You'll have to wait a while sweetheart. He's been and had his breakfast, and he's gone off for a walk. I watched him set off. He went up the hill towards the nursing home.'

Cassie frowned, 'You don't think he's…some sort of official?'

'No, why should he be?'

'Then why did he go that way? He must have a reason.'

Dave put his arm around Cassie and drew her to him. 'Who says that he has? He could have dozens of reasons for taking a stroll. Like wanting to take a breath of country air for a start, so will you stop getting your knickers in a twist? You've got to let me do the worrying.'

'Yeah,' Cassie patted his stomach gently, 'and look at

what the worrying's got you, a flaming peptic ulcer. You made that appointment yet?'

Dave nodded, 'I'm seeing Doctor White at three this afternoon.'

Cassie kissed him lightly. 'Good boy. And I'm coming with you.'

'I am over twenty-one, sweetheart.' There was a hint of reproach in Dave's voice.

Cassie giggled and kissed him again, 'Yeah, you're eighteen going on eighty, and I'm still coming with you. Then, once we've got you sorted, we're going to do something about the oldies business.' She looked up at him and her expression became serious, ''Cause I got a feeling that it ain't right what's happening round here.'

'Now Cassie, don't go jumping to conclusions,' Dave warned. 'We've got our livelihood to think of.'

'Don't you give me that. If push comes to shove I can work anywhere; we'd not starve. I tell you this: what I'm not having is turning a blind eye to something that is wicked.'

'We don't know that for sure!' Dave protested, 'Cassie, we're just guessing.' He looked about him anxiously and lowered his voice. 'We all know what happens to "whistleblowers" even when they've got it right. God help us both if we should blow the whistle and we've got it wrong.'

Cassie's mouth tightened into a stubborn line. 'But I'm not wrong, lover. Women know these things, and if you won't do anything, well I just might.'

'Cassie! Will you leave it? Please? At least for now?'

Cassie watched as her husband's face turned drip white and her anxiety increased. Have some sense, girl, she told herself, get your priorities right. Dave is in agony. See to him first. She forced herself to sound calm.

'Okay then, darlin', seeing as it's you that's asking.' She smiled, took hold of his hand and led him towards the kitchen. 'Come on, let's go and have a nice warm cuppa. You could have some more cocoa if you like?' She suggested teasingly. 'And how about a bit more of that nice dry toast?'

TWELVE

BEN PAUSED IN his walk and looked about him. It felt good
to be out in the country away from the traffic and noise.
Here all was quiet except for the occasional twittering of
the birds. He walked on, pleased that the morning was
sunny and warm, a fine day for late October.

He was not quite so happy about two things, however.
One, he had assumed that the nursing home was only a
few minutes away. He had been walking for more than
ten minutes and he could still see no sign of it. Two, the
girl had failed to mention that the walk was all up hill. He
knew that this was not a problem for an energetic teenage
cyclist, but for a newly retired and slightly portly pensioner? Ben stopped again, pulled out a hanky from his
jacket pocket and mopped the sweat from his forehead.
How much further? He peered at the skyline; there to his
right in the distance he could see two chimney stacks.
Perhaps that was the place? At least he could take a look.
He took a deep breath and strode on.

Noon

BEN HESITATED as he peered through the ornate glass
doors, then with a friendly smile he pushed the door open
and strode towards the area marked reception.

An immaculately dressed woman was seated at a desk.
She looked up as he came through the entrance. The corners of her mouth twitched into a half-smile, which dis-

appeared as soon as Ben approached. She looked down at her notes and, ignoring Ben completely, continued making entries into a ledger.

Ben was having none of this. He cleared his throat and said loudly. 'Good morning, miss. Might I have your attention?'

The receptionist put down her pen slowly, and with a bored expression looked up at him. With a beautifully manicured finger she pointed towards a small ornate table on her right. 'You will find the brochures on the rack over there, sir. I assume that that is what you want, isn't it?'

Ben studied her. It was like looking at a painted doll. He sighed. With make-up like that it would crack her face if she smiled. 'I had intended to ask for the details of this nursing home,' he said quietly. 'My aunt is looking for suitable accommodation in this area. I wondered—'

'As I said before, all of the brochures are over there, sir.' The receptionist interrupted. 'Now if you'll allow me to continue with my—'

Ben said coldly, 'In my part of the world, miss, it is customary to greet clients politely, and to at least bid them the time of day.' He leaned over the desk and added, 'When I was a lad I was taught that it is very rude to point.'

'I beg your pardon!'

'I granted you that three minutes ago,' Ben snapped, 'some folk just don't know any better. Now what I wanted to know was, is it possible to inspect these rooms? I take it that they are all en suite?'

Without a word the receptionist stood up and marched round her desk to the small table where the brochures were. She picked one up and handed it to Ben. With a voice that could cut ice she said, 'I'm afraid that an in-

spection is not possible as we have no vacancies. The
brochure should answer all of your queries. You will find
the price list on the back page. I must advise you that the
waiting list is already full, and that it may be some time
before any vacancy occurs. I feel that perhaps your aunt
should seek accommodation elsewhere.'

Two minutes later Ben came out of the nursing home
and tried to calm his indignation at the rudeness of the
receptionist. He opened the brochure that she'd given him
and stood for a while reading it. Turning to the back page
he whistled softly when he read the price list; they sure
knew how to charge.

He strolled down the steps and onto the gravel driveway and paused and looked about him. To his left the
driveway led off round to the back of the nursing home.
To his right there were several large greenhouses and at
the rear of them were woodlands. One thing was clear;
the nursing home wasn't short of land.

As he walked along the driveway towards the gates,
Ben felt puzzled. Why was that receptionist so snobby?
Okay, he'd been casually dressed and he had a northern
accent, but these days even a person of limited intelli-
gence knew not to judge a book by its cover. She was not
interested in encouraging new customers, but why? Waiting lists could diminish suddenly, especially with elderly
patients.

Ben stopped as he reached the gates and, turning round, looked back at the building. No, dammit,
he thought, he'd come all this way, may as well have a
good scout round the grounds. He strode back towards
the building and followed a path that led to the rear of
the nursing home. After all, that receptionist had refused
him permission to inspect the interior, not the grounds,
Ben grinned, not that he'd asked for it anyway.

Ben's gaze took in the state of the nursing home as he walked along. Upon close inspection the white paint on the building was peeling. The guttering was of the old metal variety, and he could see the rust even from this distance. Even if the nursing home was prosperous, for the reception area had been luxuriously furnished, whoever owned it didn't spend any money on exterior maintenance.

As he turned the corner and reached the rear of the house he could see a rusty-looking fire escape; he wouldn't trust his weight on that. A few yards further along were three large garages. He walked towards them. The doors of two of the garages were closed, but the one nearest to him was open and in it he could just make out the tail end of a grey car.

He quickened his pace and hurried towards the open doors. As he drew closer he saw that the car was a grey Jaguar. Could it be the same one that he and Rosa had seen yesterday? Ben looked about him: not a soul in sight. Taking a deep breath he darted into the garage. He couldn't remember all of the registration number of the earlier car, but he knew that it began with HXT, and that the car had black upholstery, just like this one.

He peered in through the open car window and saw to his surprise that the keys were still in the ignition, which meant…

'Are you aware that you are trespassing?' enquired a deep voice from behind him.

Ben spun round to see a burly-looking man and the receptionist standing at the entrance of the garage.

'You see, I was right about him, Jeff. I told you he was behaving suspiciously,' the receptionist said.

'I've not done anything!' said Ben, 'I was only—'

'Trying to steal a vehicle,' the security guard growled as he strode up to Ben.

Ben tried to edge round him but the guard blocked his path. Ben searched for words, but the right ones wouldn't come. 'Look, I can explain,' he began.

The man took Ben firmly by the arm, 'You come with me, sir,' he said. 'I think that we'd best discuss this further.'

SEVERAL MILES AWAY in the city of York, Veronica Smithson closed the shop door, locked it, and with a sigh of relief waddled back to her desk and eased herself onto her chair, grateful that it was lunchtime. She took a swig from a bottle of water, unwrapped a low-fat energy bar and chewed upon it listlessly. It had been a clammy morning, with the customers few and far between, and even then those that did wander in wanted only itsy bitsy tattoos, like flowers or butterflies on their shoulders, or their bums.

Having finished her biscuit, she got up, washed her hands and stood for a while allowing the cold water to run over her wrists and cool her down. She sighed, as she was not looking forward to this afternoon. In this humid weather the tattooing of bums and the piercing of nipples was hardly the most pleasant of jobs. Then she glanced down at the locked drawer of her desk and her plump cheeks softened into a smile. It was good that she had found something far more rewarding than this.

She gazed at the drawings of tattoos that papered the walls of her shop. Pictures of pythons and galleons and rock stars surrounded her. They were all offered up as examples of her work. Work that she was good at that, work that had taken her many years to perfect. But what had been her reward? Were there any takers? Any punters brave enough these days to commission such work? Not any more.

She leaned over and checked the calendar; next week the rent had to be paid and the week after that the electric was due. Had she relied solely on the profits from her tattoo work she would have been worried, but not now.

Oddly enough, it had been her tattoo work that had led to the source of her additional income. It had started with an infected tattoo, one of the hazards of this business, and it had led to the meeting with 'The Doctor' and incredibly, through him, a new career had opened up for her. Veronica chuckled; what one might call the chance of a lifetime. It was all so simple, all of that money for just a few hours work. Just so long as she kept the tattoo business running, the Inland Revenue happy, and her mouth shut.

She unlocked the drawer, pulled out her bankbook, stared at the figures inside it and felt a warm glow of comfort. Soon she would be able to have that makeover and the liposuction; the doctor had told her that he had the connections. Soon she would be slim and beautiful and look young again, as long as she did exactly as she was told.

She put the bankbook away then reached further into the drawer and pulled out a folder. She switched on the spotlight and examined the documents therein with interest. Then she picked up her pen.

THIRTEEN

Wednesday, midday

'ROSA, WILL YOU STOP staring at the phone. You can't force it to ring; it's not a question of mind over matter. Ben will call you when he's ready.'

'He's not answering his mobile,' Rosa said. 'All I keep getting is the voice mail.'

'Perhaps he's got it on silent. Besides, with mobiles it could be anything.'

Rosa still looked doubtful. 'He should have rung by now.'

Anna scowled at her sister in irritation. Why did she worry about Ben all the time? She'd been a nurse and in the past she'd had to deal with life and death situations? She could never have held down a job in the police force; Rosa was far too soft for that. Anna tried again to reassure her sister. 'Look, it's only just past lunchtime. And, speaking of which, is there any chance of some food around here?'

'Should I make a few sandwiches?' Rosa asked distractedly.

'Somebody should. I've come all over dizzy. I bet my blood sugar's having one of its turns again.' Anna stared at her sister hopefully, then on getting no response, she bustled over to the fridge and the bread bin, and made a start on the sandwiches. She glared at Rosa and said loudly, 'You might at least switch the kettle on.'

Startled, Rosa picked up the kettle and went over to the sink. 'This is not like Ben. I mean, he'd have rung even if he'd not found out anything new. He's always on that mobile of his, keeps it with him in his overcoat pocket, just in case.'

'Precisely!' said Anna. 'So if there'd been an accident you'd be the first to know. Now will you stop panicking? Here, sit down and have a bite to eat. It'll make you feel better. Tell you what; if we've not heard from Ben in a couple of hours I'll get onto that hostelry.'

BEN STOOD AT THE WINDOW of the room and stared out bleakly. Once more he tugged at the handle of the window but it was no use. Judging by the layers of old paint on the frame this window hadn't been opened in donkey's years. Of course, he could take off his shoe and smash through the glass but then where would he go? He looked down at the distant gravel path. By his estimation he was two floors up and that was one hell of a long way to jump. As for attempting to climb down these crumbling walls? He shook his head; that would be suicidal. He turned and surveyed the room again, nothing much here except an old desk and a few chairs. In the corner there was a small washbasin, he had tried the taps and there was running water, so it was unlikely that he would die of thirst.

In exasperation he strode over to the door and tried it yet again even though he knew that it was locked. He leaned against the door and listened. No sound of approaching footsteps, no sound of even a distant tea trolley; in fact, no sound at all.

His stomach rumbled and he looked at his watch: ten past one, lunchtime. He sniffed the air hopefully, but not even the merest whiff of boiled cabbage entered his nostrils. He sighed and walked over to the desk, sat behind it and glared at the locked door. This was not right! How could they do this to him? What had he done that justified him being locked up in here like a prisoner? Were they really going to call in the police and charge him for trespassing and attempted theft? He gave an indignant snort and wondered just how long he would be in the slammer if that were so. As if he'd try to steal that Jaguar? In broad daylight? Were they crazy?

He reached in his jacket pocket for his mobile. Best phone Rosa and tell her what had happened. He would try to be diplomatic about it, so as not to alarm her. He'd just say that he was being detained, well sort of. He searched all his pockets and felt a growing sense of alarm. Where was the bloody thing? Had he lost it? Then he remembered. He cursed loudly, he knew exactly where it was... in his overcoat pocket in his room.

He felt frustration seep through him and he jumped up, marched over to the door and pounded on it again. Nothing. He returned to his chair and placing his elbows on the desk tried to force himself to relax. But it was no use, his mind flitted like a demented wasp, his thoughts darting from door to Rosa to Anna, to the Jaguar, to the old man, and to the root of it all, Miss McGuire. He stared up at the green lamp shade, his mind flashing back over the years, back to the time when he was a schoolboy and Miss McGuire his maths teacher.

Even then Miss McGuire had never seemed young, but by golly, she did know her arithmetic. It wasn't that he liked her. It was not possible to like Miss Macguire, no one ever got that close to her, but he respected her for her discipline and her dedication, and he was grateful to her for her help in the past. If only she'd given him the chance to speak on Sunday. What had happened to the

woman? What had she been doing on that coach? She
had a mind as sharp as a razor; she must surely have had
a reason.

Ben sighed and toyed idly with the handle of the
drawer in the desk. It opened without resistance. He
leaned over and peered inside it, empty except for a startled spider that scurried for cover. What had he expected?
This room looked as if it hadn't been used for years.

Out of boredom he tugged at the lower drawer but it
would not open. Ben scowled down at it. He'd met with
drawers like this before and he knew just what to do with
them. He got out his pocket knife and, leaning down,
began to work on it.

FOURTEEN

Dr White's Consulting Room

CASSIE SAT IN Dr White's consulting room and listened whilst Dave related his symptoms to the doctor. She sat with her hands resting in her lap and her ankles neatly crossed, yet every muscle in her body felt tense. She tried to keep her expression pleasant, if only for Dave's sake, but there was something about Dr White that made her uneasy.

As Cassie studied the young doctor's face she realized that most women would see him as handsome. His features were well balanced, his hair dark and lustrous; his skin, though waxen, was clear. Yet it seemed to her that there was something about the blue eyes that glinted behind his rimless spectacles, a certain coldness in their expression that sent a chill through her. Her gaze drifted down to his generous mouth…a distant memory stirred, and then she knew. That was it, she thought. It was not so much the doctor's appearance, but the coldness of his expression and the sensuous mouth that so reminded her of Rob and her former lover's lips. She gave an involuntary shiver; lips that in a second could turn into a cruel snarl.

The doctor laughed loudly at some remark that Dave had made and a startled Cassie watched, as if by magic, his face become even more attractive, almost beautiful. Yes, beautiful as an angel, some would have said.

Like a fallen angel? The thought leapt into her mind...
like Lucifer?

'I've written you a prescription for some antacids and
some sedatives, Mr Hodgson,' Dr White said as he strode
round the desk and handed it to Dave, 'but please remember when you're taking the sedatives, no champagne, in
fact no alcohol at all.' He winked at Cassie, 'You'll have
to keep an eye on him.' He reached out and touched her
hand and she jerked back sharply. She felt as if an icy
chill had shot through her.

'Thanks, Doc,' Dave said as he got up and made for
the door. 'I'll take it to the chemist's straight away.'

'If things don't improve, come back and we'll investigate further.'

As the door closed behind them, Cassie hesitated. She
looked down the long well-polished corridor and listened.
For a few moments she stood silently and yet no distant
voices reached her ears.

'What's up girl?' Dave asked. He tugged at her sleeve,
'Come on, we can't hang about. We got to get to the
chemist's and chef can't hold the fort forever.' He saw
her tense expression. 'Now what's the matter?'

'It's just,' she trotted along beside him, stiletto heels
tapping loudly on the polished floor, 'that I don't hear
nothin'. This is supposed to be a nursing home, ain't it?
So where the hell is everyone?'

'It is after three; they'll be having their afternoon kip.'

Cassie stopped dead in her tracks, 'Not all of 'em,' she
looked around her. 'I feel as if I've strayed into Sleeping
Beauty's castle. Let's hope that some prince'll come and
kiss them and then they'll all wake up.'

Dave looked irritated, 'Cassie, you've got an over-
worked imagination. Stop harping on, will you. All I

want is to get this medicine down my neck. Now let's move it, shall we?'

'And I'm not sure I trust that medicine that he's prescribed, either,' Cassie protested as she trotted along behind him. 'I'm sure you're not telling me everything.' She saw her husband's back stiffen at this remark, but he increased his pace and made no reply.

Cassie's thoughts returned to Dr White and her sense of unease increased. Was she being silly? Just because he reminded her of her former partner, it didn't mean… What would be in that medicine? Would it help Dave? Or make him worse? Who could she talk to who knew about such things? She racked her memory. There was that Dr Harrison. True, he was a bit doddery, but still practising part-time here at the nursing home, and a good customer at the pub too. He often called in on his way back from the nursing home. What was it that he drank? Double malt whisky, yeah, Glenfiddich. And usually three bags of crisps to go with it. No wonder he looked like a butterball; he didn't half like his grub.

She knew that he had a surgery in the afternoons in the village; perhaps if she begged him he would see her today? She would try. She could phone whilst Dave was in the chemist's and if she got an appointment, she could make the excuse to Dave that she was tired and going to put her feet up when they got home. She gave a wry smile as she looked along the still silent corridor, since napping seemed to be the order of the day.

DR ROBERT HARRISON bustled into his consulting room and looked down at his desk in bewilderment. He was baffled. He knew that he had put them on his desk not more than ten minutes since. Now they'd vanished. He sat down and peered over his glasses at the stacks of papers that covered his desk. Hopefully he lifted up the pile of folders that were in front of him, but still there was no sign. He paused in his search and stared at the connecting door in his office with suspicion...what if nurse...

His intercom buzzed, startling him. He pressed the button.

'Cassie Hodgson to see you, Doctor.'

'Ah yes. Cassie. The young lady from the pub.' He smiled. 'Send her through.'

He pushed the folders aside and made a space in front of him, and then he remembered. Quickly he opened the top drawer, and there they were...his chocolate biscuits. Relief filled him. He should have remembered that he'd put them there for safekeeping and so that nurse wouldn't get to them. He snatched up a biscuit and munched greedily on it. What was wrong with his short-term memory? He should at least remember where he'd put his food.

He saw the door open and he closed the drawer quickly, wiping his fingers on a tissue.

'Ah! Mrs Hodgson, isn't it? Please sit down.' He watched as she perched herself nervously on the edge of the chair opposite him. She was such a jolly young woman when she served him at the pub, but today she looked wary and ill at ease. He smiled reassuringly, 'Now, my dear, what can I do for you?' He polished his spectacles and waited.

Cassie cleared her throat and began, 'Thanks for squeezing me in, Doctor. When your receptionist said you had a cancellation, I lied and said it was an emergency.'

'Really? Now that was most selfish. As I recall, you're not even one of my patients. However, if you are

in pain?' He watched as the young woman's face turned
bright pink.

'It's not me that I've come to see you about, Dr Harrison. I know that I'm not one of your customers, er sorry,
I mean patients. Nor is my Dave, my husband, Mr Hodgson, that is. But he has this problem, see.'

Dr Harrison leaned back in his chair and wondered
why husband Dave had not put in an appearance. Nevertheless, he nodded at Cassie encouragingly.

'You see, we've just been to see Dr White up at the
nursing home and he's given him a prescription but—'

He leaned forward, 'Dr White? He's a colleague of
mine, a fine doctor.' He stopped as he saw the fear in
Cassie's eyes. He probed gently, 'What exactly is the
matter, my dear?'

Cassie sniffed, 'It's just, I don't know, he's prescribed
this stuff for Dave and he's taken some already, but it
don't seem to do no good. I don't trust the stuff. I'm worried sick, and my Dave, he daren't say nothing because...'
She hesitated then blurted, 'I reckon my Dave knows a
heck of a lot more about certain things and the goings on
round here than he tells me about.' She opened her bag,
got out a tissue and dabbed at her eyes.

Dr Harrison toyed with his pen and studied her carefully. 'What could possibly be wrong with Dr White, my
dear? He does a fine job up at the nursing home. I do a bit
of work up there myself, as you well know,' he chuckled.
'At my age it helps to keep the old grey matter ticking
over.'

Cassie looked at him, 'But you're only up there part-time, you're not there all day like Dr White, and it's him,
or the medicine that he's prescribed for my Dave, what's
worrying me.' She hesitated and then said cautiously, 'I
just wondered if you could give me something safe for

Dave's stomach ache, just in case. Something that would help. I don't want to cause any bother.'

Dr Harrison pursed his lips, 'It's probably just a case of severe dyspepsia.'

Cassie shook her head, 'Dave did have a peptic ulcer once. It was a few years back.'

Dr Harrison raised his eyebrows, 'Really?' He looked thoughtful. 'As I'm not your GP I can only issue you with emergency medication.' He got up and ambled over to a cupboard that he unlocked. From it he took a small bottle and handed it to her. 'But this might be of some help. And I have to say, my dear, that I'm sure your suspicions about Dr White are unfounded. It would be most unwise to repeat them to anyone without absolute proof. As I'm sure you are aware, such remarks could be interpreted as being scandalous.' He paused and his cherubic face creased into a grin and he chuckled loudly, 'But then no harm's done. I know its just over-anxiety about your husband's health.' He touched her arm. 'Although on a more personal level, I would recommend that you take up yoga, it might help you to relax.'

Cassie put the bottle into her handbag and got to her feet. 'Thanks ever so, Doctor.' She made for the door, 'I feel less worried already.' She smiled at him. 'As for the yoga, yes, I'll have a go at that too, just as soon as I've got my Dave sorted.'

His smile vanished the instant that he closed the door. He went back to the cupboard and relocked it. That ought to do the trick, he thought. He hoped that she'd got the message about the dangers of gossiping. What were things coming to when people couldn't trust doctors?

He returned to his desk, sat down, opened the top drawer and ate some more biscuits. When he'd finished he wiped his hands and mouth, and then he unlocked an-

other drawer. With a smile of satisfaction he brought out
a large manila envelope and examined its contents with
interest.

Wednesday, Nursing Home Security office,
late afternoon

BEN'S CAPTOR SAT at the reception desk and for the third
time that day keyed in the usual number. 'Hello? Yeah,
it's Jeff Stokes from security. I've been trying to reach
you all afternoon but I couldn't get through. We've got a
problem here, yeah, an intruder. I caught him snooping
around the Jag. So I put him upstairs in the old accounts
room. I told him we might get him for trying to nick the
Jag and for trespass, just to scare him a bit, but he seems
harmless enough. He's an oldie, so I don't think he's top
brass or anything. I thought I'd better tell you before I
let him go. Did I get his name? Yep, I've got it all written
down in front of me.' He picked up a sheet of paper and
read out loud, 'Mr Ben Hammond, retired, lives in West
Yorkshire, in Halifax.' Jeff hesitated. 'Do you want his
full address? No? Okay then, that's it, boss. You heard
right. Hammond, Ben Hammond's the name.'

Jeff stopped short and listened to the agitated instructions coming from the other end of the phone. 'Okay,
okay. No worries. He's still locked up in there. Yes, right,
I'll do that. Special tea and biscuits, and a nice humble
apology.' Jeff grinned, 'That'll sort him. You'll be here
tomorrow? Bye.'

Jeff put down the phone and walked over to the mini-
kitchen that was in the corner of the room. Why on earth
did the boss want to keep the old boy here? He shrugged;
his was not to reason why. He switched on the kettle and
prepared the special tea.

BEN EASED HIS POCKET KNIFE into the top of the locked drawer and applied some pressure. Nothing. He slid the knife along the edge trying for more leverage.

The blade started to bend and he stopped. Breaking the blade would do him no good at all. Patience was needed. He got up, went over to the window and looked out. Not a soul about. Where was everybody? Again he tried to open the window, but it was useless. He walked across the room to the sink. No sign of a glass, or cup or anything, and he was thirsty. He turned on the tap and a stream of brown water spluttered out. It must have been some time since this was used. Ben waited until the water ran clear, then cupping his hands under the tap, drank from them. That was better. it was not as if the room was warm but it smelt of old wood and the air was dry and dusty.

He returned to the desk and stared down at the locked drawer. He didn't think that there'd be anything of value in it, but then again the drawer was locked and he wanted it open. He was not going to let a simple thing like that get the better of him. He picked up his penknife again; opening the drawer would help pass the time.

Five minutes later, with the faint sound of breaking wood, the lock on the drawer surrendered. Ben beamed in satisfaction, folded his knife and put it away. Gently he eased the drawer out until it was half open, then, full of curiosity, peered at the pile of yellowed papers that were in it.

He was about to lift the papers out of the drawer when he heard a distant door slam. He froze and listened intently. Yes, he had heard right. He could hear footsteps approaching. He closed the drawer, sat still and waited.

FIFTEEN

Wednesday 5.30 p.m.

DAVE WAS SEATED at the kitchen table eating a ham sandwich when Cassie returned. He looked up in surprise. 'Where did you spring from? I thought you were taking a nap.'

Cassie slipped off her jacket and put her handbag on the table. 'Changed my mind, didn't I? I thought I'd best get a second opinion from old Doc Harrison.'

'What? About me, you mean?'

Cassie fished in her handbag, brought out the bottle of medicine that Dr Harrison had given her and placed it in front of Dave. 'He said for you to take this.'

He picked up the bottle and examined it. 'Doesn't say what it is. Besides, I've already taken some of that stuff that Dr White prescribed and I'm feeling a bit better.' He gestured at the sandwiches. 'Chef left those out for us; they're very tasty.'

'Good, should tide us over 'til suppertime.' Cassie looked at her husband and felt a sense of relief; maybe soon he would be all right. 'I'm glad that you are feeling better, darlin', just as long as that stuff helps,' she walked over to the telephone and studied the message pad.

Dave frowned, 'Look, sit down a minute, love, and have a drink and something to eat before you start on that. Anyway, I've already dealt with the laundry query.

And I've agreed to a late delivery on the soft drinks. We can manage with what we've got for a while.'

Cassie said sharply, 'It says here that a Mrs Hammond phoned. Wasn't that the wife of our guest from last night?'

'Yeah, she and another woman were with him yesterday, only they left. I was a bit surprised at that, him booking a single room. It seems he hasn't phoned home when he should have, the naughty boy. I went up and checked his room but he's not there.'

'Then where is he, Dave? Last I remember he'd gone for a walk this morning, but that's over six hours ago.'

'Stop panicking, love. He's probably been back here and got a taxi while we were out.'

'But he should have checked out,' Cassie said.

Dave got up, put his arms around her and kissed the nape of her neck tenderly, 'Who knows what the man's got up to? He might well be having an away day from his missus.' He looked down at her, 'Not that I'd ever want an away day from you, lover.'

With a smile she brushed him aside and continued reading. 'Chef says that the woman sounded anxious, that she kept on saying that he'd promised to phone her.'

'She's fussing about nothing.'

Cassie looked thoughtful then she turned to Dave, her face taut with worry, 'You don't think? It's not another one?'

'Now don't be silly. That Hammond feller was fit and well, not frail like—'

'What's that supposed to mean, Dave? Frail like what? What do you know?'

He said quickly, 'Nothing, nothing at all. You've got to trust me.' Cassie stared at him for a long time then said quietly, 'How do you trust someone that won't tell the truth?'

'Why do you always jump to the worst conclusions?'

'Because I hate what's going on around here.' She marched over to the door and picked up a bunch of keys.

'Where are you going?'

'To check out Mr Hammond's room again and see what I can find.'

CASSIE WALKED INTO Ben Hammond's room and looked around. Claire was certainly a good little worker; everything was clean and tidy. On an impulse Cassie slid back the wardrobe door and her sense of unease increased, for hanging inside it was a dark-brown overcoat. She reached in, grabbed the coat, and checked the pockets. Two packets of tissues, half a tube of mints, and one mobile phone. For a long time she stared at these items in silence. Most people would not go out for a stroll in October without a coat, though this morning had been mild. But to go off for the whole day without an overcoat and phone was careless to say the least. She switched on the phone and, as she'd thought, there were several messages waiting, all coming from what she presumed was Mrs Hammond's number.

She hurried down the stairs and went back into the kitchen.

Dave looked at her. 'Is he back?'

She shook her head. 'No sign of him, but his coat was still in the wardrobe and this,' she held out the mobile, 'was in the pocket.'

'That rules out him pulling a fast one on us,' Dave said as he picked up the mobile. 'No one would leave their coat and phone behind if they were planning on doing a runner.'

Cassie walked across the room and picked up the message pad again. Dave followed her and put his arms about her reassuringly, 'Try not to worry, love. It'll all work out.'

She leaned against him. 'Chef told her that we'd call back. We've got to do something. A man's missing and his poor wife's…' She picked up the phone book. 'I know, I'll start by phoning the hospitals, deal with the worst-case scenario first, then once I know all's clear there, I'll call Mrs Hammond and try and calm her down.'

Wednesday 5.50 p.m.

'HERE, HAVE ANOTHER CUP of tea,' Anna said as she placed the mug in front of Rosa.

Rosa looked irritated. 'Why is it that people think that the cure for everything is a cup of tea?' Her gaze returned to the telephone.

Anna watched her sister and tried to control her impatience. So okay, her brother-in-law was late in phoning Rosa, but there was no reason for her to sit there as if mesmerized.

'Will you stop staring at the bloody phone?' Anna blurted. 'You've called the man at the hostelry and he's told you they'll get back to you as soon as they can.'

'We all know about folk that are going to call us back, and I'm not holding my breath,' Rosa said. She started to reach for the phone.

'Rosa! Will you leave it alone?'

'I was going to phone the hospital, in case Ben's had a funny turn.'

'Then your line won't be clear. You gave the man at the pub this number and if you start phoning round he won't be able to get through. What we might need is a

list of the numbers of the A&E Hospitals in the North
Yorkshire area. We could ask directory enquiries,' Anna
held out her mobile, 'Use my phone if you like.'

Rosa looked doubtful, 'Better not,' she said. 'I'll wait a
bit longer 'til I've heard from the pub.' She got up, walked
over to the living-room window and looked out.

Anna fought back her own sense of unease. In police
terms, being a few hours late in phoning home was nothing to worry about. People often had memory lapses, or
something unforeseen had turned up. Unforeseen? Something niggled at the back of Anna's mind. What if Ben
had found Miss McGuire? The darker side of her mind
kicked in. Or worse, what if he'd found the remains of
Miss... She dismissed that thought briskly. Be practical,
woman, stay focused. It was not that she disliked Ben.
He was a stubborn old goat to be sure, he was also ar-
gumentative, and there'd been times when she stormed
out of this house unable to tolerate any more jibes from
him, especially since her divorce. But she had to admit
that he'd been a good husband to her sister. She stopped
short. Why was she thinking of him in the past tense?
She joined Rosa at the window. 'It's no good looking.
Even Ben can't walk that distance.'

'I know, I just thought he might have got a lift.' Rosa
turned away from the window and walked back to her
armchair, disappointment etched clearly on her face.

Anna followed her and touched her arm. 'It'll be all
right love. You know what your Ben's like. He'll turn up
like the proverbial bad penny.'

Rosa's lips trembled. 'Something's gone wrong. I can
feel it.'

Anna sighed and said, 'All right then. I'll just wash
these mugs and clear away, and then I'll try phoning the

pub again.' She looked at her watch, 'It's close to six. They should have got back to us by now.'

ROSA SANK DEEPER into the armchair and watched her sister clear away, although her mind was focused on Ben. Where had he got to? Something had happened. Had he got into an argument with the landlord and made some wild accusations? Once Ben's temper was up he often let his mouth run away with his brain. What if he'd found something that he didn't like? He was not the type to stay silent. What if he'd found Miss McGuire? What if he couldn't use his phone? What if he'd got involved in some kind of scam? The 'what ifs' spun like a kaleidoscope through her head until she gripped the arms of the chair and forced common sense to the fore. There had to be a practical answer. There always was. And it wasn't doing her any good letting her imagination run away with her.

Throughout their marriage Ben had always phoned when he said he would. She smiled gently; even back in the days when she was a young nurse and they were courting, Ben was always reliable. She'd been the one who was often late. She became involved with her patients and she would not leave them when they needed her.

Ben had understood. 'The strong can take care of themselves,' he'd said, 'but that doesn't mean we can forget about the weak.' She smiled again as she thought about her big blustering husband. All bark and no bite, as they said in these parts. But what if her Ben had become weak? He could be lying out there in the middle of nowhere. She thought about the possibility of a heart attack. She knew that first aid as soon as possible in such cases was crucial. And her Ben so loved his food.

The phone rang. Rosa snatched it up eagerly. 'Mrs

Hammond speaking. Is he—?' She listened. 'No sign of him, you say?' She brushed her hand across her forehead. 'Yes, that is worrying. I'll phone the hospitals. You've done that already? That's some relief. That is kind of you, but I'm still worried. I'll get up there as soon as I can.' She looked at her sister, who was signalling urgently from the kitchen doorway. 'Oh, and just in case you need to reach me, I'll give you my sister's mobile number.' She gave the number then stood up. Her jaw tightened as she put down the phone. She looked across at Anna. 'Right then! Go and get your car out. I'll have no peace now until I find my Ben.'

SIXTEEN

CASSIE PUT DOWN THE PHONE, chewed on her fingernail, and for the first time in years wished that she'd never stopped smoking.

'What did she say, then?' asked Dave.

'That's she's coming up here to look for him, as of now.'

'Oh Lord,' Dave groaned. 'This is going to turn out to be a right bloody circus. Where the hell has the man got to? He can't just disappear.'

'Why not? There are plenty of others that did. And why did no one ask after them, eh?'

'What are you going on at me for? I know nothing.'

'Yes, you do! You just turn a blind eye, like ninety per cent of the population. None of my business, they say. And that excuses everything.'

'They're quite right. We have to look after ourselves.'

'Until something happens to us. Then what?'

Dave got to his feet and said angrily, 'What do you expect me to do? I'm not Superman. And I'm not responsible for what goes on up there.'

'Just do something! A man's gone missing. He's a guest of ours, it's nearly dark, and his wife's forming a search party and is on her way up here. You heard me say that you'd look for him, and it might be good if you were to start right now.'

'It'll be hopeless trying to find someone on—' Dave's face turned white and he winced.

'Dave! What's the matter? What is it?'

'Me gut. All this rowing don't help.'

Cassie watched him with concern. She picked up the medicine bottle from the table and handed it to him. 'Try this. Hang on, I'll get a spoon.'

Dave unscrewed the cap. 'It doesn't say what dosage.'

She gave him the spoon, 'Just try a spoonful then.'

She watched as her husband took the medication and the colour slowly returned to his face. 'Better?'

'A bit. It was like a knife cutting into me.'

Cassie put her arm round him. 'Sit down for a minute. You sure you're okay?'

He nodded.

She studied him for a while then went to her handbag and got out her car keys. 'Shan't be long.'

'Where are you going?'

'To look for our Mr Hammond. I thought I'd drive round the back roads and see if—'

'I'll do that; you go relieve Claire from the bar. It's near her home time now.' Dave got up and took the keys from her.

'You sure?'

'Stop looking so worried. I'll be fine.'

'You'd best take this with you then. It's Mr Hammond's sister-in-law's mobile number. You can ring straight through if you find him.'

'Will do.' He shoved the scrap of paper into his pocket. 'Better get a move on then.'

DAVE STRODE OUT of the pub, got in the car and slammed the door. Women!

He sat for a while in silence, his lips tight with anger. What was it about women that they felt that they had to get tangled up in other people's lives? Why were they always so emotional, as well as being downright nosy? Why couldn't they get on with living their own lives instead of worrying about everyone else? So now here he sat and instead of being able to nurse his sick stomach and get on with his job, he'd have to cruise around the back roads looking for some daft old sod, who for reasons unknown had decided to bugger off by himself.

He turned on the ignition and moved off, switching the headlights onto full beam so as to be able to see in the ditches at the sides of the road. Although the stabbing sensation had gone from his stomach it was now succeeded by a kind of burning feeling as if the whole of his gut was on fire. He pulled a face and checked his pockets, as he'd feared he'd left his medicine at home. His mobile was in his pocket though; he checked again, two mobiles? Then he remembered; one of them was Mr Hammond's.

The car crawled along whilst Dave peered through the wind-screen at the hedgerows and ditches. It got dark early now; not even a fox or a badger was to be seen. He knew it was impossible to find anything in the dark, especially in wooded areas like this. Surely it would be better to wait until daylight?

The burning sensation increased and he hunched over the wheel. At this moment all that he wanted was to get home to his medicine and to Cassie. He looked again at the two phones, his was black; Mr Hammond's was silver. In the half-light the silver shape gleamed at him. Tempting him. What harm could it do? He rummaged in his pockets, found the bit of paper that Cassie had given him then picked up the silver mobile. He keyed in the number for Mr Hammond's sister-in-law and texted a short message. It read: Everything okay. Will call soon. Love, Ben. He held the phone until he was sure that the message had been sent, then switched it off and returned it to his pocket.

Dave dismissed the feeling of guilt with impatience. All that he had done was to ease the woman's fear, and maybe buy a bit more time.

The burning in his stomach increased, seeming now to spread throughout his diaphragm. He needed some more medicine, something to ease the pain. With all thoughts of guilt and Ben Hammond forgotten, Dave pressed his foot down on the accelerator and headed for home.

Wednesday, early evening

BEN LISTENED INTENTLY, he had definitely heard footsteps. They were coming nearer. For a moment he wondered what he should do. Should he pull out a drawer, hide behind the door, clonk whoever it was on the head with it, and do a runner? The idea was tempting, but what if whoever it was turned out to be his rescuer? Ben pondered. No, it couldn't be a rescuer; if it was they would be much more stealthy in their approach. These footsteps sounded confident and…what was that? He could hear the rattle of crockery combined with the faint jingling of keys. He got to his feet and went to the door. As he did so his stomach grumbled loudly, reminding him that lunchtime was long since past and that a diet of tap water was not aiding his digestion.

The door opened slowly and the security man, bearing a tray, greeted him. 'This is for you,' he said as he came into the room. He thrust the tray into Ben's hands, and turned to lock the door, 'In case you were hungry.'

Ben gazed down at the tray; on it was a large teapot with milk and sugar, and alongside that was a plate piled high with biscuits, some slab cake and some parkin.

Without speaking he walked over to the desk and placed the tray upon it.

The man followed him. 'Look, my name's Jeff and I'm sorry to have to keep you here like this, but we've had so many prowlers around the nursing home lately and we don't want to put our patients at risk.'

'I wasn't even in the vicinity of a patient,' Ben blurted. 'All I was doing was having a good look at that grey Jaguar. What was wrong with that?'

'Cars like that cost a lot of money; you were leaning inside it, about to take the keys. From where we stood, we were sure you wanted to steal it.'

'Then you should have called the police. Where are they, by the way?'

The man shrugged. 'That's not up to me. That'll be up to the boss, but you did know you had no right to be there.'

Ben felt his temper rising, 'You can't go locking people up just because they're having a bit of a walk-about.'

'You should do your walkabouts in parks and not on other people's premises. My instructions are that you should stay here until…er…somebody comes to talk to you.' He walked back towards the door.

'Can't I at least make a phone call?' Ben pleaded.

The man reached automatically towards his pocket, then hesitated, his face reddening. 'I'll have to ask about that.' He gestured at the tray. 'You drink your tea before it gets cold.' He opened the door, slid through it quickly and locked it again as Ben ran across the room.

Ben heard the click of the lock as he reached it. He swore loudly and for a while he pounded on the door in frustration, but he knew that it was no use. Slowly he walked back to the desk and eyed the tray. The fruit-

cake looked tempting and he sure could do with a decent
cuppa; might as well make the best of it. Resignedly he
sat down and poured the tea.

IN THE CORRIDOR outside the locked room Jeff stood
mopping his forehead and listening to the hammering.
That had been close, he'd almost gone and lent the bloke
his mobile; then the shit would have hit the fan. He just
hoped that the old boy would drink the tea, then at least
he wouldn't be hammering on the door all night.

He tried not to think too deeply about having to lace
someone's tea. The drug was harmless in moderation and
besides; he didn't dare disobey the boss's instructions.
The last thing that he needed was to lose this cushy job.
The money was terrific and the work was a doddle. It just
wasn't wise to ask too many questions.

He thought about his partner waiting at home. Stella
always wanted to know everything. She'd be sure to nag
him like hell when he got back because he'd had to do
some overtime, but as he kept reminding her, she liked
the extra money. Stella always wanted more money,
and now she'd got this grand idea about buying a bigger
house.

Jeff sighed as he walked along the corridor. With the
new baby on the way, their flat did seem cramped, but
if Stella wanted a bigger place she'd have to put up with
the fact that he worked odd hours, and stop being so nosy
about what went on up here.

As he rounded the corner and reached the lift, Jeff
stood for a while and listened yet again. Yep, it was quiet
now, which meant that the old boy was enjoying his tea
and cakes. Jeff smiled; soon the drug would kick in and
the old man would be in the land of Nod, and that meant
a peaceful night.

Jeff looked at his watch, he would look in on the man in an hour or so, perhaps take him a blanket, and then hey ho, he could toddle off home to his lovely Stella.

AFTER A WHILE Ben stopped pounding on the door and with a sigh of frustration sat down, drank his tea, and eyed the door that imprisoned him. He knew that the lock was difficult to open but he would have to try, even though the only tool that he had with him was his old pocket knife.

Thoughtfully he poured himself another cup of tea, took a large gulp and then took a bite from the slab cake. He sat back relishing the taste of the rich, moist fruit, and felt a sense of enjoyment seep through him. That felt better, he hadn't realized how hungry he had been.

As he drank the tea he focused on the door and thought back to his school days, as he tried to remember what he'd learned about locks in his metalwork classes. He stared again at the old-fashioned lock, which for some reason now seemed blurred. He fished inside his jacket pocket and brought out his spectacles, put them on; still blurred. Had he got the wrong glasses? He removed them, rubbed his eyes and thought about the yellowed papers that were in the bottom drawer. He'd been meaning to have a look at them and then there had been this interruption with the... he stifled a yawn and leaned forward. He felt tired; it was so hard to think, perhaps another cup of tea might... He began to pour, then stopped and with an unsteady hand pushed the tray away and rested his head on the desk. He'd just have a quick five minutes, he thought....

ROSA HEARD THE CAR STOP outside and looked anxiously at the door. She was pulling on her coat as Anna came into the room. 'Ready to go?' she asked.

Anna shook her head, 'You want the good news or the bad news?'

'The good news, for crying out loud. I don't think I can take any more that's bad.'

Anna waved her mobile in front of Rosa's face. 'Calm down, I've got a text from your Ben.'

Rosa let out a soft sigh of relief, 'What's he say?'

Anna squinted at her mobile and read. 'Everything okay. Will call soon. Love, Ben.'

'Is that all? That is it?'

'Yep,' said Anna. 'So we're not going nowhere. We've just got to wait until later. ''Course we don't know when soon is. It could be any time.'

'All right, don't go on. Still, a message is better than nothing. At least we know he's okay and there's no need to rush. You said something about bad news; what's that?'

Anna frowned and glanced down at the car keys that she was clutching, 'I'm a bit bothered about my old run-about. I started her up just now and she made a knocking noise. It's not like her, but we did put in a lot of mileage yesterday and, like us, she is getting on a bit.'

'That is worrying,' Rosa said. 'Should we take it along to the garage and have it checked? I mean, we might as well, whilst we're waiting.'

Anna looked at her watch, 'I'll not get a mechanic at this time of night.'

'First thing tomorrow then, and I'll pay for any repairs. That's what Ben would want.'

'Now don't start on about money, Rosa. It might just be a hiccup, and there's nothing we can do about it to-night. Either way we're going to have to wait until tomorrow.' Anna flopped down on the sofa and reached for the television remote. She looked at her sister's worried face,

'Although I think I'd better stay the night with you, just to be on the safe side?'

'Yeah, of course you must.'

Anna licked her lips and eyed the kitchen door. 'Didn't you mention earlier that you'd got some of that sponge cake left over?'

'That's right. Should be enough for two slices.' Rosa took off her coat and headed for the kitchen. 'That'll do nicely for supper.'

SEVENTEEN

Thursday

ANNA SAT IN HER CAR and revved the engine again. She looked up at her sister. 'What do you think?'

'Sounds perfectly all right to me,' said Rosa, who was standing in the driveway. 'You have checked your oil and water?'

Anna nodded.

'And your tyres?'

'Rosa! You don't get knocking sounds from your tyres, not unless one's fallen off. I think we'd have noticed that, don't you?'

'Don't get cocky with me.' Rosa stared at the car and thought for a moment. 'What do you think? Will it be all right? Or should we take it down to the garage and get it checked.'

'It's not knocking now. It might just have been a bit of grit. If we take it down to the garage they'll not deal with it straight away, we might have to wait a couple of hours.'

Rosa looked anxious. 'But we should be setting off for that pub.'

'Tell you what,' Anna reached for her mobile. 'Let's try and short circuit this. I've got an old mate who's a mechanic, I could get him to come and have a look-see.'

With an impatient sigh Rosa watched Anna key in a number. Nothing seemed to be going right lately. Still no more news from Ben. What on earth was the man up to? She stifled a yawn, her eyes felt gritty, and her head ached. She'd spent a sleepless night worrying how Ben was, what he'd found out, and how they'd managed to get themselves involved in this Miss McGuire thing.

'That's sorted, then,' Anna said as she switched off her mobile. 'Stan won't promise what time he'll get here, but I know him. He'll do his best to come as soon as he can.

Rosa eyed her sister with suspicion. She knew quite a few of Anna's police pals. She said cautiously, 'That does mean he's planning on coming today, doesn't it? I mean, you did say that the matter was urgent?'

Anna's face reddened, 'Well no, you can't say that an intermittent knocking sound on a car is urgent. That wouldn't be true.'

'I meant the situation with Ben, not the bloody car.'

'Calm down, will you. No, I did not mention that. Did you want me to tell everyone that for some reason your Ben's gone missing and that you're going looking for him?'

Rosa gave an exasperated sigh and marched back into the house. Anna got out of the car and followed her into the kitchen. 'Now what are you doing?'

'Making up some sandwiches and a flask for the journey. Might as well. We can't sit out there in the car all day waiting for your friend to turn up. In fact, I was thinking about phoning the station and finding out if there's a train that'll get us there?'

'Now you're being silly. You know that pub's in the middle of nowhere. There can't be that much wrong with my car. Stan will soon fix it when he gets here.'

'Yes, but that is the big question, isn't it. When will he get here?'

'He's not going to be all day.' Anna hesitated and looked doubtful. 'Could be early afternoon though.'

'That is not good enough!' Rosa shouted as she slammed the ham down onto the buttered slices. She waved the bread knife at Anna. 'And if anything has happened to my Ben...'

'Just you be careful with that.' Anna stared warily at her sister then got out her phone again and keyed in a number. 'That you, Stan? Sorry to bother you again. Yeah, look I think I've managed to sort that problem with my car. Yeah, I know how busy you are. Well, I think I'm going to chance it. Yes, I'm sure. Okay then, catch you later, bye.'

Rosa paused in her work and looked at her. 'Now what have you gone and done?'

'Finish making up the flask and sandwiches, then we'll go.'

'But what about—'

'I've cancelled Stan. You don't want to be hanging around waiting, and after all that knocking sound might be nothing. We'll just have to go for it.'

'If you're sure?'

'Look, if push comes to shove I've got my AA card, so don't worry. I'm just going to nip down to the petrol station and fill up. Shan't be long.'

'Okay then.'

Anna looked back at her as she opened the door. 'Try not to look so stressed, Rosa. Soon we'll have all systems at "go".'

EIGHTEEN

Thursday morning

CASSIE EASED THE bedroom door open and tiptoed into the darkened room. As she approached the bed she listened to Dave's breathing, glad that at least he was resting. She looked at him then placed the mug of tea gently on the bedside table. Reassured, she was about to turn away when a hand clasped her wrist.

'Where do you think you're off to, missy?' In the half-light Dave squinted up at her. 'Why are you prowling around in the middle of the night?'

Cassie smiled down at him, 'It's not the middle of the night. It's daytime, lover. Least it was when I got up.' She walked over to the window and drew back the curtains and Dave screwed up his eyes as the sunlight streamed in.

He pulled himself up in the bed, 'Bloody hell,' he muttered grumpily 'Where's the alarm clock gone? Why didn't it ring? Why the hell didn't you wake me?'

'The alarm clock didn't ring because I hid it. You've been up most of the night with your gut ache, and I thought I'd best let you rest once you'd gone off. There's no need to look at me like that. I can manage! Now you drink that tea and calm down a bit.'

She walked back to him, sat down on the edge of the bed and watched whilst he drank his tea. After a while she said, 'Do you feel any better?'

Dave didn't speak. He put the mug back on the bedside table and got out of bed. He swayed for a moment then headed for the bathroom. Seconds later there came the sounds of vomiting.

An anxious Cassie hurried into the bathroom and watched as he wiped his mouth with a towel. He turned towards her and leaned heavily against the sink. 'Must have been last night's cocoa.' He held out the towel, 'It sort of looks that colour.'

'Dave! I'm phoning the doctor right away.'

'Stop panicking, love, it's just an upset stomach, I'll be all right in a while.'

'You're going straight back to bed. No more arguing.'

White faced, Dave looked at her. He seemed about to protest then he changed his mind and stumbled back into bed.

Cassie watched him and tried to control a growing anxiety; although Dave had taken Dr Harrison's medication, he didn't seem to be getting any better. She had to stay calm. She spoke in a matter-of-fact manner. 'You just rest there, darlin'. I'll bring you a bowl, just in case.'

Dave flopped back against the pillows. 'I can't leave you to cope on your own downstairs. Get young Claire to do a bit of overtime. Tell her I'll sort it with her later.'

Cassie smiled at him reassuringly, although she doubted whether they could afford the extra wages if Dave was sick. Perhaps she could negotiate with Claire and give her extra time off once Dave was better. Aloud she said, 'Yeah, I'll talk to her; I'm sure she'll oblige. Now don't you move a muscle. I'm going to call the doc. I'll bring you that bowl and some tissues.' She reached the door and called, 'Back in two ticks.'

Dave lay back against the pillows, wiped the sweat from his forehead, and stared blankly up at the ceiling.

He listened to the sound of Cassie's high heels tip tapping along the corridor then gradually fading away. He frowned; in a decently furnished inn you shouldn't be able to hear footsteps walking along corridors. He'd already been on to the brewery about the furnishings, but they, as ever, were being tight fisted. Still, he would have another go at them once the takings improved. The sharp pain returned and he curled up into a foetal position, as that seemed to help. After a while the pain eased and he relaxed. Try not to think of it. Try and focus on the business. His business. His and Cassie's. That was all that mattered. Cassie deserved the best. The pain struck again. Dave winced and his lips tightened. He eased himself into a sitting position and looked at the bedside table. Where the hell had she put that bloody medicine?

Downstairs, Cassie stood by the phone and pressed the redial button yet again. She listened to the ringing tone whilst her fingers drummed an impatient tattoo on the wall. After a while the ringing stopped and a recorded voice cut in asking her to leave a message. Cassie sighed and said. 'This is Mrs Hodgson, of the Full Moon Inn on Green Lane. Could Dr White please call me back as soon as possible as my husband has been ill with stomach pains throughout the night. My number is 07854 6745.' She replaced the receiver and looked doubtful. She had never trusted answer phones, and she disliked leaving urgent messages on them. If Dr White didn't call her back within the hour she would try again.

She picked up a bowl, a box of tissues, an air freshener, and went back upstairs. She tried to force back the fear that was making her edgy and to use her common sense. Dave's gut problems could just be an attack of food poisoning. Maybe she was jumping to the wrong conclusion, but should the pain go on all night, especially when Dave had only had a sandwich the night before? She reached their bedroom door and hesitated. Had she done the right thing in phoning the doc? Wouldn't it have been better if she'd called an ambulance? A mental picture of a blue light flashing, the sound of a siren, and paramedics bounding up the stairs sprang into her mind and she cringed as she thought about Dave's reaction to that scenario. She nodded; she had done the right thing.

She opened the door and, forcing a smile, went in. 'Here we are then; wasn't that long was I? The doc will be here soon.' She looked down at her husband as he lay against the pillows. The shadows under his eyes seemed to have deepened and his skin had taken on a yellowish tinge.

He scowled up at her. 'Wouldn't need no doctor would I, if I could find the bleeding medicine. Where'd you put it?'

Cassie said quietly, 'Where you left it at six o'clock this morning, on the bathroom shelf over the sink.'

Dave made as if to get out of bed.

'Stay there, lover, I'll get it.' She hurried into the bathroom and picked up the small brown bottle that Dr Harrison had given her. She sat down on the bed and poured out a spoonful. 'Open wide.'

Dave swallowed then flopped back against the pillows. 'That help any?'

He licked his lips, 'I'm not sure. They do say some medicines take a while to work.'

Cassie returned the bottle to the bathroom. 'It's in there in case you need some more.' She thought that as Dave had been taking the stuff since yesterday, it should have some effect by now, but she said, 'Here's your bowl and tissues.' She picked up the air freshener and went into the bathroom, 'I'll just have a quick spray round.'

'Sorry about snapping at you, love,' Dave called. 'But the pain was getting…'

Cassie came out of the bathroom and leaned over him, 'I know, I know, that's okay, darlin'.' She kissed him gently on his forehead. 'We'll soon have you better, you'll see.'

Dave stroked her cheek, 'Everything all right downstairs?' Cassie nodded.

'Good.' He managed a smile. 'I take it that by now the old boy, the happy wanderer, has managed to come back into the fold?'

Cassie looked blank, 'Crikey! I'd forgotten all about him.' Another thought came into her mind. Where the hell had that man's wife got to? Hadn't the woman said last night that they were setting off straight away? She glanced at her watch. It was almost midday.

'Cassie! What's up, girl?'

'Sorry, love. I don't know if that man's returned. Maybe he's slipped back in here this morning, but I'll check and make sure.' She headed for the door.

'When you find him don't forget to give him back his mobile,' Dave ordered. 'And don't forget to bill him for an extra night as well.'

Cassie slid through the door, then with a grin looked back and saluted. 'Yes, sir! Right, sir! Three bags full, sir!' She giggled and the door closed behind her.

In spite of his discomfort a faint smile flickered across Dave's face. 'Cheeky little thing,' he muttered, 'where would I be without her?'

NINETEEN

Thursday, midday

CASSIE FINISHED SERVING her customer then hurried out
of the bar and checked the answer phone again. Still no
message from Dr White. She looked at her watch, not
quite an hour as yet, so give it another five minutes. She
returned to the bar and found Dr Harrison waiting.

'Ah! There you are, young lady. I was almost getting
ready to serve myself.'

'Sorry about that, Doctor. What would you like?'

'A double malt please, and a packet of barbeque crisps
to still the hunger pangs until lunchtime.'

Whilst Cassie served him her mind was racing. Perhaps Dr Harrison would take a look at Dave, but get
the man his order first. She gave him his drink and
fussed nervously with the towelling bar mats whilst she
watched him consume his Scotch and munch happily on
the crisps.

Again she looked at the clock. It was now over an hour.
She could wait no longer. 'Doctor Harrison,' she blurted,
'can you help me?'

His round eyes opened wide. 'Whatever is it that you
want, my dear?' He beamed, 'I'd be useless as a barman.'

'It's not that, Doctor, but my husband has been ill all
night. I don't know what it is. Maybe it's food poisoning.
I left a message for Doctor White over an hour ago, but
he's not rung back, and I'm so—'

'Would that be the same person you came to see me about yesterday?' Dr Harrison's bright eyes gleamed at her. 'I seem to remember giving you some medication for him.'

'Yes, that's right,' Cassie hesitated, 'but it don't seem to have made much difference. I know I shouldn't ask when you're off duty, but could you have a look at him? Please. He's been sick and I'm really worried, see.'

Dr Harrison picked up his bag, 'Of course, my dear. Lead the way.'

Cassie peered round the bedroom door and called, 'A visitor to see you, Dave.'

Dave nodded but didn't answer.

She walked over to the bed and touched his forehead gently. It felt hot and damp. She smiled down at him. 'Doctor Harrison is going to take a look at you. Do you mind?'

'I usually have Doctor White,' Dave muttered.

'So then,' Dr Harrison said briskly as he looked down at Dave, 'what seems to be the problem?' He bent over him and examined his eyes and tongue.

'My gut,' Dave replied.

'Tongue's quite white. Let's have a look at your tummy.' Dr Harrison leaned over, pushed back the duvet and prodded Dave's stomach.

Dave winced.

'Tender, is it?' Dr Harrison completed his examination and turned to Cassie. 'You did say he took the medication that I gave you?'

'Yes, it didn't seem to help though; in fact, he's got worse.' She looked at the doctor. 'Perhaps it takes a while to kick in?'

Dr Harrison looked down at Dave, his face expressionless. 'Is there any of that medicine left?'

'A spoonful or so; it's in the bathroom.' Cassie moved
to get the medicine, but Dr Harrison brushed past her,
'I'll get it.' he said.

Seconds later he returned holding the bottle and a
spoon. He beamed down at Dave. 'Let's try one last
spoonful, shall we?' He administered the medicine then
placed the spoon on the bedside table. 'There, that's the
last drop. It's probably a bad bout of food poisoning, so
I should stay off solids for a while.' Casually he slipped
the empty bottle into his pocket and turned to Cassie.
'This could well be the turning point, you know. Now I
must be off. Keep him warm and lots of fluids. Bye,' he
called as he bustled off to the bedroom door.

'I SHOULD THINK THAT would clear it. If I see Dr White I'll
have a word with him, save him the journey,' Dr Harrison said as he strode across the forecourt.

Cassie walked with him to his car. 'I don't know how
to thank you, Doctor; you've been ever so kind.'

'Only did what was necessary, my dear. There's no
need for thanks.' Dr Harrison beamed at her, gave a quick
wave and drove off. Once he was out of sight of the pub,
he pulled in to the side of the road. With a whimsical
smile he brought the empty medicine bottle out of his
pocket, and opening the car window tossed the bottle
into the deepest part of the hedgerow, then he drove on.

Thursday 12.30 p.m.

DR WHITE STOOD NEAR his office window, took a hasty
sip from his coffee, and looked down at the car park
below. He watched as a large woman dismounted from
her scooter and made her way towards the entrance. She
had just reached the door when a green Audi drove up

and the driver tooted on the horn. The woman turned in surprise and walked back to greet Dr Harrison as he got out of his car. She seemed very pleased to see him and Dr White wondered whether she could be some relation. At that moment the phone rang, distracting him; he was about to take the call when the answer phone kicked in. He relaxed, finished off his coffee and looked again at the scene below. He saw that Dr Harrison now had a large manila envelope under his arm and that the woman was making her way back to her scooter. She waved cheerfully at Dr Harrison and drove off.

Ian White shrugged, returned to his desk and wondered just where he had seen that woman before. A distant memory stirred but he pushed it aside briskly. Back to work, he told himself, there was much to do.

He listened carefully to the messages on his voicemail, then picked up a scrap of paper and wrote down the number that he'd heard. He was about to ring back when the door opened and Dr Harrison came in.

'Brr,' he said with a shiver, 'the sun might be shining but there's a distinct nip in the air.' He beamed at Ian, 'How's things with you?'

Ian scowled. 'Like a madhouse this morning. I've had three emergencies in here already, and now it looks like there's another one as well. I'm just going to call her.'

Bob Harrison looked down at the phone. 'If that's in response to a call from the bouncy blonde landlady at the Full Moon Inn, you don't need to. I've dealt with it.'

Ian looked at him in surprise, 'How come?'

'I'd just nipped in there for a bag of crisps because I'd missed my coffee break, and she asked me to take a look at her husband, so I did.' Bob Harrison grinned. 'I gave him some more of the medicine that you'd prescribed, so that should do the trick.' He removed his jacket, pulled on his white coat and continued. 'If you ask me, that young woman's inclined to make a fuss over nothing. She looks the type. You know? The "worried well" sort?'

Ian leaned back in the chair and felt relief wash through him. He was glad that he didn't have to go to the Full Moon Inn. Cassie Hodgson always made him feel self-conscious. Pretty, confident women always paralyzed him; they brought back too many bitter memories. He saw Bob Harrison looking at him quizzically and forced a smile. 'Thanks, that's saved me a journey. At least I'll have time to finish off my paper work.' He glanced anxiously at the intercom. 'That is, if I don't get any more interruptions.'

He picked up a sheaf of papers, leafed through them, then paused and frowned. For a while he read on silently, then looking up remarked. 'Mrs Green died last week? She seemed so very sprightly when I last saw her.'

Bob Harrison, who was standing at the open drawer of the filing cabinet, turned to look at him. 'Mrs Green? That nice old girl with the dyed red hair? Yes indeedy. Went out like a light, she did. Him upstairs pressed the off switch, I suppose, and by the time I got there she'd gone. As you were away I asked the locum to corroborate the death certificate.'

Ian continued to scowl at the document. 'So I see.'

'Oh come on, Ian, she was eighty-nine. They go like that at times.'

'Still, I would have thought,' Ian hesitated and read through the attached notes, 'it says here that she's to be cremated. She always insisted that she wanted to be buried. "I want a proper job" she used to say, "with black horses and plumes, and wreaths with yellow tulips".'

'You know what they're like at eighty-nine. They're

not with us most of the time.' Doctor Harrison smiled consolingly. 'But I should imagine she'll get her yellow tulips.' He chuckled, 'Her relations can easily afford them now.'

Ian rested his elbows on the desk and stared worriedly at his notes. Going through them again he counted silently and said. 'But Bob, that makes four we lost last week.' His shoulders slumped. 'It's not as if we've had a flu epidemic.'

Dr Harrison fished a squashed-looking cellophane-wrapped cookie out of his overall pocket, removed the wrapper, and took a large bite from the biscuit. He walked over to the desk and peered down at the papers. 'What you've got to remember is that this is a place for old sick people. We do what we can to make them... comfortable. But there comes a time when the heart gives in, either that or it's a stroke, or a cancer.' He paused then pushed the remainder of the cookie into his mouth and said, 'Something will get us all one day, that's for sure.'

Ian wiped the spray of biscuit crumbs from his face and tried not to feel irritated. He looked up at Bob and thought, no prizes as to what is going to get you. Five years down the line and you'll just be one ball of blubber. He said, 'What I don't understand is that lately they all manage to die whenever I'm off duty, or away somewhere.' He tossed the papers aside, got up and stared out of the window. 'You know what? I'm starting to dread taking a day off.' He turned to look at Bob Harrison. 'Don't you find it...unusual?'

'No, not at all, dear boy. You're not working in geriatrics in a general hospital, you know. There, patients come and go. Working here takes some getting used to. Remember how grateful you were to get this job. How it helped you out of, how shall I put it, certain indiscretions?'

Ian White's face flushed, 'I'm not being ungrateful.'

'Of course you're not, dear boy,' Dr Harrison chuckled. 'I'm fully aware of how depressing it can be in here at times. We're both fortunate that we can work as GPs as well, otherwise we really would get the blues.'

'Blues?' Ian frowned.

'Whoops, sorry, that's just an old-fashioned term for depression. You remember Elvis, don't you?'

'Sorry, I've heard of him but I was an infant when he died.'

Dr Harrison's berry-brown eyes stared at him blankly for a moment. 'Yes, of course. I keep forgetting how young you are.' He chuckled loudly, 'Call it an age thing.' He turned back to the filing cabinet, pulled out a file and walked towards the door. 'Try to look on the lighter side, Ian. Thanks to our generous proprietor our patients here are getting the best possible care, nice surroundings, good food… Ah! That reminds me. I must have a shufty at what's on today's lunch menu before I do my rounds.' He gave a cheery grin. 'You'll see. You'll find there's always something to look forward to.' The door closed behind him.

Ian smiled briefly as he watched the door close. He was about to continue reading, when a thought occurred to him and he reached out and picked up his desk diary. Leafing back, he found last week's entries. At the start of that week, it confirmed the days that he'd been on holiday. It also stated that Dr Robinson, locum, would be away on a course during that same week. What had happened here then, he wondered. Had Bob Harrison brought in a supply doctor or had he mixed up the dates of the entries. He stared at both the entries for a long time, and then he closed the diary and, picking up the papers, checked the handwriting on last week's documents. There, plain as day, was the signature of Dr Robinson.

TWENTY

BEN STIRRED AND became aware that his cheek was pressed against something hard. Yes, that was it, something hard and round and painful. Something that made a creaking sound whenever he moved his head. What was it? Where was he? And why did his cheekbone ache so? He raised his head and like magic the pain went. Something clattered down onto the desk in front of him and he squinted sleepily at the object. His reading glasses! How did they get there? He leaned back against the chair, yawned and rubbed his eyes, then he remembered; he'd been about to inspect that lock again and he must have nodded off for a minute.

More than a minute, his mind told him. You don't get a king-size headache, a mouth like a sewer, and your knees feeling as if they've got rigor mortis if you've just had a few quick zeds. Blearily, Ben gazed at the shiny metal teapot in front of him and enlightenment dawned. There must have been something in that tea. He sat bolt upright with indignation. That bloody security man had gone and slipped him a Mickey Finn.

He stood up, then stumbled as a pale blue blanket fell from him. He turned and stared down at it. Where the hell had that come from?

Groaning, he walked stiffly across the room to the sink and felt the fear grow within him. Why this? What was happening? He leaned over the sink, splashed his face with water, then cupping his hands together, drank thirstily. Having eased his thirst, he turned and looked around. He stared at the desk with the tea tray on it. Then with a puzzled frown he stared at the floor where the pale blue blanket lay in a crumpled heap. How that had got there was still a mystery.

Ben walked over to the windows and looked out. He felt a sense of relief; it was still daylight so he couldn't have been asleep all that long. His throat still felt bone dry, his limbs ached and he became aware of an urgent need to visit the lavatory. Earlier he'd managed to relieve himself in the sink, but now his bowels were ready to move and he needed to find a toilet fast.

He hurried over to the door and hammered on it. Surely someone must hear him. He paused, listened and thought that he could hear footsteps. They'd got to hear him. He kicked relentlessly on the door. It brought results.

There came a jangling of keys and the door swung open.

'Where's the fire then?' the security man said.

'I need the loo,' Ben blurted.

'Right,' the man said, 'I hadn't thought about that. I'll go get you a commode.'

'You'll hell as like.'

'Okay then.' The man placed a hand firmly on Ben's shoulder, 'This way.'

They hurried along the corridor. Not a soul about, thought Ben, although he did glimpse a few open doors as they passed by.

'Here we are then,' the man said, and he shut and locked the door behind him. 'Be back soon,' he called through the door.

Later Ben stood at one of the sinks and gazed at his reflection in surprise. The face that stared back at him was badly in need of a shave, which was strange; he had never needed to shave twice in one day. Perhaps it was the poor lighting? He looked at his watch and sighed in exasperation, ten past four! Either the battery is on the blink or I've knocked the bloody winder. He rubbed at the dusty mirror and again peered closely at his image. No doubt about it; he definitely needed a shave.

He stripped off his jacket and looked around. His gaze took in the three washbasins and the four cubicles. Instead of the usual hot air dryer there was a linen roller towel fitment from which hung a worn-looking towel that had not been used. It was a big room, designed for the use of several patients. It seemed odd to Ben that no one else wanted to use the facilities. No one had even tried the outer door.

Ben looked up at the windows that were of frosted glass and placed near to the ceiling. They were quite large in size; with any luck he might be able to squeeze through them. He hurried over to them and, placing one foot on the water pipes that ran along the wall, and one foot on the edge of the sink, he climbed up and grasped the window handle, pushing with all of his might. Nothing happened. The window remained shut. Ben cursed loudly. He inspected the window frame and saw that the thick layers of paint made it impossible to open. At this close range he could see the cobwebs stretched over the corners of the windows and he realized that they had not been opened in years.

With a sense of frustration he climbed down. No chance of escape there. He went to the sink to wash his hands and checked his watch again. Now it read four fifteen. He slipped it from his wrist, checked the winder was in place, and shook the watch. That couldn't be right. He remembered having looked at the time just before he'd had his tea. Then it had read five thirty. I must have bust it somehow, he thought. He held the watch up to his ear, then looked at it again in confusion; it was ticking steadily.

For a while Ben stared at the watch in disbelief then looked again at his reflection as realization set in. Incredibly, he had lost a day! His stomach churned and he wanted to vomit. He'd heard of situations like this. He'd often seen them in the spy dramas on the telly, but such things didn't happen to ordinary folk…unless someone thought that he knew something. But what did he know? More importantly, what did they think he knew?

With his mind still searching for answers he turned back to the sink and struggled with the stiff hot water tap. It gurgled and groaned, but after a while water spluttered out. Ben thumped down hard on the soap dispenser and began to wash himself.

He dried his hands, slipped his watch back on his wrist, and was pulling on his jacket when he heard the key turn in the lock and the door opened again.

The security man came in. 'All bright eyed and bushy tailed, then?'

Ben strode up to him and yelled, 'Just what the hell is going on? You've drugged me and you've kept me here against my will for over a day now. Boy oh boy! Am I going to get the law on you! Just you wait 'til I get out of here. My solicitor is going to have a field day. When I've finished with you lot, you won't have a rag to your arses.'

'Now, now, sir.' The security man held up his hands, 'Calm down a bit. We're doing our best to look after you, considering your circumstances. All that we have to do now is to wait for authorization. The usual red tape, don't you know.' He smiled at Ben reassuringly. 'And once that is authorized, well then you'll be free to go.' His smile faded. 'But for now I've got to ask you to return to your room.' He raised an eyebrow. 'So, if you'll come with me?'

Fuming, Ben walked beside the security man in silence. He should try and make a bid for freedom, he thought, but he still felt weak and dizzy and, as he eyed the burly young security man, he knew that in his condition he'd not have much chance. He had to try to do something, though, so as he passed each open door, he hesitated, either forcing a cough and stopping, or pretending to fix his shoelace, trying to see if there would be a opportunity later of an escape route through the wards.

He saw quickly that some of the wards seemed empty, except for what looked like one or two bedridden patients who were asleep. He also saw that in the other rooms most of the patients, whether sitting or sleeping, had a drip stand beside them. They seemed totally uninterested in the passers-by in the corridor. Ben was puzzled. Why were they so damn quiet? They must have heard him shouting, and it wasn't as if it was night time. Surely at least some of them should be listening to the radio or watching the telly?

The security man halted and frowned at him, 'Why do you keep stopping? Can't you walk a bit faster?'

'I've got cramp in me legs, see,' Ben grumbled. 'Comes with all that sitting down.'

The man forced a smile, 'Now come along, sir. I've got a nice pot of tea and some fruit and sandwiches waiting.'

'Another poisoned chalice,' Ben muttered.

'Sir?'

'Look,' said Ben, 'Get me a bottle of water, untouched and sealed. That's all I'm going to drink.'

'Okay, sir,' the man nodded as he ushered Ben back

into the room. 'I'll be back in a few minutes.' With that he closed and locked the door.

Ben wandered into the centre of the room and stared again at the desk. Why did he have an uneasy feeling that he'd forgotten something?

He strolled up to the desk and examined the fresh tray that was there. On it were sandwiches, some chocolate biscuits and some fruit. There was also another large teapot but Ben decided to ignore it. He picked up an apple, bit into it, eased himself down onto the chair behind the desk and stared blankly at the wall. What was it they thought he knew? He swivelled in the chair and his leg caught against the desk drawer. He winced and rubbed his shin and looking down, remembered the yellowed papers.

Relief flooded through him. This was what had been bothering him. He'd been about to examine these and he'd gone and fallen asleep. Eagerly he opened the drawer and brought a sheaf of papers up onto the desk.

TWENTY-ONE

Thursday afternoon

'Now,' SAID ANNA. 'When you see the sign for the B road near Malton, just before Wombleton, let me know in good time. Not like you did twenty minutes ago when you told me to fork left just as we'd passed the junction.'

'I would have told you earlier,' protested Rosa, 'except that you were rabbiting on about the Force again. Once you get started on that, you never stop.'

'The reason that I was talking so much was because I could see that you were listening for that knocking sound, which, touch wood,' Anna tapped her head, 'has not re-occurred.'

'Ah, but, it could have.' Rosa said sagely 'And if we're talking non-stop, we might not hear it.'

'Believe me, Rosa, if that starts up again, we will definitely hear it. So, you keep on checking with your road map and admiring the scenery.' She reached out and switched on the radio. 'As for me, I'm going to listen to some music.'

Rosa clicked her tongue and looked out of the car window. She tried to mask her annoyance. Now she would have to listen to that rock and roll stuff blaring away. She shot a sidelong glance at her sister; even worse, Anna might decide to join in with the singing. Rosa shuddered at that thought; her sister had a singing voice like a frog with laryngitis. As for her ability to hold a note!

Rosa pulled up her coat collar and slid deeper into the seat. She didn't want to listen to any pop music, although a bit of classical might have been soothing. Most of all, she wanted to hear from Ben. Surely he could have managed to text her again by now? She felt in her coat pocket for Anna's mobile, brought it out and checked it again.

'Any more messages?' asked Anna.

'Nothing.'

'Did you think to check your own mobile?'

'No point in that,' said Rosa, 'That thing's useless. It's not been right since I dropped it into the spin dryer; you'd think they'd make them a bit stronger these days, wouldn't you. It was only in there a minute. Now every time I switch it on, all I get is "No signal".'

'Why doesn't that surprise me?' murmured Anna.

Rosa shrugged, slipped Anna's phone back in her pocket and stared blankly at the lorry in front of them. 'Well Driven?' it asked on its rear doors. Rosa wanted to write, 'but not well washed' over its number plate. She thought about Anna's instructions, 'Admire the scenery', she'd said. For the last five minutes they'd been stuck behind this mucky three-ton truck. Some scenery. Why didn't Anna put her foot down and overtake it?

As if reading Rosa's mind, Anna pressed hard on the accelerator and drove past the truck. That's better, Rosa thought. She glanced down at the map again. Still no sign of that road, but it must be close by now. She tried to listen to the radio, but for Rosa the miles seemed to inch by. She wanted to shout, go faster Anna, drive quickly so that I can find my Ben, but common sense ruled and she remained silent. Upsetting the driver wouldn't achieve anything.

'There it is! The B road.' Anna shouted above the music. 'Fine navigator you turned out to be.'

'I would have seen it,' Rosa protested. 'That junction is still over a mile away.' She eased herself upright in the seat, stared at the road signs and did a mental calculation. 'So that would make it just over one and a half hours before we get there?'

'Just about,' Anna said, 'unless we get stuck behind a tractor on these country roads.'

'Don't even go there,' Rosa said.

Anna looked at Rosa and smiled. 'Well, love, if the worst comes to the worst, it isn't as if you're not prepared. You brought the thermos and sandwiches, if you remember.'

'I've told you before, you should never go on a long journey without a drink and something to eat,' Rosa said. 'I should know, I've lost count of how many times I've been stranded.'

'Rosa, this will only take a couple of hours unless, as I just said, we get stuck behind some lorry.' She laughed loudly and patted the steering wheel. 'Ease up Sis, there's nothing at all to worry about.'

Half an hour later, after they had driven a few miles down the country road Rosa eyed the dashboard and asked tentatively, 'Why has a red light just come on?'

'If you mean the ignition light, that can't come on, not when we're moving,' Anna said. 'It's probably just the sunlight beaming down on the dashboard. You just sit back and relax. Oh look over there. There's still a few wild flowers growing in the ditches.'

'You look at your ignition, never mind the ruddy flowers,' snapped Rosa. 'And I've never yet seen sunlight that was a luminous red.'

Anna looked at the ignition light and scowled. 'It's probably a loose wire.' She thumped the dashboard in an attempt to make the red light disappear. 'What you've got to remember is that my little Ford Escort is nearly twenty years old, and at her age wire and bits and pieces are inclined to fall off.' She slapped the dashboard again but, stubborn as ever, the red light stayed on.

Rosa enquired cautiously, 'Would this have anything to do with the knocking sound?'

Anna looked at her in disgust and did not deign to reply.

After a while Rosa said, 'Well, whatever it is, hadn't you better stop and fix it. I mean, something's not right.'

'All right, all right, but I'm not an electrician,' Anna grumbled. Nevertheless, she slowed down and looked for a safe place to pull over. She found a lay-by and stopped the car. For a while both women sat in silence staring at the offending red light. Anna leaned forward and switched off the engine. The light vanished. She started up again and the red light reappeared.

'If it's a wire, don't you think you'd best look under the bonnet,' Rosa suggested.

Anna frowned. 'Now what?'

'I'm trying to remember which button it is. I don't often look under there. I leave that to the mechanics.'

Rosa gave a snort of exasperation and sprawled back in her seat. She said evenly, 'Then try the process of elimination. It has to be there somewhere.'

'Should be near my seat,' Anna muttered. 'That one there's for the petrol, so this must be it!' There was a loud click, 'Ah, I was right.'

Both women got out, walked to the front of the car, lifted up the bonnet and gazed down at the machinery beneath.

'The bonnet felt hot.' Rosa said. 'Could it be the radiator?'

Anna crouched down and looked underneath the

car. 'No sign of a leak.' She touched the radiator then snatched her hand away. 'Rosa, go back into the car and switch on the ignition.'

'Who? Me? You know I don't drive.'

'Just turn the key. I want to see.'

Rosa obliged. The engine started, but the fan behind the radiator remained motionless.

'Got it.' Anna closed the bonnet and returned to the car.

'Now what?'

'Give me my mobile.' She reached across Rosa into the glove compartment, got out her AA card and keyed in the phone number.

Rosa listened whilst Anna gave the AA instructions as to their whereabouts. After a minute she keyed off and gave the phone back to Rosa. 'They're on their way.' She smiled, 'They shouldn't take too long.'

Rosa felt annoyed. 'I told you we should have hired a car. There's always a problem with these old b—' she stopped as she saw her sister's expression. 'I'm sorry, love,' she said in gentler tones, 'but I can't stop thinking about my Ben. We seem to be taking forever to go and help him. He's in trouble. I just know it. If only I knew what's gone wrong.'

'Try to be patient,' Anna said. 'The AA man will be here soon, he's only got to come from York. And if it's what I think it is, he can fix that in a few minutes.'

'What is wrong with the car?'

Anna hesitated, 'If my guess is right then I think it's the fan belt.'

'Is that serious?'

'Oh yes, but it's easy to put right.' She looked thoughtful, 'In fact I read somewhere that a man's tie or a pair of tights would do as an emergency repair.' She grinned at Rosa, 'So come on then, you want to see your Ben. You're in a rush. So get your tights off, woman.'

Rosa looked sheepish. 'You get your tights off. It's your car.'

'Your husband!'

Rosa's mouth turned down and she folded her arms across her chest. 'I can't.'

'Why not?'

'I don't wear 'em.'

'What. Bare legged in October?'

'I never said that,' Rosa said huffily. 'I wear stockings.'

'You're joking? Wow-ee! You don't, do you?' Anna reached across to her sister's knees and tried to lift her skirt.

'Gerroff,' Rosa pushed her away. 'I'll wear what I want.'

Anna stifled a laugh but her shoulders shook. After a minute she said, 'I have a question,' she slid a glance at Rosa.'

'What?'

'Do you wear garters?' Anna giggled loudly.

Rosa thumped Anna on her shoulder, 'No, I do not. If you must know, I wear stockings because my Ben likes me to, and that's why I don't wear trousers. Ben likes to see me in skirts, see.' She gave a coy smile. 'He says I've got nice knees.'

'I see,' Anna looked at her sister with a straight face. 'And do you wear black suspenders?'

Rosa turned bright pink and gave her a swift cuff round the ear, 'You mind your own ruddy business; that's got nothing to do with you.'

Anna fought back another laugh, 'All I can say to that revelation, big sister, is that every day I learn something new about you two.'

'Well, thank you for that,' Rosa said stiltedly. 'It might help if in future you were to learn how to be tactful and stop letting your mouth run away with your brain. As for me,' she opened the car door and got out, 'I'm going for a little walkabout. I feel like I need some fresh air.'

ANNA WATCHED HER SISTER walk along the road and felt a sense of guilt. She really shouldn't have teased her like that, not when she was stressed already. She wanted to get out of the car and apologize, but she thought that Rosa might need some time alone. She sat in the car and waited for her sister to return; there was nothing more that she could do. Then she remembered the thermos and the ham sandwiches.

'You really must have second sight,' Anna said as she and Rosa finished off the first packet of sandwiches, and she put the wrappers away.

'Always best to be prepared, especially as you were worried about the car.' Rosa took a last sip from her coffee then stowed the cup away.

Anna peered out of the window. 'Wonder what's keeping them? It's over an hour since I rang.'

Rosa sighed and turned to look out of the rear window.

'Let me have my mobile again, Rosa. Did you check for messages?'

'Yes. Not a word.'

Anna keyed in the AA number again and listened impatiently to the ringing tone. Then as she glanced in the car mirror she saw the familiar yellow van approaching and felt a huge sense of relief. Switching off the phone she said, 'Cheer up, Rosa, looks like our rescuer is here and we'll soon be on our way.' And they got out of the car to greet him.

TWENTY-TWO

Thursday afternoon

CASSIE CLOSED THE bedroom door and hurried along the hallway to the guest bedrooms. As she reached Ben Hammond's room she stopped and knocked politely on the door. There was no response. With a sigh she used her master key and went into the room.

Just as she expected, she found it exactly the same as it had been the night before. So the elusive Mr Hammond had still not returned. Just to be certain, she peeked into the bathroom, then once again checked the wardrobe where the solitary overcoat still hung. She hesitated and looked about her. What on earth was going on here? Where had the old boy got to? What had happened to his 'trouble and strife' and her sister? They should have arrived last night. Had the two women done a disappearing act as well? Perhaps there was a simpler solution. Perhaps Mr Hammond had turned up at his home, and his wife hadn't felt the need to let her know.

At this thought Cassie drew in her breath and felt the indignation grow within her. After all that she'd done last night. She'd phoned them and even sent her poor sick Dave out looking for the old man. Wait! Phone? What had happened to Mr Hammond's mobile? She'd given it to Dave. So where was the bloody thing? She swept out of the room, down the stairs and into the kitchen and checked all the work surfaces and drawers for any sign of the phone, but it wasn't there. Dave must still have it. She glanced up at the clock. Right now the last thing that she wanted was to disturb her sick husband. Best to let him sleep for a while. With a start she remembered that Claire had still not had her lunch and she hurried into the bar to relieve her; she would look for the mobile later.

CASSIE SMILED CHEERILY at the few customers, polished the bar for the umpteenth time, and tried not to look anxiously at the door that lead upstairs to the Inn's bedrooms and the private accommodation. She'd sent Claire home for a late lunch and a few hours off, so she'd have to stay in the bar until she returned. She had to stop worrying. The good doctor had examined Dave and given him the medicine and now she must let nature take its course. She'd nipped upstairs a few minutes ago and sneaked a look at Dave and he seemed to be fast asleep. She walked over to the coffee maker and poured herself another cup. She was just about awash with the stuff but at least it kept the tiredness at bay.

A customer rapped sharply with a coin on the bar and, startled, she turned towards him. She forced a smile. 'Yes, sir. What'll it be?'

'A pint of Tetley's, love. And is it too late to order a lasagne?'

'It's never too late, sir,' she smiled. 'We serve food all day.' Thanks to the invention of the microwave, she thought. She wrote down the order, then drew the man his pint. As she did so, Cassie was reminded of the last guest who'd ordered a lasagne, the missing Mr Hammond. Just where the hell was he?

She took the food order into the kitchen then stopped dead at the sight of her husband slumped over the kitchen table. 'My God! Dave! You look dreadful.' She hurried over to him and put her arms round him reassuringly, 'Sweetheart, whatever's the matter?' Leaning back a little she frowned at the large brown stain on the lapel of his dressing gown. 'What's that?'

'Sorry, luv,' he murmured. 'Been sick again. Didn't make it to the bathroom.' He tried to smile. 'Don't know what it was that I ate, girl. But whatever it was it must be bloody lethal.' His head slumped onto his chest.

Cassie stood transfixed. Her Dave was really ill. She had to do something, but it was as if her mind was frozen. She ran and picked up the phone.

THE LITTLE BLUE Ford Escort came to a halt in front of the Inn and Anna got out, stretched, and with a self-satisfied smile addressed her sister. 'Told you I'd get you here.'

'The Pony Express would have been quicker,' Rosa snapped as she hurried towards the entrance. 'Come on, don't just stand there, I want to know what's happened to my Ben.'

Rosa looked anxiously about her as she came into the pub, there didn't seem to be too many customers, and none of them looked remotely like her husband. She headed straight to the bar to enquire but, except for a lone customer, there didn't seem to be anyone serving.

'She's gone to fetch me lasagne, I think,' the man said. 'But that were a while since.' He rapped again on the bar. 'Happen she's had to lasso the cow first.'

'Where is everyone?' Anna asked as she joined Rosa at the bar.

'Dunno,' Rosa said, 'but the man here reckons the girl's been gone for some time.'

'That doesn't seem right.'

'Maybe she's tripped or something,' Rosa hurried towards the kitchen door, 'I'd best go have a look.'

'I'll stay here,' Anna said. She stared at the man standing at the bar with suspicion. 'And keep an eye on things.'

Rosa tapped politely on the door to the kitchen, and, on hearing no response, entered cautiously. 'Hello' she said, then on seeing the young woman bending over the landlord, moved swiftly towards them. The man looked very ill and Rosa's training took over.

Cassie looked up at her anxiously.

'Sorry to barge in on you, I'm Rosa Hammond,' she said calmly. She looked closely at the sick man. 'I used to work as a nurse. How long has he been like this?'

'Not sure,' Cassie said. 'He came downstairs and said he'd been sick, then he passed out. I've lost track of time. I've dialled 999. They should be here any minute. Only Dave, he's my husband, keeps coming round and being sick. I daren't leave him in case he chokes. Claire should be back soon.'

Rosa knelt down beside Cassie. 'May I look at him?'

Cassie nodded and watched whilst Rosa looked at Dave and then examined the stains on his dressing gown lapel.

She turned to Cassie. 'Your husband needs urgent medical attention. I don't want to alarm you and I'm not one hundred per cent certain, but this looks like a perforated ulcer to me. I could be wrong,' she said quickly on seeing Cassie's expression, 'but I would like the doctors at the hospital to see him, just to be sure.' Rosa stood up and hurried over to the phone. 'I'll check where that ambulance has got to.' She spoke briefly to the operator then turned to Cassie, who knelt as if frozen, with both hands pressed over her mouth.

Rosa went to her and bending over her put an arm around her. 'There now. Not to worry, my dear. The operator says that the ambulance should be here at any minute. Help is on its way.'

'I thought it was food poisoning, least that's what doc—' Cassie broke off and began to sob.

Rosa said gently, 'You've done all that you can.'

Cassie shivered, 'I'm so scared.' She looked at Rosa. 'I'm not usually soft. When it's me I'm as tough as old boots. But it's my Dave, see. He's all I've got, I should have known.'

Rosa held her close. 'No one knows everything. Just try to stay calm. Tell you what, you go and keep an eye out for the medics, and I'll stay with him. I'll come with you in the ambulance if you like? My sister can keep an eye on things.'

Rosa watched as Cassie hurried out of the kitchen then her thoughts returned to Ben. Where was he? She looked down at the grey-faced landlord. This poor soul was in dire need of help. Wherever Ben was, it would have to wait.

Thursday afternoon

BEN REACHED DOWN into the bottom drawer, gently eased the papers out and placed them in front of him. They might well be nothing much but at least he could be nosy. It would keep his mind occupied and the cold sense of fear at bay. Sooner or later he would get an answer on what was happening, meanwhile...

He picked up the first sheet of paper and read it. It was some sort of invoice, dated 2001. As he perused the bill his spirits sank. It was boring stuff really, just the pricing for care and food for one particular patient. Wait a minute...*one* patient? Ben looked again. Even allowing for the necessary nursing care, the charges stated seemed far more appropriate for a luxurious hotel than that of a nursing home. His gaze continued down the page to the hand-written comment of the payee. It read; 'For easing my burden, and with grateful thanks for the care of great aunt Mary. May she rest in peace.' This was followed by an indecipherable name.

Ben's gaze moved on to the 'Final payment received with thanks', scrawl, below which there was also a signature. Ben blinked. Perhaps if this 'final payment' was for the time that the patient had been treated here, then that might justify such a large amount? Quickly he shuffled through the other invoices, checking the dates.

It didn't take him long before he found a similar bill for the same patient; this time dated a week earlier. He compared the totals, then sat back and shook his head in amazement. The pricing was outrageous. How were they getting away with overcharging like this? They must be feeding the patients gold dust.

Ben thought back to the time that he'd entered the reception area. True, that had been fitted out expensively. And then he thought about his visit to the toilets and the dust and threadbare towels. It didn't make sense. Another thought came into his mind; was it possible that Miss McGuire was a patient here? Perhaps she was having some kind of treatment. He started to rifle though the other letters and invoices and then he heard the footsteps.

Quickly he shoved the papers back into the drawer and closed it just as the door opened and Jeff came in with a bottle of water.

'You thought I'd forgotten 'bout this, didn't you?' Jeff said as he placed the bottle on the desk. 'Will that be enough?'

Ben eyed the two-litre bottle with suspicion, 'Depends on how much longer you're keeping me here.' He stood up and checked that the bottle's seal wasn't broken. 'Don't think for one minute you're getting away with this "kidnapping". I'm gonna sue the pants off this firm, believe me.'

'Now, now, sir, I'm sure it's going to be all right in the end.'

Ben said sharply. 'Do you have a patient by the name of McGuire staying here?'

'Can't say, sir,' Jeff blustered. 'Me. I'm only an employee, and it's not my business to discuss patients. It'd be more than my job's worth.'

'Ha,' Ben snorted. 'The classic answer throughout history. You're one of the hear all, see all, say nowt brigade, then?'

'I have to hang on to my job, don't I?' Jeff turned, made for the door and unlocked it. 'It isn't as if I'm doing anything wrong.' He looked back at Ben. 'I just obey orders.' He slid through the door, locking it quickly behind him.

Ben stood for a while and listened as the sound of the departing footsteps faded away. He felt a sense of confusion well up within him. If Miss McGuire was a patient here there had to be a way of finding out.

He opened the drawer and again brought out the pile of papers, again placing them on the desk in front of him. Picking up the first sheet, he scrutinized each line carefully. He needed to know more.

Some time later Ben took off his glasses and rubbed at his eyes. Reading in this light made them feel itchy. He saw the darkness outside, then looked at his watch. Ten past six. That figured, the watch couldn't be far out then. It usually was dark about this time in October. He stacked the yellowed papers into a neat pile, replacing them in the exact order that he had found them. Then he returned them to the bottom drawer. He sat back and, lacing his hands behind his head, started to think things through.

The papers, most of them invoices, were in many ways informative. They told him that no matter how dilapidated this building appeared to be, it was, judging by the service it provided, hugely profitable. What really bothered Ben was exactly what it was that this nursing home did provide. And how the hell did they manage to find clients that were prepared to pay such outrageous charges. Judging by some of the comments on the invoices, not only did the clients seem to be more than grateful, some of them were most effusive in their praise. Again the questions niggled at Ben's brain. What were they doing to the patients? Why were they doing it? And how on earth did they manage to earn such gratitude from the patients' relations? There had to be an answer.

With a tired sigh he got to his feet and walked stiffly over to the sink. Turning on the cold tap he allowed the water to wash over his wrists, then he splashed it over his face, cooling him down, helping him to think clearly. If only he could shake off this weariness. He needed to think straight and try and work things out.

His thoughts went back to some hours ago when he was on his way back from the toilets, how he'd had a glimpse of the frail and the elderly patients and the silence that surrounded them. He realized now that he should have looked more closely. What if one of them had been Miss McGuire? He straightened up and, after drying his hands and face with a tissue, stood for a moment trying to do a mental replay of what he had seen earlier. After a while he shook his head. No, he felt sure that Miss McGuire had not been in the rooms that he'd seen. The patients there were much frailer than she was, but the question remained, where had she got to? Rosa claimed that she had seen someone fitting her description outside the Full Moon Inn, but where had she gone from there?

Perhaps it would have been better if he had left well alone. He should have minded his own business like most people did and then he wouldn't have ended up in here. But to his mind it seemed so out of character for Miss Macguire to scurry away and avoid him. What was it that had frightened her? What if, like him, she was not here of her own free will? Wherever she was, he would find her.

With a scowl Ben crossed the room and stared at the door. His scowl deepened as he eyed the old-fashioned lock. Before he could find anyone he had to get out of here. He felt in his inside pocket for his wallet, checked his jacket pocket and found his pocket knife. He pulled out the contents of the other pocket and discovered a used tissue, a piece of wire, and the bar bill from the Inn.

Puzzled, he looked down at the wire then remembered that last week he'd snipped a bit off the fencing down by the sweet peas. Rosa had been complaining that she kept catching her arm on it. He tossed the items onto the desk and looked down at them. 'Thank God for one small mercy, or maybe it's two small mercies?' he muttered as an idea occurred to him; it was worth a try. He picked up the wire and the pocket knife and walked over to the door. Leaning against the door, he listened. Not a sound. He could begin.

TWENTY-THREE

Thursday evening

IT WAS DARK outside when Anna saw Cassie and Rosa coming in through the pub doors. 'How is he?' she asked as she got up from her chair and went towards them.

'In good hands, I think.' Rosa placed a reassuring arm around Cassie's shoulders, 'The doctors up at the hospital have seen him. It is a perforated ulcer and they're keeping him in for a while. He should be all right now.'

'I'd have liked to have stayed with him,' Cassie said, 'but they said to go home and phone through later. They wanted to know what medicine he'd been taking. I gave them the bottle from Dr White, but for the life of me I can't remember what I did with the bottle that Dr Harrison gave me, and that's the stuff Dave took, see. I'll check again upstairs.'

'Don't worry about that for now, Cassie. What you need is a nice sweet cup of tea.' Rosa looked around and smiled. 'Or perhaps a good stiff brandy? We're in the right place for it.'

Cassie smiled at her, 'I don't know how to thank you. If you hadn't turned up, I daren't even think about what would have happened. Look, I'll have a quick word with young Claire and get her to hold the fort for a bit longer, then I'll make you two ladies something to eat. You must be starving.'

'I'm not bothered about eating. I came here to find my Ben.'

'You speak for yourself,' Anna said quickly. She looked at Cassie, then gave an embarrassed grin. 'Well, I did try one of your treacle puddings whilst you were gone. I must say it was delicious. In fact I did try two.'

'I might have known,' Rosa muttered.

Cassie grinned. 'You can try a dozen if you like, darlin'. It's all on the house for you two.'

WHILST ROSA WAS EATING she listened carefully to what Cassie said about searching Ben's room and finding his overcoat and his mobile. She realized that if Cassie had the mobile, Ben could not have texted Anna. Her mind began to race as this fact registered and she knew that everything was far from all right as far as Ben was concerned. Her sense of alarm increased, but she pushed back the fear and tried to take things through step by step. 'When was the last time that you saw my husband, Cassie?'

Cassie put down her knife and fork and looked thoughtful. 'To be honest, the last time was on Tuesday evening when you two ladies left and Mr Hammond booked a room here. If I remember rightly, it was Claire who told my Dave that Mr Hammond had been asking about the nursing home, so that would be Wednesday morning. Yeah, that would make it almost two days since....'

Almost two whole days! Rosa felt the blood drain from her face. She hadn't realized how much time had passed until Cassie said it out loud.

Anna stared at her. 'You've gone drip white. What's the matter now?'

'We've got to find my Ben,' she whispered. 'Nearly two whole days.'

Anna touched her arm. 'That's counting today. Now don't start to panic. After all you've been through today, we've got to treat this logically and deal with the facts.' She looked from Rosa to Cassie. 'To my mind the one thing that keeps coming up time and again is that nursing home, so that's where we'll make a start.'

'Too right,' said Cassie as she got up and cleared away, 'and I'm coming with you.' She saw that they were about to protest and insisted. 'I'm helping you as you helped me. I'll just ring the hospital and make sure my Dave's okay, and then,' she tapped her nose, 'not only do I know the way to that nursing home. I know one or two short cuts as well.'

Thursday evening

IAN RETURNED TO HIS OFFICE, removed his white coat, walked over to the window and stared at the darkness outside. It had been a long, hard day. He turned away from the window and flopped down into his chair behind his desk. Now he had to enter up the patients' notes. For a while Ian worked conscientiously until this task was completed then, pushing back his chair, he yawned and switched off the computer.

He was about to put on his overcoat when he noticed that the files from this morning were still on his desk. He sighed as he remembered; he had left them out for a very good reason.

He returned to his chair and switching on the desk light began to re-examine the suspect papers. The problem had not gone away. How could it be that the locum was in two places at once?

Ian peered once more at the signature of the locum, Doctor Robinson. To the casual observer it appeared to be exactly the same as it had been in earlier reports, but now he knew that this could not be. He picked up the paper and held it under the desk light. Looking closely, what he saw was a very faint lightening underneath and around the signature just as if someone had made a small erasure before signing. Yes, that was possible. It could well be that the doctor had made a mistake and rubbed it out. Yet surely it would have been simpler to have crossed out the error and initialled it?

He thought for a while. There was only one way to settle these mysteries and that was to go straight to the horse's mouth; he'd phone Pete Robinson. Ian reached for the phone, and then hesitated, his thoughts going back to the threatening remarks that Bob Harrison had made yesterday.

Slowly he replaced the receiver and stared down at the suspect documents. If he were to kick up a fuss about this then it could well ricochet back onto him and it could cost him his job. Bob Harrison had not only got him this position, but he also knew much, perhaps too much, about his past history. Still, Ian told himself, he'd been drug free now for over two years and even if Bob Harrison had pressurized him into taking the odd back hander for one or two insurance medicals, that wasn't all that bad. It wasn't as if it was… He stared again at the documents and his mind froze. Just what was happening in this place? How was he to deal with a locum who seemed to be capable of being in two places at once and dodgy-looking signatures? Just what had he got himself involved in?

Abruptly he got up, strode over to the filing cabinet and pulled out the folders with the weekly reports, going back several months. He carried them back to his desk and, pulling out the appropriate papers, began to go through them in reverse order, checking the signatures of the locum against his diary. As he did so he could not escape the feeling that something here was wrong. If he was right, one thing was certain. He would need more evidence, more proof, before he could confront anyone.

He paused at one particular paper and studied a signature from an earlier month. Nervously he flicked back the pages in his diary and compared dates. There it was again! The same signature on the document, and here in black and white, his diary confirmed the fact that he'd been on leave and the locum had been off sick. He recalled that at the time he'd been reluctant to take leave, knowing that they were short staffed. His lips tightened as he remembered how Bob Harrison had insisted that he do so, assuring him that if necessary he would call in a doctor from another area. Ian's heart sank as he realized that in that same week three of the patients had died.

Ian's mind raced as he checked and double-checked the entries on the papers. Again and again he held the suspect signatures under the lamp and always with the same result; there had been erasures.

He stood up and paced the floor, collating and digesting the information. He thought about the frequency of deaths that occurred whenever he was absent and he stopped in midtrack as realization set in. There were far too many coincidences. Bob Harrison was up to something. Something that was wrong!

Ian's heart pounded, he felt strangely weak and he went back to his chair and sat down. How was he to deal with this? He would have to question Bob, but that could be dangerous, especially if, as he suspected, Bob was involved.

He thought for a while then reached a decision. Yes, he would have to tackle Bob. He would go to see him tonight, but there were other things that he, as a doctor, would need to do first. He opened the drawer, got out some notepaper, and picking up his pen, began to write.

CASSIE PARKED THE CAR close to the nursing home gates and for a moment the three women sat in darkness, staring along the drive at the large white building.

'Right then,' said Rosa. 'Which way is it to reception?' She made as if to get out of the car and Cassie turned to her.

'Rosa, would you mind if I was to go in there first and ask about your husband? You see, I reckon that the receptionist will have finished work for today and the security man will be on duty.' She laughed softly, 'Jeff is one of our customers and I happen to know that he fancies me. He might be a bit more obliging if I were to ask a few questions.'

'We could all go in there together,' said Anna.

Rosa thought about this, 'No,' she said sharply, 'then we'd seem like invaders and that would get us nowhere.' She touched Cassie's arm. 'You go and have a try, and see what you can find out, but do take care, love.'

'I'll just take us back a bit so that you can see the drive better and we don't block the gates.' Cassie said. Having done that, she got out of the car and turned towards the two women. 'We'll call this plan A,' she whispered, then she set off across the road.

Anna and Rosa watched Cassie walk towards the building until she disappeared from view and all they could hear was the distant crunching of her heels on the gravel.

'I still say that we should have all gone up there

together,' muttered Anna, 'even if the two of us had to wait outside. There's safety in numbers, as I keep on telling you.'

'You should have said so before. She's gone now, so it's no good arguing.' Rosa stared at the building. Although she assumed that the house was painted white, in the darkness it appeared to be a greyish-blue amongst the trees and shadows.

Perhaps it was her anxiety over Ben, but it seemed to her that there was something sinister about the place. Brightness shone from the downstairs windows, but no such welcoming glow came from the top floor, only the palest glimmer of light.

Her thoughts returned to Ben and her heartbeat quickened. Where was he? He could be anywhere. This was not like him at all. Would they know about Ben in that place? Perhaps he'd been taken ill whilst he was there? If so, could it be that they were looking after him? But if they were, why hadn't they contacted her, or even phoned the landlord at the pub? She sat up straight and stared ahead of her. Of course she was thinking the worst; she should try to be positive. Ben might not be anywhere near here. He could have set off on a different trail altogether. He could even be making his way home....

'The wind's getting up,' said Anna. 'Look how the branches on the trees are moving. I'll bet this is the end of this mild spell.'

Rosa nodded absently but continued to stare fixedly in the direction of the house.

Anna watched her sister then muttered, 'Might as well talk to the moon.' She leaned over in her seat and rapped Rosa firmly on her shoulder. 'Here, have a crisp.'

'What?' A startled Rosa looked at her and gaped at the

packet in front of her. 'How can you? Here's me worrying myself sick and you…where'd you get them from?'

'Cassie said I could, so I—'

'Anna. We've only just had dinner.'

Anna fidgeted in her seat. 'Got to do something to pass the time. I always liked to nibble when I was on surveillance.' She sniffed. 'I should have brought a drink along as well; these crisps are salty.'

Rosa snatched the packet from her. 'Give me those. You're just plain greedy. Cassie's not been gone five minutes. My husband's gone missing, for all we know he could be at death's door, and there's you munching away. It's no wonder your hips are—'

'Head down,' Anna hissed, 'there's a car coming down the drive.'

Without thinking, Rosa slid down in her seat until the car headlights had faded and darkness returned. She eased herself upright and took a quick swipe at her sister. 'What did you make me do that for?'

'You never know who it might be.' Anna frowned. 'I was trying to get the number, but he was too fast.' She looked at her sister. 'After twenty years on the Force old habits die hard.' Her gaze returned to the driveway. 'It always pays to be cautious.'

WHEN CASSIE SAW the car headlights she stepped into the verge of the drive. As the car went past she recognized the driver as Dr White. He hadn't returned her phone call yesterday, which in a way was a relief because Dr Harrison had turned up and looked at Dave. Still, he should have checked it out. Dave was one of his patients. Cassie's lips tightened; she'd give him a piece of her mind when she next saw him.

Cursing softly, she eased her stiletto heels out of the

mud, went back onto the driveway and tried not to think of the damage that had been done to her shoes. A small price to pay, if she could get things sorted.

She thought about her Dave and felt a sense of relief. At least he was safe and the doctors had got to him in time, thanks mainly to Rosa Hammond. When she had phoned the hospital earlier the staff nurse had sounded positive and reassuring. Mr Hodgson was comfortable, she had told her. She could visit him tomorrow, but, the nurse had added, could she possibly bring the medication that Dave had taken prior to his admittance. Cassie frowned at this request; she still could not remember what had happened to the bottle that Dr Harrison had given her. She would search for it again once she had helped Rosa find her husband.

She reached the lighted entrance and her thoughts returned to the task ahead. 'Focus, girl,' she told herself. She wiped her shoes with a tissue, looked at the ornate glass door and peered at her reflection in an appraising manner. She fluffed out her blonde curls, straightened her jacket, licked her lips, and made her entrance.

Jeff looked up from the desk and she saw him do a double take. 'Hello, Cassie,' he said, as he got to his feet and straightened his tie. 'What on earth brings you here?'

Cassie widened her big brown eyes and smiled seductively up at him. 'I'm looking for your help, Jeff. We seem to have lost one of our customers.'

Jeff gulped as he gazed down at the pretty blonde woman and tried hard to stop himself stammering like a schoolboy, 'Well, I've not got him, Cassie,' he forced a laugh, 'and it's not like you to lose customers. They flock to you like moths to a flame. I mean to say, we'd have hell's delight trying to get them out of your pub, and dragging them up here.'

Cassie blushed. 'It's more the good beer than me, I reckon. I'd be fooling myself to think otherwise.' She frowned up at him. 'Nevertheless, I am very worried, Jeff. You see, our customer was last seen heading up the hill in this direction, and well, the state of play at the moment is that the family is kicking up one hell of a fuss. Who knows what's gonna happen next. I'm worried that they might call in the police.'

She looked around and peered into the corridor behind him. 'So I thought I'd have a word with your receptionist; she might have seen...'

'She's long since gone home for her tea,' Jeff said quickly. 'Besides, if anyone had been here I would have known about it.' He drew himself up to his full height. 'After all, I'm in charge of security.'

Cassie fluttered her eyelashes and smiled at him, 'I guess I must have hit lucky then, finding you on duty. You're the one that would know everything. Although... it might be possible that your receptionist saw someone whilst you were having a break?'

'Not a chance,' Jeff said firmly. 'I miss nothing. She has to report everything to me.' His eyes roved thoughtfully over Cassie's hourglass figure. 'Which reminds me, didn't I see you and your hubby coming out of here yesterday?' He watched as Cassie's face took on a serious expression, 'Sorry. Did I say something that I shouldn't?'

Cassie looked at him. 'You must have the eyes of a hawk. Yes, of course you did see me and my Dave.' She wrinkled her nose. 'We'd been to see that Dr White.'

'What's that face for?' said Jeff. 'He didn't give you any bad news, did he?'

Cassie shook her head. 'Not me; it's my Dave that's ill.' Tears welled up as she looked at him. 'Oh Jeff, you do know that my Dave's in hospital, don't you?'

'What! When?'

'Sorry.' Cassie pushed back her hair from her fore-head worriedly, 'I thought I'd mentioned it but so much has been happening lately that I don't know at times if I'm coming or going.' She took a deep breath, 'As for my Dave, they got to him in the nick of time.' She bit on her lip, 'I nearly lost him, Jeff, and no thanks to your Dr White.'

Jeff walked round the desk and put his arm on her shoulder. 'There, there, love, don't upset yourself.' He watched whilst Cassie took out a tissue and dabbed at her mascara. 'Would you like a glass of water?'

'No, I'm okay, thanks. Dave's fine now, I'll be visiting him tomorrow, but when I think that Dr White never even returned my call. If I'd done nothing and waited for him…it don't bear thinking about.'

Jeff looked over his shoulder at the corridor behind him and said, 'To tell you the truth, that doctor is a bit of a weirdo.' He leaned closer and his voice dropped to a whisper, 'and though I says it, strictly in confidence mind, he should never have been employed here.'

Cassie stared up at him, 'What do you mean, Jeff? Who said so?'

'Not exactly said,' Jeff hesitated and then said softly. 'I heard he'd been a bit of a naughty lad, been messing around with drugs, see. I mean to say, you know of folk that take one drink too many. Well, you must have in your line of business?'

Cassie nodded. 'Alcoholics, you mean?'

'Yeah, same with him, only drugs.'

Cassie took a backward step and stared up at Jeff in horror. She said loudly. 'Hells Bells! You mean to tell me you've got a practising doctor working here who's a junky?'

'Sssh! No, no, of course not! And you don't have to shout like that.' He looked warily over his shoulder. 'You never know who might hear you. What I'm telling you is only what I've heard old Doc Harrison say when he's had a drink or two. He knew Dr White a few years back and he helped him out. Helped him get this job, so he says. 'Course Dr White's clean now. There's even some that say he's a fine doctor, but,' Jeff paused and said quietly, 'with junkies you just never can tell.'

'I always get this weird feeling when I see him,' said Cassie. 'He never looks straight at you, if you know what I mean. So maybe it was a blessing that my Dave got old Doc Harrison instead.'

The phone at the reception desk rang, startling them both.

'Damn!' said Jeff as he looked towards it. 'I forgot to switch the answer phone on.' He looked apologetically at Cassie. 'It might be important.'

'You'd best answer it then,' said Cassie as she moved towards the door, 'and I'd better get back to my pub. Bye for now, but if you do see anyone, don't forget to let me know.'

Jeff hurried towards the phone, 'I should reckon the daft old sod's got himself lost in the woods somewhere,' he looked back and grinned at her, 'but if he turns up here, you'll be the first to know.'

CASSIE EASED HERSELF through the door and closed it softly behind her. She looked back through the glass and gave a little wave to Jeff who was still talking on the phone. Then she set off back down the driveway with a thoughtful smile curving her lips. Her visit had been worthwhile, for Jeff had made two mistakes. One thing was clear. Jeffrey Stokes was lying.

As Cassie approached her car the passenger door opened and Rosa got out and hurried towards her. 'What did he say?' she called. 'Did you find anything out?'

'A bit,' Cassie took Rosa by the arm and together they walked back to the car. 'Let's get out of this wind first, Rosa,' Cassie glanced back up the drive, 'and away from these gates before Jeff sees us. He thinks I came up here by myself. He'd wonder what was going on if he saw you.'

They got into the car and drove off down the road until they were a safe distance away from the nursing home.

'Cassie, will you please pull over,' said Anna, 'before my sister bites her nails down to her knuckles. For crying out loud, will you tell us what happened?'

Cassie stopped the car, then turned to Rosa and related the gist of her conversation with Jeff to her.

'Then he's not been seen there either?' Rosa said, her voice sounding close to tears.

'That's what Jeff said,' Cassie replied. She paused and patted Rosa's hand reassuringly, 'but I don't believe him, and I'll tell you for why. See, when I went in there, Jeff seemed flustered. Whether it was me or not, I don't know. But when I asked if he'd seen anyone he came out with, "Well, I've not got him". See what I mean? Because I'd never mentioned that it was a bloke I was looking for.'

'So Jeff knows something?' Rosa said.

Cassie nodded. 'Just to be sure, as I was leaving I asked him to let me know should he see anyone, note the "anyone", mind. And Jeff's reply was, and I'm quoting this, "I should reckon the daft old sod's got himself lost in the woods somewhere".'

'I'll give him daft,' said Rosa angrily. She seemed about to get out of the car, 'calling my Ben an old sod, just you—'

Anna reached over and grabbed her sister's shoulder. 'Cool it, Rosa,' she said. 'Let Cassie finish.'

'Sorry,' Rosa muttered, 'but why is it that anyone over the age of sixty is classified as an idiot these days?'

'Rosa, will you calm down and let Cassie do the talking. You do want to find your Ben, don't you?'

Rosa clicked her tongue. 'Now it's you that's being stupid.'

'Will you just listen?' said Anna. 'Carry on, Cassie. Tell us all.'

'Those were the two most important things,' Cassie said. 'To my way of thinking Jeff must have seen Ben, but why was he lying? If everything was above board, why didn't Jeff admit that Ben had been wandering around in the grounds and such. There's no harm in that.' She hesitated and the worried expression returned to her face. 'There's only one reason that I can think of, and that is that Ben's already in the nursing home. Why else would Jeff say "I've not got him?" What bothers me is *why* Ben is there?'

She paused and for a few minutes there came a silence whilst each of the women pondered over this question.

'He should never have gone after that Miss McGuire,' blurted Rosa. 'That was the start of it all.'

'Miss McGuire?' There was a puzzled note in Cassie's voice.

'Yes, she was his old schoolmarm from donkey's years back, and well, he saw her on the coach, didn't he. But she wouldn't speak to him, darted away every time he got near her. Then she…just disappeared. Come to think of it, last time I thought I saw her was outside your pub.'

Cassie sat up straight. 'The name don't ring any bells, Rosa. Describe her to me.'

'Ben said she was about eighty,' Rosa replied. 'Small,

thin, sort of wiry. Grey haired, wore specs.' She paused, thinking back over Ben's words. 'He said her face was sharp, and that she had a pointed chin, and that she'd got thin lips, like a line.'

'No beauty queen then,' Cassie said thoughtfully, 'but I've seen a woman who looked like that a couple of times, it might not be the same person, though. She talked to the coach drivers sometimes, but she never stayed as a guest in our pub.'

'Then where else would she stay?' Anna said. We know that Miss McGuire lives near us and we live over a good two hours drive away.'

'If you're lucky!' snapped Rosa.

Anna seemed about to defend herself, but thought better of it and continued. 'All we are getting is more and more unanswered questions. People can't keep disappearing. There has to be a connection.' She looked over her shoulder through the back window of the car, 'I'm sure that the link is the nursing home.' She looked from Rosa to Cassie, 'And I think it's time we did something about it.'

Cassie stared at her. 'You mean…go in?'

Anna nodded. 'Yep, but we'll go in through the back way. See who, or what, we can find.'

'What if you're wrong?' asked Cassie. 'If I get caught for…what do you call it?'

'Breaking and entering.'

'That's it. But I could lose my licence, Anna. I'd have a criminal record.' She stopped short as she saw that Anna was shaking her head.

'It's your husband's name over the door of your pub, and he's safely in hospital. You'd be all right.'

'Always assuming that we ever get out again,' piped

up Rosa. 'As you said, folk keep vanishing round here. Same thing could happen to us.'

'Be brave, Rosa. Think about your Ben.'

'Oh, I'm going in, all right. Just let anyone try and stop me.' Rosa glared at her sister. 'I am thinking about my Ben, and I'm thinking about Cassie here as well. Hasn't she got enough problems without getting involved in breaking into a nursing home?'

'That decision's up to me, Rosa, if you don't mind,' Cassie said firmly. 'I've not decided yet what I'll do, but I'll take you as far as the back of the building. It means you'll have to go through the woods.'

IAN WHITE WAS STARTLED as his car headlights picked out the figure of a blonde-haired woman on the driveway; she had appeared from nowhere. As he drew closer he saw that it was Mrs Hodgson, the pretty landlady from the Full Moon Inn. He remembered hearing her message on the answer phone that morning and he'd been about to deal with it when Bob Harrison had walked in and said that he'd already dealt with Mr Hodgson.

Vaguely Ian wondered if all was well with her husband, or if further complications had developed? Surely she would have telephoned again if that were the case. What was she doing here? She would hardly need to visit the nursing home.

He peered again through the rear-view mirror at the retreating figure; these days, like all attractive blondes, she made him nervous. They reminded him of Fiona. He thought back to when he had first met Fiona; she too had been blonde. To him she had looked just like an angel. He shuddered. Some angel! Through her conniving and with the help of her super-rich friends she had driven him to the very edge of hell. Even after all these years Ian felt his face flush as he thought about how foolish and how gullible he'd been. 'All my friends think you're just wonderful; you're their favourite medic, Ian.' And 'Darling, if you play your cards right, we'll have you in Harley Street in no time. You just have to be a bit more flexible.' Flexible indeed, thought Ian. What she had really meant was do what you're told, and hand over some of your prescription pads. And he, keen to impress her, had done so. Even worse, like an idiot he'd joined in on the drug taking as well until he'd come within a hair's breadth of ruining his career, not to mention his life.

He gave a tired sigh and his thoughts returned to Bob Harrison. For some reason he'd never quite understood, Bob had been the one to offer him a job when all others had shied away. And now here he was on his way to confront him. It seemed so ungrateful, but he had to know the truth.

As the car approached the junction leading to the turn-off for Bob's house Ian's mind focused on the immediate problem. His hand slid inside his overcoat and he touched the two envelopes that were in the inside pocket and felt reassured.

What would he say to Bob? Where should he begin? He would tell him about the forgeries, of course, he had proof of that. But as to whether he should mention his other suspicions? Coldness grew within him as he thought this through. He had no proof; only his gut feeling told him that Bob was involved in something evil.

He felt sure that Bob would be outraged; he would see him as a traitor and an ungrateful one at that. In a way it was true. Bob Harrison had used his influence in getting him this well paid position. At the time it had seemed like a godsend to Ian, yet now the doubts returned. 'Why did he do it?' he said out loud. 'There were plenty of other doctors to choose from.' Ian voiced the question again 'Why?' and stared blankly at the road ahead as the answers formed a queue in his mind. Because I would be grateful. Because I would be too intimidated to ask questions. Because I would be too frightened of losing my job to be inquisitive. He gave a bitter smile; he'd fallen into a trap that had been well baited. Now it was up to him to put things right. It was the only way if he were to continue to practise his profession in an upright and honest manner. His car's headlights lit up the number eighty-nine on the white-painted gatepost. He'd reached Bob's home. Ian turned the car into the drive and stopped. Taking a deep breath he got out and rang the doorbell. As he waited, bizarrely, a schoolboy rhyme came into his head. 'The time has come,' the Walrus said, 'to talk of many things.'

'GOOD LORD!' SAID BOB as he opened the door. 'Ian! What a surprise. Oh, do come in out of the wind.' He looked at Ian anxiously. 'There's not an emergency, or anything wrong up at the Home is there?'

'No, it's just that I wanted a word.'

'Of course, but let me get your overcoat. It's quite warm in here,' he grinned. 'At my age I tend to feel the cold a bit more than you young 'uns.'

'I'd rather keep it on, thanks. I won't stay long.'

'As you wish.' Bob smiled, 'But for heavens sake sit down.' He watched as Ian perched himself nervously on the edge of an armchair.

'Let me offer you a drink. I've got brandy, whisky, vodka?' He paused as Ian waved his hand dismissively.

'Not right this minute, Bob.'

Bob raised his eyebrows. 'Later then?'

Ian nodded. 'We'll see.'

Bob stared at him for a moment then returned to his chair. 'So, all right, you don't want a drink and you've just missed supper. What can I do for you?'

Ian took a deep breath and said, 'I hate to say this, but there seems to be…' He stopped, stared hard at Bob and continued, 'no, not seems to be. There are discrepancies on the death certificates of some of our patients.'

There was a long silence and then Bob said quietly. 'So? Somebody's made a boo-boo. Shit happens.'

'Not as often as this.'

Bob got up, went to the drinks cabinet and poured himself a large whisky. He turned to Ian. 'Elaborate.'

Ian leaned forward. 'Several of the documents have signatures that are forgeries and, yes, I know because I've checked and double-checked. Our locum, Doctor Robinson, often appears to be in two places at the same time.'

Bob grinned and took a cautious sip from his whisky. 'Perhaps he's another Houdini?'

'This is no joke,' said Ian. 'If anyone from the GMC should check these papers, they'd close us down.'

'Why ever would they want to check up on us? Unless, of course, someone blabs.'

'Bob! Don't you see? I cannot let this go unreported. Any fool can see that these signatures have been tampered with. You must have noticed it?'

Bob shrugged. 'Why would I? My job is to treat the patients. I'm not paid to be a penpusher, nor are you.' He finished off his drink then continued. 'I do think that you are getting a bit overzealous about this, Ian. Discrepancies happen; errors do occur.' He beamed at him. 'So calm down and let me get you a drink whilst we talk about this.' His expression brightened. 'In fact, I almost forgot, there is something that I'd like your opinion on. Bear with me for a moment. I'll be back in a second.'

He bustled off out of the room and after a few minutes returned carrying two full liqueur glasses. He handed one to Ian. 'You really must try this. This is special. Only a sip if you wish.' He watched as Ian drank the liqueur. 'What do you think?' he asked eagerly.

Ian nodded, 'Not bad.' He licked his lips, 'Not that I'm an expert on liqueurs, but to get back to—'

'I think it's delicious,' interrupted Bob. 'One of my patients gave it to me. It's made from orange peel, don't you know.' Bob's eyes glittered as he watched Ian drain his glass. He gave a laugh. 'Sure beats "crack", don't you think?'

Ian's face flushed, but he stared back at Bob. 'It has a sort of bitter-sweet aftertaste, though.'

Bob smiled in agreement. 'As have most addictions.'

Ian frowned then got up and walked towards the door. 'Bob, I came to see you so that I could get to the root of these forgeries. You've got to realize that the situation is serious. Something is wrong up at the nursing home and I'm sure that you know all about it.'

'What would I know? Except that you are getting over-anxious. Why this mad rush? Why can't we look at your evidence tomorrow in the clear light of day?'

'You know that I'll have to report it?'

'Yes, of course, but can't it wait a few more hours?' Bob looked at him thoughtfully, 'I know you. You're going to be lying awake worrying all night.' His face brightened. 'Before you go, though, I've got something that might put a stop to that.' He went over to a drawer, brought out a small bottle of pills then pushed them into Ian's coat pocket. 'Those are herbal, they're quite harm-less, and they might help you get some shuteye.'

'Really Bob,' Ian fished out the bottle of pills, looked

at the label, then shook his head. He opened the door and walked outside, 'I don't need anything.'

'Just humour me.' Bob followed him. He watched as Ian got into his car.

Ian turned to him, 'We'll definitely talk tomorrow?'

'First thing.'

Bob smiled and called, 'Sleep well, dear boy, sleep well.'

Still smiling, Bob Harrison waved until Ian's car was out of sight, then he walked back into the house. As soon as he reached the living room he poured himself another stiff measure of whisky and sipped it slowly, taking time to think things through. He thought about their conversation and Ian's suspicions. Would Ian really have written to the GMC and ruined everything as he had threatened? A sly smile creased Bob's lips. Not any more. That liqueur that he'd given him would work quickly. Bob grinned to himself. In fact, he doubted that Ian would even reach his home safely.

He looked at his watch, just to be on the safe side he'd better drive over to the nursing home and lose those files, but first things first. He went to the phone, dialled a number, heard the engaged signal then slammed the receiver down in annoyance. 'Damn it,' he muttered. He stood glaring at the phone impatiently. He would just have to wait a minute. He tried again. 'It's me,' he said when the call connected. 'Something's gone wrong. I think I've dealt with it but just to be sure I'd like to get rid of the evidence at the nursing home...if that's all right with you? We've got to do something. When can you get there then? As late as that? He clicked his tongue in annoyance, 'Well, all right, I'll wait. Just as long as everything's taken care of by morning. I'll meet you there then.'

TWENTY-FOUR

CASSIE BROUGHT THE CAR to a halt in the back lane and for a moment all three women stared out at the six feet high mesh fence that the cars headlights illuminated. In front of the fenced off area was a deep ditch, but there was no sign of any gateway.

'You sure we've stopped at the right bit?' Rosa asked.

Cassie gave a confident nod. 'Yes, this is where the gardener told me.' She pointed through the window. 'See where that white-striped post is? That's the way in. He said he cuts through there, then he runs down the hill at the double to our place so that he has time for a quick lunchtime pint. He swears blind he'd never make it if he were to go the long way round.'

Rosa peered doubtfully out at the fence. 'I don't know about that. I'm not sure I can climb such a high fence.'

Cassie tapped a finger to her nose. 'Trust me, Rosa. There's more than one way to skin a rabbit.' She got out of the car and pulled on her jacket. 'Follow me, ladies,' she said, and then she stopped, stared down at her sandals and muttered, 'Dammit. Just a minute, first things first.' She opened the car boot and removed her shoes. 'These have taken enough punishment for today.' She got her wellies out of the boot and put them on. 'Another thing,' she said as she locked the car. 'I do hope that one of you has got a torch, 'cause I'll need mine.'

Anna tapped her shoulder bag. 'Always got one with me,' she replied. She walked a few paces along the lane and took a brief look around then, turning back, jumped over the ditch and scrutinized the fence. She ran her hand over the post that supported the fencing, 'If that white-striped post is the marker, the opening must be some-where about...' Part of the fencing moved towards her. 'Aha! Thought so!' She looked over her shoulder and grinned at the other two. 'Amazing what a bit of putty can do, if it's in the right place.'

Rosa looked at Cassie, 'It's her criminal mind, you know. She can always figure out how to break in. I reckon in the next incarnation she's going to be a master crook.'

Cassie giggled, 'It's a useful gift to have these days.'

Rosa sighed. 'I just wish she was just as good at find-ing people, and that we'd hurry up and find my Ben.'

Cassie gave her a hug. 'Patience, Rosa, we'll find him.' She hesitated, peered uneasily at the dense woods behind the fence and said defiantly. 'At least we'll have a bloody good try. Now stay close to me, darlin'. Your sis-ter's through the fence already, but once we get through we'd better be sure to close it. Don't want to give my cus-tomers' secrets away.'

Rosa followed Cassie over the ditch to where Anna waited, and they eased themselves through.

'Now where?' Anna asked as she watched Cassie ease the fencing back into place. 'Can't see nothing from here.'

'Half a mo,' Cassie said. 'I'll just fix this in case some passing motorist notices.' She walked over to Anna and said, 'You'd best use your torch now, but keep the beam low, in case someone over at the nursing home spots the light. I was told there's a pathway over to your left.' She watched as Anna swung the beam of the torch round until it finally picked out a narrow track. 'There we are!'

With Anna leading the way, they followed the torch-light until they reached the path.

'Right,' said Cassie, 'stay on the path until you see two greenhouses, then you'll know that you've reached the nursing home grounds.' She stopped and glanced at her watch. Having noted the time she hesitated and looked at the women uneasily.

'What's the matter?' Rosa asked.

'Nothing. It's just…' She walked a few paces in front of them and pointed. 'Look! Over there, to your left. You can just see the lights from the nursing home.'

'Just about,' Rosa said who was behind her. 'They look pretty dim though, hardly a welcoming beacon.'

'Let them guide you,' Cassie said, 'least you'll know in which direction to go.' She hesitated again and looked embarrassed, 'Look ladies, I'm sorry but I'm going to have to leave you. I'd have liked to have stayed, but the hospital might ring, and there's the pub and Claire too… I've gotta get back, see, just to make sure.'

Rosa touched her arm and stretching up kissed her soundly on her cheek. 'Of course you have, my dear. You've already done more than we could hope for, and I'm very grateful to you. You go and see if your Dave's okay.'

Cassie turned to walk away. She looked over her shoulder at the women. 'I will try and get back as soon as I've checked things out. I will, I promise.' She hurried back towards the fence.

Rosa and Anna stood silently and watched Cassie's trim figure disappear into the darkness.

'Now what?' Rosa said after a while.

'We've got to get going,' Anna said. She looked up at the sky. 'Pity there's no moon tonight.'

'It can't get much darker. Just you keep shining that

torch in my direction.' Rosa looked about her nervously. 'It's black as ink back here.'

Anna eyed Rosa and hoped that she wasn't starting to panic. Best try and keep her focused. Aloud, she said, 'Now do as I tell you and stay on the path.'

'I am on the path.' Rosa retorted angrily, 'Did you think I'd be swinging from the trees like Tarzan?'

'Don't you start getting sarky with me, otherwise I'll just leave you right there.'

There came an angry snort from Rosa in reply and for a while there was silence broken only by the occasional snapping of twigs as the women made their way through the wood.

Several minutes later Rosa said, 'Anna!'

'What?'

'I can hear something!'

'Like what?'

'Like running water.'

'Hmm! Could be a stream or a lake.'

'Could be a pond. A deep pond.'

Anna stopped in her tracks and turned the beam of her flashlight onto the face of her sister. 'Will you stop being so pessimistic. Do you think that if you fell into a pond I wouldn't notice? You know I'd fish you out.'

'It's not me that I'm worried about. I can't help thinking about my Ben. He might be out here lying in some stream somewhere, all wet and shivering and cold and who knows what else.'

About 7.30 p.m.

BEN'S FACE FELT HOT and he was glad of the cooling sensation of the sweat that trickled from his forehead down to his neck. He heard the soft click of the lock as the tumblers slipped into place, and with a trembling hand he slowly eased the door open.

With a sigh of relief he took a backward step, wiped the sweat from his face and regained his breath. That job had been much more difficult than he'd expected. In the old days he could have had that door open in no time at all; now it had taken ages. He listened. Had anyone heard him? He stood in the doorway, looked both ways along the corridor and listened again. Nothing. Not a sound.

Tiptoeing into the corridor he gazed up at the passage ceiling; the lighting here seemed much dimmer than in his room, and it gave off a cold eerie glow. Something else seemed wrong; this place was a nursing home, it looked like a nursing home, it had that antiseptic smell of a nursing home but... Ben sniffed the air. Where was the food? Surely it must be near supper time, yet no tempting aromas drifted past him.

Once more he listened. Nothing! Not even the sound of a distant television. Just silence.

You're free! He told himself. Don't stand there as if you've taken root! Move it! Get yourself out of here. Now! He surged forward but some inner instinct urged him to stay cautious. He stopped to remove his shoes, and, tying the laces together, hung them around his neck.

At the far end of the corridor he could see the standard green symbols for the escape route in case of fire. Cautiously, he crept along in that direction. He could not remember on which side of the building the fire escape was situated, but as long as it got him out of here he didn't much care.

As he went past the wards he glanced into them, he wanted to go in and ask the patients if any of them knew of a Miss McGuire, but they all appeared to be sleeping. Keep moving, he told himself, and he focused on the distant fire symbols. With relief he spotted the fire door and he increased his pace. He was within a few yards of the fire door when he heard the sound. His pulses quickened and he stopped dead in his tracks. Please, no! Not now, he thought, as he identified it. It was the unmistakable rattle of a trolley. It seemed to be coming from one of the side wards behind him. Ben pressed himself up against the wall. Perhaps the trolley would go in the opposite direction. It might not be coming his way at all. If he stood very still with any luck they just might not see him. His optimism faded as the sound of the trolley became louder. He waited, holding his breath. If only he could reach that bloody door. He froze, eyes and ears straining.

Then came the other sounds, the lighter, higher pitch of a woman's voice and the deeper tones of a male. As he heard the latter, Ben's hopes sank; it was the voice of his captor, Jeff.

Hope vanished and desperation took control. He had to get out of here. He had to try. He rushed towards the fire door, not turning, not thinking, as the voices behind him grew ever louder.

He made it! He'd reached the door! He was seconds away from freedom! He pushed against the door. 'Open, damn you! Open!' He cursed. The door remained closed.

In desperation Ben turned to face his former captor. He would at least put up a fight and give Jeff a good thrashing. He braced himself against the door.

'What the hell do you think you're playing at?' Jeff shouted as he grabbed Ben's arms.

'I'll give you three guesses.' Ben yelled as he kneed at Jeff's groin. At that precise moment, Ben felt the fire door latch open behind him.

TWENTY-FIVE

IAN DROVE OUT of the drive and turned right onto the road. He peered through his rear mirror at the chubby figure of Bob Harrison standing in the doorway, waving cheerfully. What was wrong with the man, he wondered. He'd just been given some frightening news, and how had he reacted? By playing the genial host, and by plying him with booze. And the result? He now had a blinding headache.

He rubbed his forehead. That bloody liqueur! Added to the tension, it was making him feel really ill. The snide remarks that Bob had made about 'crack' hadn't helped either. How was he going to get through to Bob? Didn't he understand what he'd told him?

After a few minutes he felt the nausea build within him, he blinked. The road ahead seemed to blur. He'd better slow down. He'd soon be home and then he could get some food inside him; that might help. The dizziness increased. The car swerved and he clutched the steering wheel tightly. What was happening to the road? Why was it zigzagging? It was heaving like a rollercoaster ride. He was going to be sick. Desperately he wrenched on the wheel. If he could just pull over....

CASSIE HURRIED BACK to her car, got in and switched on the ignition. She tried to dismiss the guilt that she felt having to leave those two ladies. They were hardly in the first flush of youth and if one of them stumbled and was injured it would add to her list of problems, as if she hadn't enough already. I should have gone with them, at least guided them through the woods until they reached the drive, she told herself, as she drove along the narrow lane. But she hadn't been able to stop worrying how Dave was, or whether the hospital had rung. She fished her mobile out of her pocket, checked it, and breathed a sigh of relief as the words 'no new messages' came up on the screen.

Her thoughts moved on to the running of their pub, and she wondered if Claire was coping by herself. She knew it was asking a lot of a young girl, but in an emergency it was all she could do. As she drove on through the night Cassie's thoughts raced. So okay, Dave should be safe now, and hopefully he was being well looked after, but what if by helping Rosa and Anna she had unwittingly brought yet more trouble down upon them both?

What if the nursing home was bona fide and they then discovered that she had been the one who had helped the two women break into the grounds. They could, in fact, sue her for aiding unlawful entry and trespass.

Cassie sighed; she had no proof but her sixth sense told her that there was something evil up at the nursing home. She thought about the oldies that had gone missing over the past few months. What had happened to these people? Why had no one come looking for them?

Her thoughts came back to the present; what had become of Rosa's husband? She felt sure he was being held at the nursing home, but the big question was, what had he done? Or, more likely, what had he discovered? Was there, in fact, a very good reason for them to keep him there?

She recalled the events of the last two days and her mood darkened; there were so many questions and no answers. She tried to push her bleak thoughts away. Get a grip, woman, she told herself and she pressed down hard on the accelerator.

She had not driven far before she saw a car sideways in the ditch with the headlights full on. Was it joyriders or an accident? As if she hadn't had enough aggro for today. She slowed to a halt, picked up her torch and cautiously got out to investigate.

It was a dark-blue BMW and the engine was still running. She approached it slowly and peered through the car window. With a start she saw that someone was slumped over the steering wheel. With horror she realized that the driver was Dr White.

She wrenched the car door open. 'Check the breathing, stop the bleeding,' she muttered, recalling the age-old rule. The stench of vomit made her shrink back, but taking a deep breath she leaned into the car again and looked at him. There was no sign of blood, but from what she could see, Dr White looked to be unconscious.

Cassie examined his face carefully; apart from the traces of vomit around his mouth, and the fact that his glasses had fallen off and were hanging precariously on the edge of the steering wheel, she could see no signs of bruising. She picked up the glasses, switched off the engine, then putting both glasses and keys into her jacket pocket, looked at the doctor again. She shook his shoulder and called out 'Doctor White' in a gentle attempt to rouse him, but it had no effect, and, as she listened she noted that his breathing was slow and shallow. Cassie gave a deep sigh, got her mobile out of her pocket, and dialled 999.

She stood on the dark and lonely road and waited for the ambulance. And whilst she waited Cassie pondered the irony of her situation. How strange it was, she thought, that she, of all people, should be the one who was rescuing the man whose careless diagnosis had just about killed her husband.

'ANNA!'

With a snort of exasperation Anna turned round and scowled at her sister. 'Now what?'

'I've lost my shoe! It's got stuck in the mud.'

Cursing under her breath, Anna looked at Rosa. 'Let's see.' She shone her torch down into the muddy undergrowth. There, sure enough, half submerged, was Rosa's shoe. 'Don't just stand there!' Anna said, 'Pull it out.'

'Have you got some tissues?'

Anna drew upon her reserves of patience. 'Yes, I have, but I've only a few left and I'm not letting you use them up just to get your shoe out of the mud. Use some leaves or something, and try to stay close in future.'

'Don't walk so fast, then.' Rosa called as she eased her foot back into the shoe, 'I keep slipping with all of this mud.'

Anna looked down at the path, 'It's the stream that's causing the mud.'

'I could have told you that five minutes ago. I'm not daft, y'know.'

What is wrong with her, Anna thought. Is it the worry that's making her so tetchy? 'Look,' she said, 'Try to walk in my shoeprints like we used to do when we were kids, remember?'

'I could hardly forget. Not with your big feet. And even in those days you never stopped trying to boss me. Of course I—' Rosa broke off as there came the sound of a loud splash, then a churning as if something was wading towards them. 'What the hell is that?'

Anna hissed. 'Freeze!' She switched off her torch and

she and Rosa stood in total darkness whilst the sound of something or someone wading through water came nearer, then gradually faded away.

Rosa gulped and after a while said, 'What *was* that, then?'

'Dunno,' Anna was puzzled, 'Whatever it was it must have been quite a size.'

Rosa's voice trembled, 'It was probably a deer. They do say there are lots of them in these parts.' An owl hooted nearby and she spun round nervously. 'I've never liked woods, y'know. There's always something sinister about them, 'specially at night.'

Anna switched the torch back on. 'All the more reason to get out of here, but just try to move quietly. If we make too much noise someone might hear us.'

'You don't happen to think that it might have been *them* just now, coming looking for us?'

'Look!' said Anna. 'Stop thinking. Just move…as quickly and as quietly as you can.' She tried to hide her own anxiety as she added, 'The sooner we're clear of these woods the better.' Under her breath she murmured, 'Once in the open we'll stand a better chance.'

They ploughed on silently for a while then Rosa said, 'The trees are thinning out and, oh look, there are the greenhouses, the ones Cassie mentioned. Anna, we're there!'

They climbed through the wire fence and made their way round between the greenhouses until they reached the gravel drive.

'Watch it now,' Anna said. 'Stay on the grass verge. If you walk on gravel you can hear every sound.' She stood without moving, peering up at the building.

Rosa looked at her, 'Why have you stopped?'

'I'm looking for security cameras. Looks like there's

one over the entrance and one just there at the corner, but let's see what they've got round the back.'

Cautiously they picked their way along the grass verge past the garages and further along past what appeared to be a little-used delivery entrance. They were approaching an ancient-looking fire escape staircase when they heard the sound of a car coming up the driveway. 'Quick, get back into the bushes,' Anna said, 'the car might be coming into the garages.'

As they crouched in the bushes Rosa looked up at the dimly lit windows and said wistfully, 'I wonder where they're keeping my Ben?'

'We're not even sure that he's here,' Anna replied as she turned to watch the car come up the drive and park on the far side of the entrance. She heard the car door slam and the crunch of gravel, but could see no one. 'Damn!'

Rosa seemed uninterested in the arrival of the vehicles. 'Cassie must have thought that Ben was here,' she insisted, 'and that they were keeping him, otherwise she'd not have helped us out.'

'Agreed,' Anna said. 'But he might have been moved, or they might even have let him go by now.'

Rosa turned to her sister and when she spoke there was a tinge of steel in her voice. 'Well, yes, let's hope he's free. But we are still going in there to look for him, aren't we?'

Anna repressed a sigh. 'Of course we are, only...' Her gaze travelled over the building and its many windows, then came to rest on the delivery door. 'Stay put,' she ordered as she hurried over to the door and, shining her torch, examined the lock and padlocks that were on it. After a while she turned and walked back to where Rosa waited.

'Any luck?' Rosa asked.

Anna shook her head. 'I thought that we might have stood a chance there, but there are two padlocks on the door and the lock itself is rusty and covered in cobwebs. They must make all the deliveries through the main entrance.'

'Can't you open it?'

'Perhaps I could,' Anna said thoughtfully, 'but it would take up too much time. That door has not been opened for years.'

Rosa said anxiously. 'We've got to get in somehow. I can't leave Ben. We can't give in. Not now. Not after all this.' She sniffed and fought back her tears.

'Hey!' Anna said, 'Don't lose your bottle.' She put her arms round her sister, pulled her close and said gently, 'Remember that old saying? "The impossible we achieve immediately...miracles take a bit longer".'

Through her tears Rosa hugged Anna and giggled, 'Right on, Sis, right on.'

They stood closely together for a while and surveyed the building, then Anna said, 'I think we'd best rule out the ground-floor windows. They're sure to have security locks on them.'

Rosa nodded. 'We don't want to be climbing in and scaring any poor patients.'

'Let's try here, then.' Anna strode over to the fire escape stairs.

Rosa followed her with reluctance: she looked up at the stairs and gulped. Finally she spoke. 'I feel dizzy when I look up there and I've got to say I don't like the look of them stairs very much. You know how I feel about heights.'

'Oh come on now, do try and be brave. You're scared if you've to jump off the edge of a carpet. You've got to get over it, Rosa. There are handrails.'

'But are you sure these are safe? What I mean is we don't want to get half way up and then fall through them. They look mighty old to me. They've probably got, what do they call it? Metal fatigue.'

Anna clicked her tongue. 'That's what airplanes get, not fire escapes.' She gestured at the steps. 'Besides, they've got to be safe, otherwise Health and Safety would be after them.'

Rosa was unconvinced; she took a backward step and stared upwards. 'It's still a long way up to the top.'

'Yes, I know, but we've got to try the fire doors.' Anna studied her sister and said, 'Although, at your age, if you don't think you can manage it?'

'If you can, I can,' Rosa said indignantly. She stared meaningfully at Anna's hips. 'I'm nothing like your weight.'

'But you are two years older, and you do get short of breath.'

'If I run out of puff, then I'll stop for a while, so let's have no more dawdling. Are we going to stand here all night, or can we go?'

'Hold on, hold on,' Anna said. 'First things first. Listen to what I'm telling you. These metal stairs will echo the slightest sound, so we've got to be quiet. So take your shoes off and put them in your pockets.'

'One's still covered in mud.' Rosa protested.

'Just do it!'

Grumbling softly, Rosa did as Anna asked. ''Course you do know I'll have to take this coat straight to the dry cleaners tomorrow?'

'Will you shut up for a minute?'

Anna took off her own shoes and then checked her shoulder bag. 'Just so as I've got something to "do" the lock with, if we can find a way in.' She waved a nail file at Rosa.

'Will you get a move on then, my feet are getting cold.'

Anna started to climb and turned to look down at her. 'They'll be colder still in a minute. Now follow me and try to put your feet at the sides of the steps; that way there's less creaking.'

'Orders, orders,' Rosa muttered as she followed her. 'If there was an honours degree in giving orders, you'd have got it.'

Anna looked back at her. 'Sssh!'

Silently, Rosa and Anna began their climb, pausing occasionally whilst Rosa regained her breath.

'How many doors are you going to try?' Rosa asked breathlessly.

'As many as it takes,' said Anna, 'If I could just ease one of them open.'

They reached the top of a flight of stairs, stopped and looked about them.

'Phew,' Rosa gasped. 'It's a long way down from here!'

'Try not to look at the ground too much. You might get vertigo.'

Rosa grabbed the stair rail with both hands and said nervously, 'I've been too busy climbing to think about that, but now that you mention it....'

Anna groaned, 'Could you manage to unpeel one of your hands from that rail for a minute, and hold my torch for me?'

With a sigh Rosa held on grimly to the rail with one hand, then clutched Anna's torch.

'I've told you before, hold it steady, so as I can see.' Anna opened her shoulder bag and fished out the nail file again.

Rosa stared at it doubtfully.

'Don't worry,' Anna reassured her, 'I do have other little gadgets, should this fail.'

'It's not so much you failing as me falling that's bothering me,' Rosa said as she tried not to look down. 'Hurry up, will you.'

'Shine the light on the door then.' Anna looked at the door, and then said casually, 'Could you try to shine the light a bit higher, yeah, that's nearly it. Just up a bit more and over to your right.'

TWENTY-SIX

WITH A SENSE of relief Cassie watched as the ambulance approached with blue lights flashing. It had seemed like an eternity standing there on this bleak road waiting for them, especially as she'd had to call upon their help earlier that day.

As the ambulance halted, and the paramedics got out and came towards her, Cassie peered in the car again at the slumped figure of Dr White. She'd checked his breathing every few minutes but now it seemed ragged and uneven, and she thought that he needed urgent medical attention. That was the number one priority.

For the moment she had to put all thoughts of Dave to the back of her mind. The hospital had said that they would contact her if there were any problems or queries, although once she'd dealt with this she would ring them and check again just to be sure.

'Mrs Hodgson? You phoned earlier? You've had an accident?' the paramedic said.

'Not me,' Cassie said quickly, 'I'm okay,' she gestured at the figure inside the BMW.

'I came across him as I was on my way home. I thought it best to call you as he's unconscious and he's been sick. I don't know how badly injured he is.'

The paramedic pulled open the car door again, sniffed the air and climbed inside. He called to his colleague, 'Give me some light, Steve.'

His colleague handed him a torch and he shone the

light on Dr White's face, just as Cassie had done. He tried gently to wake him but it was of no avail. He turned to Cassie, 'Do you know this man?'

'It's Dr White. He works up at the nursing home.'

'What's his first name?'

'I think it's Ian.'

The paramedic leaned over the doctor again and spoke loudly, 'Ian, can you hear me? It's all right, you're going be okay… Ian?' There was no response. The paramedic turned to Steve, 'Get the stretcher.' He watched as Steve returned to the ambulance then spoke to Cassie. 'Looks like we'd better take him to A&E, Mrs Hodgson. You're a friend of his, then?'

'Not really. He's my husband's GP.'

Steve brought up the stretcher and as they eased Dr White onto it, the paramedic leaned over him, placed an oxygen mask over his nose and mouth, and spoke reassuringly. 'Ian! This is just to help you breathe a bit better, okay? We're going to move you now, get you to the hospital, you're going to be fine.' He glanced at his colleague and nodded. 'Steady, Steve. Right? One, two, three, here we go.' He looked down at Ian. 'Soon we'll be off.'

Cassie stood silently whilst they moved the doctor into the ambulance. She saw with concern that his face was still a deathly pale. Whilst the paramedics were securing the stretcher, a police car drove up, and Cassie watched as the policeman got out, consulted with the paramedics, and then walked over and made a cursory examination of Dr White's car. She lingered and wondered if he was going to question her, but he merely placed a 'police aware' sticker on the BMW windscreen and drove off, following the ambulance down the lane. She watched as the tail-lights of both vehicles faded into the night then got into her own car and drove home.

When she got back to the pub Cassie went through to the kitchen, checked her mobile again, then, as there were still no new messages, decided to call the hospital. Whilst she waited for the ward to answer, she tried to calm her nerves. It had been a hectic and worrying day but there was no point in getting over anxious.

'Hello? Blue ward, Sister Mullins speaking.'

'Good evening, Sister. It's Mrs Hodgson here. I'm just ringing to enquire about my husband, Mr David Hodgson. He was admitted earlier today, this afternoon it was. They told me then that he'd be on the Blue ward.'

'Ah, yes.' Cassie heard a rustling of papers. 'I've got his notes here. We've stopped the bleeding and we're giving him a transfusion.' There came a pause, 'Mrs Hodgson, he's awake now and he's comfortable.'

'Oh that's great,' said Cassie with relief; at least something was going right. 'What time should I visit tomorrow?'

'Anytime would be fine.'

'Thank you,' said Cassie. She was about to replace the receiver when the Sister said, 'Mrs Hodgson?'

'Yes?'

'I've just been reading your husband's notes. Do you think you could bring in the medicine that he'd been taking? That would be helpful.'

''Course I will. Thanks again, and good night.' As Cassie put down the phone she tried to think just where she'd put that little brown bottle. Trouble was that so much had happened today she was finding it hard to focus on stuff like that. Although now that Sister had mentioned it, she remembered that the casualty doctor had also asked her to bring Dave's medication in to them. Why did they want it? She scratched her head and tried to remember. Where the hell had she put that bloody bottle?

'Is Mr Hodgson all right now?' said a voice. Cassie looked over at the door that connected to the bar and saw Claire smiling at her.

Cassie said, 'I'm sorry, my love. I should have come and told you. The hospital says that he's comfortable now.'

'That's all right then,' said Claire. She hesitated, 'Would you be wanting me to stay on until closing time?'

'No, my darlin', you've helped enough already. Has it been busy?'

'Steady like, not much doing in the kitchen. Chef went home early.'

'And you must go home too. If you'll just give me five minutes to make a sandwich and a drink, then I'll let you go.'

'Sure, I'll start clearing away then.' Claire went back into the bar.

As Cassie took off her jacket she felt the spectacles and Dr White's car keys in her pocket. She fished them out and stared at them blankly, she couldn't even remember putting them there. She felt annoyed at her forgetfulness. By rights both the spectacles and the keys should be with the ambulance men. She would have to find some way to return them to Dr White but the trouble was she didn't know where he lived. She also ought to tell someone about his accident.

The only person that she could think of was Dr Harrison at the nursing home and he'd hardly be working up there at this time of night. But she could leave a message on the nursing home answer phone. At least they would know first thing tomorrow. She went to the phone and keyed in the number.

Having left the message Cassie put down the phone, put the keys and the spectacles into her handbag for safe

keeping, and thought about Dr White. It did seem odd
that he should crash into the ditch and be unconscious.
He'd seemed all right when she'd seen him just over an
hour ago. Doubts crept into her mind. What if it wasn't
drugs that had caused that? The man could be ill? She
might be jumping to the wrong conclusion just because
she didn't like him. She shrugged; but like him, or not,
she'd done all that she could for him.

Her thoughts moved on to Rosa and Anna and her
missing husband. What on earth was going on there? She
hoped that the two women had found a way into the nursing home. She glanced at the clock again; if she hadn't
heard from them by eleven when the pub was closed she
would set out to find them.

Cassie walked over to the fridge, got out the mak-
ings for a sandwich and switched the kettle on. As she
buttered the bread her mind drifted on to the worst-case
scenario. What if the two women should also disappear?
Cassie stood stock still. Then she really would have to
take action. Then, come hell or high water, she'd call in
the police!

TWENTY-SEVEN

JEFF GASPED, and biting back his pain, grabbed hold of Ben and dragged him away from the fire door, 'Get over here you old sod and don't ever do that again!' As Ben continued to struggle Jeff twisted Ben's arm into an arm lock, then pulling a baton from his inside pocket extended it with a twist of his wrist. He leaned over Ben and waved the baton threateningly. 'Just don't force me to use this, okay? It would break your legs in no time.'

Ben stared at the weapon and his heart raced, he'd never seen a baton this close to, but he'd seen it at work on the television, and the effect that they had when the police used them during a riot. They could cripple a man; that much was certain. 'Okay, okay!' Ben said. 'Take it easy, will you, I was only trying to get home.'

'You'll go when they tell you.' Jeff waved the baton menacingly. 'Now, are you going to behave or not?'

'Let go of me, will you. All right!' He nodded at the weapon. 'There's no need for that.'

Jeff released him and Ben winced as he rubbed his arm and tried to regain his breath. Reluctantly, he trudged along the corridor beside Jeff until they reached his original room. Here Jeff stopped when he saw that the door was wide open. He turned to stare at Ben. 'How the hell did you manage that?'

'By using my brains. Something that you're short of, else you'd never work here,' Ben said defiantly. It was an effort to speak. His heart was still racing and he felt shaky, but he wasn't going to show fear.

Jeff glared at Ben. 'Don't you stretch my patience. I've had enough of you.' He hauled a bunch of keys out of his pocket, grabbed Ben's arm and pulled him further along down the corridor until they reached another room.

As they entered it Ben saw that this was some kind of examination room. There was a wash basin, a small table, some chairs and a couch.

'Ha!' he said with bravado as he spotted the couch. 'Now I get to lie down, do I?'

Jeff strode over to the couch and, bending down, tugged at some straps that were underneath it. He held up a strap and looked at Ben. 'You'll get to stay down if I have any more bother.'

Ben said nothing. He stared at the straps in stunned disbelief and felt his fear increase. Be careful, he thought, once those straps are on, you'd have no chance. Aloud he said, 'Look. There's nothing personal in this. You or your bosses have locked me up. God knows why, I don't. Look at it from my point of view. If you were me, wouldn't you try to escape?'

Jeff scowled at him, 'Just stop wittering, will you. My job is to do what I'm told.'

Ben held up his hands. 'All right, you win. How long are you going to keep me here?'

Jeff stared at him and shook his head.

'You really don't know?'

'Not part of my job to ask questions, but whilst I remember,' he strode over to Ben, 'Come on, empty your pockets.'

'Okay, okay!' Ben said, backing away.

'Get on with it, before I do it for you.' Jeff stood and watched whilst Ben placed an assortment of items on the table, until at last the pocket knife and the bit of wire appeared.

'There we are,' Jeff said triumphantly. He grabbed the pocket knife, the wire and the other stuff and walked to the door, pulling it open. 'I'm taking these with me in case you decide to have another DIY session and try to remove this one as well.' He slipped through the door locking it behind him.

With a sense of relief Ben watched him go and then as an afterthought shouted, 'Can't I at least have a bottle of water?' But there was no answer, only the sound of footsteps echoing hollowly down the corridor.

Ben looked around the room then switched off the light and walked over to the window. At least he might get some idea of where he was situated this time. It could be worth breaking a window if there was a convenient tree or even some ivy that he could cling to. He reached the window and stared out into the darkness, automatically checking if it was locked, but much the same scene as earlier greeted him. Disappointed, he made his way back to the door and switched the light back on again.

He removed his shoes from around his neck and for a while stared down at them. His gaze flicked to the couch and he walked over to it and examined the sheet that covered it. He shook his head; it was far too short for his needs. He slumped down on the couch and felt the weariness grow within him. He was tempted; his bones ached with tiredness. It seemed to be years since he'd had a proper sleep. He eased his legs up, stretched them out and lay back and felt a huge sense of relief. At least the pain in his legs was easing. He grinned in reminiscence; not that kneeing Jeff had done much to help his knee pains, but he'd felt a hell of a lot better for it.

As he lay there Ben's eyes scanned the room, it was

just as neutral as the first one had been, with pale green colour washed walls and faded looking curtains. The desk was modern and the chairs looked new, all perfectly ordinary, except for the couch, and the straps. Why on earth would anyone want straps on a couch?

In spite of his frustration and a growing sense of thirst Ben dozed off. He was just about asleep when he heard the sound. Had he dreamt it? He frowned, trying to identify it. It wasn't the jangle of keys. It wasn't footsteps. It wasn't voices. It was a rattling, tinny sound, like that of something solid ricocheting and clanking hollowly on metal. With a start he sat up, he remembered the fire door. Ears straining, he listened intently, but yet again the silence had returned.

IAN WHITE WOKE TO the mingled sounds of voices, footsteps hurrying, echoingly loudly. He heard a child cry out in pain. A phone rang, making him start. 'Where in God's name am I?' he said as he tried to pull himself upright. For a long moment he stared blurrily at the garish floral curtains that surrounded him. He was in some sort of screened off cubicle, and he could smell...

A wave of nausea hit him and he vomited. He heard the sound of a curtain being drawn back and a voice say, 'I'll get a bowl.'

Gloved hands gave him a cardboard bowl and he nodded dumbly as he watched the nurse clean up. Tissues were passed to him and he wiped his mouth.

'You okay now?' she enquired as she placed another bowl on the locker.

'Think so,' he managed.

She poured him a glass of water, 'Take it slowly. Just a little sip at a time.'

He took a large gulp, swilled it round in his mouth,

then spat it out into the bowl, trying to eliminate the taste of vomit and bile. There, that was better.

He shuffled into a sitting position in the bed and, looking blearily down, saw that his overcoat and jacket had been removed. He realized that he was in the A&E unit at the hospital and gave a grim smile. As a junior doctor he'd had to work in Casualty as part of his training for several months. Great learning experience, but not the easiest of jobs.

His stomach clenched again and he felt the nausea return. The nurse had disappeared. He reached for the bowl on the locker; better out than in. When he'd finished he breathed a deep sigh then laying back in the bed, drifted into sleep.

Ian woke again in what seemed to him to be a few minutes to find a white-coated figure staring down at him. He squinted up at the ID card on the man's lapel; and saw that his name was Dr Brendan. He shook his head; he didn't know him.

'Ah, back with us at last,' Dr Brendan said. 'Good to see that the stuff worked, thought for a while there we might need to use a stomach pump on you.' He leaned over and, taking hold of Ian's wrist, checked his pulse. He peered closely at his eyes. 'Still dilated,' he muttered. Then he pulled a chair up to the bed and sat down.

Looking earnestly at him, he said, 'Do you feel ready to tell me what brought this on? He paused when he saw Ian's puzzled expression then continued. 'What made you want to take an overdose?'

Ian stared at him. 'I didn't take anything.'

'Oh come now.' The doctor waved his chart at him. 'We've got your history on file. We know that—'

Ian struggled to sit upright and felt his vision blur. 'I *did not* take any drugs, I tell you!'

'Doctor White. Our tests show that there was a large amount of diamorphine in your blood.' Dr Brendan lowered his voice and said seriously, 'in fact you are lucky to be alive!'

'But I didn't take it,' Ian insisted.

The doctor raised his eyebrows, 'So? How did it get there?'

Ian rubbed his forehead. 'I don't know. The only thing I can think of is that Dr Harrison gave it to me in a liqueur.' He thought back to what Bob Harrison had said earlier when he'd given him the drink. No wonder he'd called the liqueur special. No wonder he'd seemed so persuasive. He was trying his damnedest to get rid of him. Permanently.

Dr Brendan leaned back in the chair and folded his arms across his chest. 'You really don't mean old Dr Harrison down in the village? *He* gave you that?'

'Yes. Who else?'

'I know him,' the doctor said, 'and you're telling me that Bob Harrison, who has been in the profession for forty years, was trying to…drug you?'

'To hell with "drugging me", as you so politely put it.' Ian tried to shout and he felt the sweat break out on his brow. 'He was bloody well trying to kill me!'

The doctor pushed back his chair, stood up briskly and strode to the curtained exit. He turned to Ian. 'What you are stating, Dr White, is that someone—'

'Not someone. Bob Harrison.' Ian groaned.

'*He* attempted to murder you?'

'Yes!' insisted Ian. 'If you have done checks on my blood, you will also have found traces of alcohol in it. The drug must have been mixed with that. The only alcohol that I have consumed within the last twenty-four hours was the liqueur that Bob Harrison gave me. The result should be perfectly clear.'

Dr Brendan pulled back the curtain and hesitated. 'There was some alcohol in your blood tests,' he said doubtfully. 'In fact, at first the paramedics thought you were intoxicated. They, and we, assumed that you were trying to OD.'

Ian shook his head. 'No way.'

The doctor warned, 'You do realize that this is a serious allegation that you are making against Dr Harrison?'

'Of course I do,' Ian said, 'and I think it's time I called in the police.'

AT THE SAME HOSPITAL on another floor, in another ward, Dave Hodgson lay quietly in his bed and stared at the plastic tubes that were connected to his left arm. He smiled to himself; one thing was sure, whatever it was that the quacks had done to him, the pain had gone.

He allowed himself the luxury of stretching his body and breathing normally. True, his stomach muscles were a bit tender and he certainly felt light-headed, but he was grateful for the absence of pain.

He snuggled into the pillows and wondered how long he had been here. From what he could see through the window across the ward, it was already night-time. He looked at his watch and felt a slight sense of panic when he found that it had been replaced by a plastic ID bracelet. Worriedly he opened the locker drawer at his bedside, then saw with relief that his watch, his wallet and other personal belongings were all there.

Vaguely he recalled being lifted into the ambulance, the sounds of the siren, then oblivion. Dave stared up at a blood pack on a stand and he followed the blood's progress down the thin plastic tube into his arm. He felt a sense of gratitude to that generous anonymous donor. Where would he be without this life force?

His mind drifted on to Cassie. What a girl, what a wife! How could he ever thank her, she'd saved his life. As for the pub? Soon as he was well again, he'd try his best to make a go of it, or, if he failed, get rid of it.

He watched as a white-coated doctor came onto the ward. He was pushing a small trolley filled with blood phials, and he smiled as he approached Dave's bed. The young man stopped, lifted up Dave's chart from the end of the bed and compared it with the notes that he had with him.

'Mister Hodgson? Mister David Hodgson?' he enquired.

'That's me.'

The doctor grinned at him, then pulled his trolley up to the bedside, got a chair and sat down beside him. 'Sorry,' he said, 'but I've come to pinch some more blood from you.'

'Feel free,' Dave replied. He glanced up at the blood pack on the stand to his left, 'It looks to me like we've got a case of demand and supply.' He laughed, 'Just so long as you don't manage to take out more than the other lot are putting in.'

The man grinned, then rubbed Dave's arm with an alcohol swab. 'Do you want to look the other way?'

Dave laughed, 'Which way would you suggest?'

The man smiled again, inserted the needle and began to withdraw some blood. When he deposited the blood into several small phials he compared his notes to Dave's chart. He studied it for a while and looked puzzled.

'Mr Hodgson, I hope you don't mind my asking, but you do have a history of ulcers, don't you?'

'Tell me about it.'

The young doctor hesitated, read the notes again, and then said cautiously. 'I just wondered. Did you forget that with your medical history you should avoid aspirin?'

'Nope, I never take aspirin. That's tempting fate in my case.'

'Sure is,' the man muttered under his breath.

Dave stared at him. 'What do you mean?'

The doctor sat up and looked Dave straight in the eyes. He tapped on the notes with his fingers. 'It says here that they've found large amounts of aspirin in your blood.'

Dave shook his head. 'That can't be right. I only took what was prescribed for me.'

'Alkaline? It's usually a whitish liquid?'

'I don't recall it being white, I think it was colourless. You see, the stuff that my doctor prescribed was whitish, but my wife seemed to think that the medicine her doctor prescribed was much better.' He sighed and looked at the technician, 'Anything to oblige the ladies, eh?'

The doctor's expression became blank. He flipped back a page or two of his notes and read through them.

'It says here that when you were admitted the A&E department asked your wife to bring your medicine along so that we know exactly what you have been taking.'

'And?'

The man's face remained expressionless. He looked down at his notes and avoided Dave's gaze. 'As yet we have not received the medication.'

Dave felt defensive. What were they implying? 'Well, she'll probably bring it in later, or maybe tomorrow. She does have a business to run.'

The doctor stood up and pushed his trolley back to the centre aisle. He smiled politely at Dave. 'That would be appreciated.' He continued along the ward.

Dave watched him walk away then he lay back against

the pillows and pondered. What was going on? Cassie would never have given him anything that would hurt him. At least, not knowingly…or would she? Doubts began to form in his mind. Was she fed up of living with an older man? At having to work like a skivvy in a failing pub for little reward? He'd be the first one to understand if she walked off and left him. He smiled as he thought about his beautiful little wife and shook his head. No, that was not his Cassie. That was not her way. She could never be as devious as that. But that left only Dr Harrison.

Why would Dr Harrison want to harm him? From what he knew of the old doctor, he seemed harmless enough, always jolly, always eating, still working up at that bloody nursing home. Wait! Nursing home? Stop right there. Dave felt his stomach muscles tighten as he thought about the things he suspected and the things that he already knew went on up there.

He should never have got involved, never have taken those backhanders, or bonuses, as the coach companies so coyly called them. That's where it had all started. He'd been so desperate for money and so keen to impress Cassie. Why hadn't he been honest, instead of letting his pride get in the way? He shook his head impatiently, there was no time for remorse. He had to get to the root of this, and the root was Dr Harrison.

How did Dr Harrison know that he, Dave, was aware that something was going on at the nursing home? Unless? Had Cassie said something? Made some remark, unthinkingly of course, but enough to alarm him. Enough for Dr Harrison to realize that the whole set-up was in danger of being exposed, and to use his expertise to prescribe medicine to get rid of…him…and Cassie.

I need to get to a phone, Dave thought. He tried to get

out of bed but as his feet touched the ground he swayed dangerously. A nurse saw him stagger and rushed over to help him.

'You should have pressed the buzzer, Mr Hodgson.'

Dave said urgently, 'I need the phone.'

The nurse eased him back into bed. 'I'll bring you the phone trolley. Just stay there. You're still too weak to walk around.' She checked the infusion tube, then hurried off and returned a few minutes later with the phone trolley.

With trembling fingers Dave keyed in Cassie's mobile number and sat listening to the ringing tone. If his life had been threatened, then Cassie was also in danger. He'd got to warn her. He listened again; 'Damn it.' He said aloud, 'I've got the blasted voicemail.' He slammed down the receiver then picking it up again, keyed in the pub number.

He tried to control his fear and his frustration as the phone rang again and again and again, but no answer. There had to be an answer. It was a bloody pub, after all.

'Sorry, Mr Hodgson,' the nurse interrupted his thoughts, 'but another patient needs to use the phone urgently.'

'I'm not through yet,' Dave protested.

The nurse smiled reassuringly. 'I'll bring it straight back. You can try again later.'

CASSIE RUSHED to answer the phone just as it stopped ringing. She looked down at the nearby answer machine and to her annoyance realized that she'd left it switched off.

Picking up the receiver, she keyed in 1471 'You were called at 21.29 hours. The caller withheld their number', came the reply. She replaced the receiver and stared down at the phone thoughtfully. The call could have come from so many people. Her first thoughts were of Dave; should she try ringing the hospital again? She looked down at the phone; if she used that she might block anyone that was trying to call her, but she could use her mobile.

She keyed in the hospital number and waited for them to answer. Several minutes later Cassie put down the receiver with a sigh. The hospital switchboard had just told her that they had no knowledge of any outgoing calls to her number; they had also reminded her that there were other outside lines situated inside the hospital. She tried asking for the ward but when they put her through she was given the same information. So, thought Cassie, even if Dave has been trying to contact me, I'd not be able to return the call.

Her thoughts turned to Rosa and her sister and she wondered if they'd been trying to reach her. She wanted to ring Anna just to check if they'd reached the nursing home and managed to find Rosa's husband, but then decided against it. It would be best to wait a bit longer. As for the unknown caller, she would just have to wait until they tried again.

TWENTY-EIGHT

ANNA AND ROSA crouched like petrified rabbits caught in a headlight. They listened in horror to the sound of Rosa's shoes rattling down the metal stairs of the fire escape. After what seemed an eternity the noise stopped and there came a silence whilst the two sisters glared accusingly at each other.

'I told you to put your shoes in your pocket!' Anna hissed. 'Right in!'

'You told me to move to the right and to hold the torch up higher so that you could see. I raised my arm, and my shoes fell out. How was I to know that would happen?'

'Forget it.'

'I mean, I'm not a contortionist.'

'Just shut it. Let me listen—'

'All of a sudden I'm expected to know everything 'bout burglaries.'

'Will you shush!' Anna looked at her sister in exasperation. She waited patiently until Rosa stopped muttering, then said, 'Look, I'm sorry, but I think we'll have to abandon this way of entry. Someone will have heard the noise. It's bound to attract attention.'

'We can't give up on Ben.'

Anna looked at her sister in exasperation. 'I'm not saying that, but we'll have to find another way in, or maybe wait a couple of hours.' She gave a deep sigh and leaned against the fire door. As she did so she felt it move. Hope returned. Cautiously she slid her fingers to-

wards the edge of the door. Fire doors always open out-
wards, she remembered. She turned and tugged at the
edge. The door opened towards them. She peered round
it then with her fingers pressed over her lips she turned
to Rosa and beckoned. Silently they slid through it.

IN HIS OFFICE three floors below, Jeff was eating his
supper when he spotted the red flashing light on the exit
monitors. He stood up and took a closer look. How long
had that been flashing? He noted that it was the monitor
on the fire exit on the top floor and tutted in irritation.
It was only ten minutes since he'd been on that floor, he
should have thought to have checked it when he'd seen
the old boy tinkering with it. He scowled down at his
mug; he'd not even had the chance to drink his tea.

Better go and take a look-see, although more than
likely it would be yet another electrical fault. The wiring
on this place was lousy, especially on that floor. Picking
up his keys, Jeff made for the door. They should have
had the electrics checked; he'd recommended it dozens
of times but the owners didn't seem to be interested. He
sighed; they couldn't half be penny pinching at times.

He walked towards the lift and thought about the cap-
tive on the top floor. Jeff still felt a sense of relief that
he'd happened to be doing a spot check and chatting up
the nurse, when by sheer chance he'd seen the geezer
at the fire door. Jeff winced as he recalled the struggle
and the kneeing that the old lad had given him as he'd
dragged him away; he still felt sore. He'd nearly lost control and punched him one, but the sight of the baton had
made the old boy behave. He sighed deeply. That bloke
was nothing but trouble; it was time that they got rid of
him.

Jeff still felt a sense of awe when he realized that the

man had managed to unlock that door solely with the aid
of a pocket knife and some wire, and that it was by pure
luck that he'd been in the right place at the right time or
else the old boy would have got clean away. He scowled
as he thought that through. If that had happened he'd have
been first in the queue at the Job Centre tomorrow.

He got into the lift, pressed the button for the top floor
and watched the green arrow indicator until the doors
opened again. As he came into the corridor he hesitated
and, as always, listened to the silence. This floor gave
him the creeps. The patients here were so frail it was as
if they were in a half-life, clinging on to this world by the
merest thread. He gave a shrug and dismissed his unease;
best get on with the work they paid him to do.

He strode towards the fire door and wondered just
what the bosses were going to do about the man. What
was so special about him? He recalled the bosses' agitation when he'd first told them about the trespasser,
especially when he'd mentioned the man's name. His
instructions had been precise: on no account was the
man to be freed. Should anyone enquire he must deny
all knowledge of this man's existence. Jeff grunted; quite
a big order, in fact. He was good at obeying orders, but
even he did feel uneasy about this case. He knew that the
bosses were on the premises tonight. He had seen one car
arrive on the CCTV monitor at reception. He sighed in
resignation; they'd probably be issuing yet more orders
later on.

TWENTY-NINE

Anna and Rosa eased themselves through the fire door into the corridor and stood pressed against the wall, hardly daring to breathe. Not a sound. No sign of anyone.

Rosa peered down the passage then whispered, 'It looks to be a gloomy old place.' She looked down at the skirting boards. 'Could do with a good dusting too.'

Anna said urgently, 'We've got to move.' She gazed along the lengthy passage. 'We're too vulnerable here.'

Rosa nudged her elbow. 'Looks as if there might be a side ward down there.' She nodded briefly to her left. 'I'll go first. Come on, just follow me and try not to frighten any patients.' She tiptoed in stockinged feet along the corridor.

Anna put on her shoes and watched her sister anxiously, hoping that she wouldn't slip on the floor tiles.

Rosa reached the entrance of the ward, disappeared into it, only to reappear a few seconds later and beckon to her sister. Anna joined her and for a long moment they both stood gazing silently at the two patients that were lying in their beds. Both of the patients were male and elderly. Both lay without moving, apparently asleep. What appeared to be a saline drip stand and a drug pump were placed by each of the patient's beds. From beneath the bedcovers a thin plastic tube led down to a bottle underneath the beds. At the end of each bed hung a clipboard.

Rosa eyed the charts thoughtfully then whispered,

'I wonder whether I should go and grab a quick look at their notes?'

Anna, however, had other things on her mind. She focused on the details of the room. Square-shaped, window at the far side, and near it a white-painted door, which she assumed was the lavatory. She frowned as her gaze took in the contents of the room, or rather the lack of contents. No television. No sign of any slippers, no dressing gowns, not even occasional towels were visible. Her frown deepened as her gaze continued over the bedside tables. No flowers, no cards, no water jug, not even a box of tissues.

Alarm bells rang in her mind. This was too neat. The room seemed more like a stage set, and the patients more like puppets rather than living, breathing human beings. She touched Rosa's arm.

'What's up?'

Anna nodded at the patients, 'You sure they're alive?'

''Course they are; they're sleeping.'

Anna's jaw tightened. She stared again at the two men, then looked at her sister and whispered, 'You certain 'bout that?'

Rosa clicked her tongue, and then looking closer, hesitated. 'I'll go and check their breathing.'

Anna nodded. 'That would be good.' She watched as Rosa walked swiftly over to the bed of the nearest patient. She knew very little about nursing and sick people; that was Rosa's area of expertise. She crossed her fingers and hoped against hope that these poor men weren't...

Rosa turned to her and gave the thumbs up signal and Anna let out a deep sigh of relief. She watched as Rosa checked out both patients and then tiptoed to the ends of the beds and collected their charts. With a triumphant smile Rosa clutched the charts to her and returned to

Anna. She looked down at the notes. 'Let's see what we can find out.'

Anna stood quietly whilst her sister studied the charts then her gaze shifted from the patients to the entrance of the ward. This place was getting to her. The gut feeling that she'd felt the other day, when she'd first visited the Full Moon Inn returned. That same sense of something wrong. The sense of something evil. The rustling of paper brought her back to the present and she looked at Rosa and nodded at the notes. 'What do they tell you?'

Rosa was disappointed. 'Not as much as I'd hoped. Oh, there's temperature and blood pressure checks, right enough, and their breathing is deep and slow.' She glanced at the stands. 'Those are saline drips…as for the other?' She hesitated, chewed on her lip and looked puzzled. 'Saline by itself shouldn't knock them out like that.' She gestured at the patients. 'Those men are in deep sleep!'

'So?'

'That isn't normal. They're being given some drug, but I don't know…' Again she studied the charts. 'There's something that I'm missing.' Rosa stopped short as Anna grabbed her arm, held her finger to her mouth warningly and they heard the sound of a lift.

Panic seized them and they clutched each other. 'I never noticed a lift,' whispered Rosa.

'Must be one round the corner.'

'Maybe it's not even on this floor?'

Anna crept back towards the entrance of the ward and peered along the corridor. She shrank back against the wall and gestured to Rosa, warning her to be silent.

Rosa joined her and mouthed, 'What's happening?'

'A man coming,' Anna whispered. She grabbed Rosa

by the arm and they scurried towards the white door and went through it.

As Anna had guessed earlier, the room turned out to be a disabled type of bathroom with a washbasin, a toilet and a shower area. She looked around the room and her sense of alarm increased. There was no sign of any soap or toiletries near the washbasin and not even a hand towel or toilet paper. The room was immaculate, as if it had never been used.

'Anna,' whispered Rosa, who had eased open the door and was peering out, 'I heard somebody go past the ward entrance.' She turned to her. 'Probably the security man.'

They both stood listening. They heard the rattle of the fire door, and then footsteps returning.

Rosa whispered nervously, 'He's coming this way.' She started to close the bathroom door but in her agitation the lock did not click into place and with a clear metallic sound the door sprung open again.

She froze and stared blankly at the door.

Anna reached past her and was about to pull the door shut again when it was dragged out of her hand and the security man stood framed in the doorway.

He stared at them. 'Who the hell are you?'

THIRTY

Rosa gulped and nudged her sister.

Anna blurted, 'We just…needed the loo.'

The man stared at them in disbelief, 'Now I've heard everything! So you're telling me you broke in here and came right up to the top floor for the pleasure of using the lavatory? It don't make sense to me.'

Anna tried to edge past him and bluff it out. 'Well, we did, and it does, least as far as we're concerned.' She pushed against him. 'Now, if you don't mind, we've finished visiting and we've a bus to catch.'

The security man grabbed hold of her arm. 'And I just saw a pig fly past that window. You're coming with me, both of you.'

Anna's mouth tightened. 'Look, we've been visiting a patient.'

The security man looked down at Rosa's feet and gave a grim smile. 'Is this the latest thing, then, visiting folk with no shoes on? I always thought they only did that in Japan.' His grip on Anna tightened. 'Now, I've had enough of your bloody lies. You're coming down to my office 'cause I want to know why you're here and what you're up to. And neither of you is leaving this building until I do!'

Rosa watched the security guard march Anna out into the corridor. Her sense of outrage grew. She knew very well that in this unguarded moment she could make good her escape, but that meant leaving her kid sister behind

and she would rather cut off her left arm than do that.
'Just you let go of her,' she shouted as she hurried after
them, 'she's not a prisoner.' She tugged at the security
man's sleeve, 'Call the police if you have to! In fact I
insist that you call them. You're breaking the law, don't
you know?'

Jeff looked down at her bleakly, then grabbed her by
the arm as well. 'You've no right to be here, so just stop
yelling and keep up with us.'

'I will not stop shouting! I will shout as loud as I like
and when the police get here I'm going to tell them all
about you and your physical abuse.' She looked across
him at Anna, who oddly enough was walking along
meekly as if all the fight had gone out of her. Why
doesn't she work her judo stuff on him, Rosa wondered.
As they marched along the corridor she heard the sound
of banging. Was that one of the patients protesting? Then
she heard a voice call out. It sounded like her Ben. It was
her Ben! She was sure it was him! What had they done
to him? She tried to break away from the guard, 'That's
my—'

'Rosa!' Anna yelled quickly, drowning her sister's
words. She tried to reach across the security man and
grab her sister's arm. 'Stop shouting, you'll frighten the
patients.'

'Here, you two,' the security man snarled as he tightened his grip on both women's arms. 'Don't you dare try
any of your breakaway tricks on me, 'cause it won't work,
see.' He quickened his pace, almost dragging them along,
'and if you two ain't gonna behave like ladies then I'm
not gonna behave like no gent either, so move it. You've
been warned.'

Rosa gaped across at her sister, open mouthed. 'But
you must have...' She stared in amazement then gave a

nod as she watched Anna place her finger over her lips, then Rosa continued to protest loudly, 'I want you to know, young man, that if I've got bruises on my arm tomorrow, I'm going to sue you for molesting me. Just you see if I don't.'

Jeff looked down at her and sneered, 'If you carry on squawking like this, you'll be lucky to see tomorrow. Now just shut your bloody gob 'cause you're giving me a headache.'

Anna marched along beside the security man and felt a huge sense of relief that Rosa had understood her warning and that she was now doing her best to distract him. It gave her the chance to memorize their whereabouts and look for possible escape routes. When they had passed the doors of what appeared to be private rooms, her keen ears had also picked up the sound of Ben shouting, but now was not the time to intervene. She felt excited; at last they had a good idea where Ben was being held, but which floor were they on? She looked around desperately, hoping to see some notice or indication, but there was nothing. She thought about Miss McGuire. Perhaps Ben had found her and they were keeping the old lady in the same room as Ben? With all of her heart she wanted to break free and go back and check, or at least talk to her sister and reassure her, but on second thoughts she decided to play stumm and not react. The last thing that they needed was to make this security guard even more suspicious of their intentions.

She tried to snatch a quick glance into the wards as they marched past them, but she could see little apart from the occasional bedridden form. She noticed that they were approaching the lift doors and she looked to see if there were any stairs nearby where they could escape, but again she could see nothing. Bide your time, she thought, as the security man pushed her into the lift. She turned to face the steel lift doors, focusing on the green arrow indicators as they descended past each floor, then saw that the man was watching her. She stared stonily back at him. Patience, woman, she told herself; everything comes to those who wait.

As Jeff pushed the two women into the lift he looked down at them. Why was this place being invaded by middle-aged women? he wondered. This was all he needed.

He eyed the taller of the two women warily. Although the little one had a mighty mouth on her, to his mind, old thunder-thighs was the one to watch. She was staring at him as a wrestler would when sizing up an opponent and it was getting on his nerves.

He stood with his back against the steel doors of the lift, bracing himself. If, when the doors opened, she decided to do a rugby tackle, he'd be more than ready for her.

BEN ALSO HEARD the sound of a lift. Funny. He'd not heard that in the other room. When they'd first caught him, they'd made him climb up several flights of stairs. He lay on the couch thinking about this new discovery and he wondered why it hadn't occurred to him before. Of course nursing homes would have lifts, much the same as hospitals did.

He paused in his reflections and pulled himself upright into a sitting position. Was someone coming? He wondered if maybe the security man had had a change of heart and decided to bring him some bottled water after all. If not? Ben eyed the wash basin across the room; well, he could try drinking from there, but if it turned out to be the same rusty stuff that had trickled out of the tap in the earlier room, he sighed, then he'd just have to put up with his thirst until things got desperate.

The sound of footsteps came closer, then went on past Ben's door, fading until he heard the distant thud of a fire door being secured. 'Damn! Damn, damn!' he cursed in frustration. Jeff must have realized that it was un-locked. Despair seeped through him and he lay back on the couch. 'Must I lose all hope?' he said loudly. 'Will I ever get out of this place?' He stared bleakly at the ceil-ing. 'There must be a way and I've got to find it! Isn't there anything, or anyone?' He broke off, listening. Foot-steps again! But more than one set. Ben strained his ears trying to pick out the rhythm. Two sets of footsteps? Not sure… He stood up and felt a growing sense of excite-ment. Something was happening. At last. Someone was coming to see him!

Above the sound of the footsteps he could hear Jeff's voice. And another voice that he knew all too well. Ben's face creased into a smile. A voice that many times had made his heart near-burst with joy. Rosa! It was his little Rosa! And true to form, she was protesting loudly. His grin stretched from ear to ear, he laughed out loud and hurried to the door.

Ben's first thought was that Rosa had come to rescue him and that perhaps she'd found Miss McGuire? His smile faded as a second thought occurred to him. If that was so, he hoped she'd brought the police with her? Knowing Jeff and his attitude, he could only pray that she had. But if she hadn't, what then? What if, like him, she'd been caught snooping around the place and was now in trouble? His anxiety increased and, with his heart racing, he pressed his ear against the door, waiting, straining to hear any word.

The echoing footsteps and the mingled voices of both

Jeff and Rosa faded and Ben stood dumbly as all of his hopes left him. He pounded on the door in disbelief, 'Rosa, I'm right here, for God's sake,' he yelled. 'You bastard, what are you up to? Don't you dare hurt her? Where the hell are you taking her?'

He banged on the door again, then listened, but there was no answer. What was Jeff up to? Ben thought about Jeff, and his fear for his wife grew. What was Jeff going to do to her? Another thought came to him. Where was Anna? Although he and his sister-in-law were rarely on the same wavelength, there was a very close bond between her and Rosa.

He tried to reassure himself; he knew that in times of crisis, Anna would not be far from Rosa's side. Despair took control. He slumped against the door dejectedly and his frustration grew. He heard the faint sound of a lift and he pounded again on the door with all of his might and then he listened. Nothing. The silence had returned. Everything was as before.

THIRTY-ONE

DR IAN WHITE lay on his hospital bed and tried to control his impatience. 'Where the hell are my glasses?' he muttered. For the life of him he couldn't remember where they'd got to, but then he couldn't remember his accident either, though doubtless his memory would return in good time.

He looked about him and scowled; he felt irritated, in spite of his angry protests that he was feeling much better and he wanted to go home, the A&E staff, in their wisdom, had decided to shunt him into the observation ward.

Earlier he had tried on two occasions to get out of bed, but each time his feet touched the floor waves of nausea and an alarming attack of palpitations overcame him. He fought against his fear. As a doctor, he knew that he must be patient and allow sufficient time for the antidote to work on his body. 'Physician heal thyself,' he muttered, as he tried to calm down. Even so, it was still bloody frightening. He tried to relax and allow his body more time to recover.

He glanced at the bedside locker and sighed. He'd asked for more water and, frowning, wondered where on earth his clothes and his personal belongings had got to; so far only the jug of water had appeared.

Pulling himself upright he poured himself a drink and sipped it slowly. He was thirsty but he knew better than to gulp it down. He leaned forward and peered shortsightedly through a gap in the screening curtains to see if he could spot anyone on the ward, but there was no one about. By the looks of things they'd probably all gone off for their supper. He smiled faintly at the irony of his situation; here he was on an observation ward, and not a soul was there to observe him.

Ian stared down at his naked wrist in annoyance. 'How the hell can I calculate the effects of the morphine when I've no idea what time it is? Think back, he told himself, what time was it when you went to see Bob Harrison. 'It was dark when I set off, but it wasn't all that late,' he muttered. And the time now was? Bloody good question. I'm snookered again; I can't see a clock anywhere. Ian shuddered; that was not his only problem. He thought about the police; he'd almost forgotten them, and they must be due here any time now. He snorted; there it was again, that word *Time*. *I've* got to find out what time it is, and then…he shuffled to the side of the bed and slowly eased his feet onto the floor. Once standing, he edged gingerly along the length of the bed until he reached the opening in the curtains and looked out.

Gripping the end of the bed, he steadied himself to ward off the dizziness and looked around for any sign of a clock. He was not disappointed; there, right above the nurse's station, was a large wall clock. He squinted at it. As far as he could make out, its hands pointed at close to ten.

He sat down on the end of the bed and at the same time realized that the palpitations had gone, so the antidote that they'd used had worked well. Ian sighed. What he still could not calculate was the strength of the diamorphine that that evil sod Bob Harrison had given him. His mouth tightened as he thought about it. Well, come what may Dr Harrison was not going to get away with this, or any of the other fraudulent scams that he'd been involved in.

'Feeling better, are we?' A nurse, carrying a large grey plastic bag, had approached silently. She smiled and handed him the bag. 'Found them. The porter must have left them in the A&E department when he moved you here.' She watched as Ian grabbed the bag eagerly, and opened it, then she added, 'Doctor says to tell you that the police will be along in about half an hour.'

Ian nodded, he checked his clothes, his watch and the contents of his wallet, but he still couldn't find his glasses. Had he broken them? And where were his keys? Then he remembered the letters that he'd written, that told the police and the GMC of his suspicions concerning Dr Harrison and the nursing home. Anxiously he fingered the inside pocket of his overcoat. As his hands touched the two envelopes a sense of relief flooded through him; at least they were still there. He looked at the nurse and smiled. 'Thank you, thank you so much.' He slipped his watch over his wrist and waited until the nurse nodded and walked away, then he pulled the envelopes out of his coat pocket, peered at them closely and saw that the seals were still intact. All was well.

Looking down at the letters, he pondered. Now he was going to have to explain this to the local police. Not only would he have to convince them that the well-respected, well-established and, to the best of the police's knowledge, totally honourable Dr Bob Harrison was at the very least involved in fraud, and, in his case, attempted murder. A doctor who lived in this area for nigh on forty years. Ian hesitated as logic intervened.

Question one. Would the police believe what he said?

Question two. How would the police see *him,* the accuser? A doctor with a history of drug taking?

Question three. When they were informed of these facts, how then would the police react?

Indignation filled him. 'It is my word against his!' he said angrily, then realized that mere words were not enough. The police would need proof. 'And I have clear proof of the fraud up at the nursing home,' he said loudly. 'It's all there, locked up in the office filing…' He broke off. 'Oh, bloody hell!' He suddenly remembered that Bob Harrison also had a key to the filing cabinet and that his own keys had disappeared. Easing himself off the bed Ian tried to dress quickly; there was no time to lose. He'd got to get up to the nursing home, even if he had to get security to open the office door.

Ten minutes later Ian stood outside the hospital entrance. He leaned weakly against the wall and waited impatiently for the arrival of the taxi that he'd ordered at reception. He still felt a bit groggy and breathless. Perhaps it had been foolish to sign himself out, but he couldn't hang around waiting for the police to arrive. It was imperative that he got to his office and the files first.

He saw the taxi approaching and stepped out into the road to hail it. As he clambered inside he tried to overcome his anxiety.

Once he had the files there would be no doubt. He thought about his car, his keys and his missing glasses and felt slightly comforted as he remembered that he kept an emergency pair of spectacles in the office desk drawer. He leaned forward and tapped the taxi driver on the shoulder. 'The nursing home at Shadwell on Green End Lane, as fast as you can, please,' he urged.

THIRTY-TWO

'COME ON, YOU TWO...ladies, in here,' Growled Jeff as he unlocked the security office door and pulled it open. He eyed Anna sternly, 'And it's no good glaring at me like that. In you go. I want to know just what you've been up to.' He herded Rosa and Anna into the room and gestured towards the chairs. 'You may as well park yourselves 'cause you're not leaving here until I get some answers.'

As Anna followed Rosa into the room, she stood still for moment and looked around, taking in all that she saw. A desk, on it a half empty mug of what appeared to be tea. Three wooden chairs, a phone. Over by the sink, an electric kettle and a microwave oven. Close to the oven, a small wall-mounted fire extinguisher. Her gaze moved on, taking in the barred windows, the CCTV monitors and the security light indicators of external doors. The security man's voice reached her. 'You deaf or what? Didn't I tell you to sit down?'

Anna looked at Rosa, who was already seated with her arms tightly folded across her chest and a stubborn expression on her face. She pulled out a chair, edged it nearer to the desk and sat down.

'That's better,' said the security man grudgingly. He looked at Rosa who was still staring stubbornly at the opposite wall. 'Now before I pick up this phone, call the police and have them arrest you two for the attempted theft of our patients belongings—'

'As if!' shouted an outraged Rosa. 'We would never take a thing that didn't belong to us.'

'Happens all the time in hospitals and nursing homes, don't you know,' the security man said. 'Evil folk get in pretending that they're visitors and they nick patients' wallets and valuables. Don't you ever read the newspapers? Why else do you think I'm here?' He leaned across the desk towards Rosa, 'Now, let's have a look-see at what's in your handbag, missus. There's no need to be shy, if, after all, you've got nothing to hide.' He snatched Rosa's bag from her and emptied its contents onto the desk. Lipstick, comb, purse and keys, spilled out in front of him. 'Ah, lets see what you've got here,' he said as he began to sort through them.

'I hope you realize that what you are doing is strictly illegal,' Anna said sharply.

'You what?'

'You have no right to search us. That should be left to the police.'

'The police ain't here, are they? So you can fume as much as you like, missus. I'm in charge.'

'We're definitely going to report you,' said Rosa as she swept the contents back into her bag, 'that's for sure.'

Anna gestured at the phone, 'Now, if you're not going to let us go, you'd better call the police.'

'Yes,' Jeff said, his voice deep with suspicion, 'I might just do that, but first let's see what's in your handbag as well.' As he reached out to pull Anna's shoulder bag from her, the phone rang, startling them all. The security man hesitated, then picked up the receiver. 'Security,' he said briskly. He listened intently then straightened up and replied, 'Yes, straight away.' He cursed under his breath, replaced the receiver and for a second stared blankly at the two women seated in front of him. 'Look,' he said,

'I've got to leave you here for a minute or two, but when I get back I want the truth from you, otherwise I will have you arrested and charged with trespassing. Is that clear?'

Both Rosa and Anna remained silent.

The security man sighed, looked at his bunch of keys, removed one of them from the ring and placed it in his pocket, then pushed the door open. As he went out he called, 'Don't even think about trying to get out. This here is a mortise lock, see.' With that he went out into the corridor and closed the door.

The second she heard the key being turned in the lock, Rosa sprang up, rushed to the door, tried the handle, then hammered on the door in a fury.

Anna stood up and watched her. 'That's not going to do any good,' she called, but Rosa carried on pounding on the door with the flat of her hand. 'If we make enough noise,' she shouted, 'someone's bound to hear us.'

Anna hurried over to the security man's desk and checked the drawers. She sighed. Just as she thought, they were locked. She bit on her lip and wondered whether to force them, then realized that their number one priority was to get out of this room. The question was, how? She rubbed her forehead, trying to think, then snapped at Rosa in irritation. 'For heaven's sake, will you stop that pounding? Even if a patient does come to help, they'll not get past that lock without a key.'

'What do you suggest, then? Do you want us to be prisoners here as well?' Rosa said. She looked at the desk phone, 'Call the police, why don't you.'

'Didn't you hear what the man said?' asked Anna. 'He'll be back at any minute. The police could never get here before the security man.' She fished out her mobile from her bag and keyed in 999, 'But I'll try anyway. Yes. Police, please. My name is Anna Sharpe; I'm calling you

from the Shadwell Nursing Home, off Green End Lane,
near Shadwell. My sister and I are being falsely imprisoned by a security guard and I have reason to believe that
others are being held here too. Yes, right, thank you,' and
she keyed off. She looked around again distractedly, then
spotted the fire extinguisher. She dashed across the room
and lifted it down from the wall.

Rosa eyed the fire extinguisher that Anna was clutching warily, 'What are you up to? Are you going to bop
him with that when he comes back?'

Anna gave a wicked smile, 'Only if push comes to
shove. Now listen, I want you to go back to that chair and
sit so that you're facing the door.'

'Why?'

Anna controlled her impatience. 'So that you'll be the
first thing the security man sees when he comes back into
the room.

Obediently Rosa returned to the chair and sat down.
'Then what?'

'When that door opens shout, scream, jump up and
down if you like,' Anna said, '*but do not* look at me.'

'You're going to tackle him?'

'Sort of, but when I shout "run" go like the clappers
and don't look back.'

'But what if—'

'No ifs or buts,' Anna hissed. 'Sssh, I hear someone
coming.'

'Bossy boots giving orders yet again,' grumbled Rosa.

'Quiet!'

As they heard the key turning in the lock, Anna
rushed to the door and switched off the light.

The door was pulled open and a hand reached in grop-
ing for the light switch.

Anna kicked the door back on its hinges and it slammed into the security man's face.

There came a yell of pain as he grasped the edge of the door and pulled it wide open. For a split second he stood silhouetted against the corridor light, then from the shadows Rosa screamed. He lurched towards her. At the same time Anna pressed the button on the extinguisher and aimed the foam straight at his face.

The man gasped and clutched his eyes.

'Run!' yelled Anna and Rosa shot out into the corridor.

'Keep on running.' Anna shouted, as she shoved the security man further into his office and pushed the door shut behind him. As Rosa raced down the corridor, Anna grabbed a chair and wedged it under the door handle. That should buy us some time, she thought, and she hared off down the corridor to join her sister.

Rosa was standing near the lift taking deep breaths when Anna reached her.

'You okay?' she asked.

Rosa nodded but couldn't speak.

Anna controlled her unease and looked about her. She didn't want to frighten Rosa but she knew that at any second someone might rescue the security man. They needed to be further away from that office door, much further. She took a deep breath and tried to sound calm. 'We've got to keep moving. We've got to find Ben.'

'Can't we use the lift?' Rosa gasped breathlessly.

Anna shook her head. 'Sorry, love, the sound of the lift might tell him where we are. We have to go as quickly and quietly as we can.' She looked along the corridor, 'We'd best start by searching this floor, and seeing if we can find another way out of here, 'cause it's too risky going through reception now.' She looked at Rosa worriedly. 'You sure you're okay?'

Rosa straightened her shoulders. "Course I am,' she said defiantly.

'Right,' Anna took hold of Rosa's arm, 'let's go.'

'What about the telephone and those cameras?' said Rosa. 'Did you get to switch them off?'

'No, I'd have needed more time to disconnect them.'

'But you should have—'

Anna stopped and looked at her in exasperation, 'Rosa! I am not Wonder Woman!' She looked around anxiously then carried on walking, 'Come on, let's hurry.'

'You did hear Ben as well, didn't you?' Rosa asked worriedly. 'We must find him.'

'Yes, he's here somewhere. Only problem is I'm not sure what floor he's on. We know he's not on the wards and we've still got to find Miss McGuire.'

'Miss McGuire will have to wait. It's my Ben I'm worried about. We were being frog-marched past some doors when we heard him,' Rosa added. She looked hopefully at Anna. 'Maybe Ben and Miss McGuire are locked up together?'

'That's what I was thinking, but we didn't hear a woman's voice and surely she'd have shouted as well,' Anna said, 'so that's why we'd best check each floor, starting from here.'

'Well, yes,' said Rosa. She gave her sister a warning look as her nursing instincts took over and they continued along the passage. 'But as quietly as you can, Anna, we don't want to frighten the patients.'

THIRTY-THREE

DAVE HODGSON SAT bolt upright in his hospital bed and glared at the youth who was lying in a bed across from him, talking on his mobile. He clicked his tongue in irritation; the lad must have been rabbiting on for at least half an hour. He'd gestured and tried to catch the youth's eye but it was hopeless. Dave had even mimed his urgent need for the use of the mobile and waved a fiver at him. But the lad had only gazed at him, given him a laconic wave back, and giggling, had continued to whisper ardently to his girlfriend.

Dave sighed in exasperation and looked along the ward to where the Night Sister was seated writing a report. He looked at the ward clock and his anxiety increased. If only Sister would leave the ward for a few minutes, Dave thought. Given half a chance he'd be out of this bed, across the room and onto the next ward. Somehow he'd drag that bloody phone trolley back in here. He gazed again at the Ward Sister hopefully, willing her to look at him, but she showed not the slightest sign of doing so.

Thoughtfully Dave looked at his bedside call buzzer. Should he summon her and demand a bedpan? That way she would have to leave the ward, but then if she got back before he'd commandeered the phone trolley he'd be in even more trouble. But he had to talk to Cassie! It was vital. Why hadn't she answered the phone earlier, that was what bothered him. They lived in a public house for heaven's sake; there just had to be someone there. He thought through the possible technical faults that phones developed, but there was a landline and she had a mobile. Surely both of them could not be out of order at the same time?

A darker thought occurred to him and he flopped back against the pillows. What if Dr Harrison had already got to Cassie? He felt his heart rate quicken; he had to warn her. He stared hard at the Night Sister and waited.

Then it happened. Sister looked up from her work and smiled straight at him. She stood up. 'I've not forgotten you, Mr Hodgson,' she mouthed silently. She hurried off to the next ward and returned almost immediately, pushing the phone trolley ahead of her. She smiled as she approached him. 'I take it you do still need to make that urgent call?' she asked quietly.

'Indeed I do, Sister.'

She wheeled the trolley up close to him and plugged it in. Dave got the small stack of coins from his locker. 'Now do be as brief as you can,' she whispered. 'It's getting rather late.'

'Too true, Sister,' Dave murmured as he keyed in the pub's number. 'Let's just hope that I'm not too late either.' He listened to the ringing tone and held his breath. Surely she must—

'The Full Moon Inn, how may I help you?' answered his wife's voice.

'Cassie?' Dave said and felt an overpowering sense of relief. 'Thank God I got through to you.'

'Dave!' she replied and he could hear the delight in her voice. 'Everything all right, darlin'? You feeling a bit better now?'

'Yes,' he said, 'but I rang you earlier and nobody answered. Where were you? I've been driving myself crazy wondering what had happened.'

Cassie laughed, 'I'm all right. That was just silly me forgetting to leave the answer phone on.'

'Listen, lover,' Dave interrupted. 'There's no time to chat. Where's that medicine bottle Dr Harrison gave you?'

'Why is everyone harping on about that bloody medicine bottle?' Cassie said angrily. She gave a defiant sniff. 'Well, you can tell them from me as soon as I find it I'll bring it straight up to the hospital.'

Dave sighed. Now she was sounding close to tears; not surprising, with the stress she'd been under. He tried to mask his fear for her and sound calm. 'Listen, sweetheart, don't get upset, just try to reel back your memory and remember the last time you saw that medicine bottle.'

'For crying out loud, it's only a—'

'Please, lover! It's important.'

Cassie's voice sounded doubtful, she said hesitantly, 'It was when Dr Harrison examined you. He asked whether I'd given you his medicine, and I said yes.' She hesitated again then said, 'And then he gave you the last of it, but—'

'But what?'

Cassie said thoughtfully, 'The bottle was empty and I was going to take it off him...but he put it in his pocket!' Her voice rose excitedly. 'Dave, that's where the bottle is, in Dr Harrison's pocket.'

Dave suppressed a groan. What's the betting it's not there now, he thought. Aloud he said, 'Listen, sweetheart, try not to worry, but I'm sure Dr Harrison is up to no good. It was his medicine that just about killed me.'

'But why would—'

'Because you and me know more about that bloody nursing home than we should,' he snapped.

'He's trying to get rid of us?' Cassie screeched.

'Permanently. Think about it, lover. After all, who would question a doctor?'

'I bloody well would,' said Cassie, sounding more like her old self again. 'Just you wait, first thing tomorrow I'll—'

'No, Cassie,' Dave insisted. 'What I want you to do is to phone the police and tell them about the nursing home. Let them deal with it. Promise me you'll not go near Dr Harrison. I mean it, lover. It'll be safer for you.'

'But Dave—'

'Look, sweetheart, I'm running out of change. Now just…' There came a click and the sound of an empty line.

Cassie stared at the phone in frustration, she replaced the receiver and thoughtfully recalled Dave's advice: 'It'll be safer for you,' he'd said. Obediently she did as he had asked and called the police. When she had finished talking to them she put down the phone and her thoughts turned to those poor women up at the nursing home, searching for Rosa's husband. Would it be safe for them? She looked around her; she'd already locked up the pub and counted the takings, not that they were much. Her anxiety increased; she'd done as Dave asked, but she just couldn't leave those women up there. She pulled on her coat, picked up her car keys and went out. Somebody had to warn them as well.

DR BOB HARRISON stared furiously at the road ahead as he drove along. Just when he'd thought that life was running smoothly, that silly young pup had to start sticking his nose into things. Why couldn't Ian be grateful that he'd got a decent job? Why did he have to start looking into other people's business and querying everything?

That was what was wrong with young people these days; they didn't appreciate what they had.

He opened the glove compartment and fumbled for the bag of truffles that he kept there. He crammed a couple of chocolates into his mouth and chewed on them ferociously, seeking comfort from their sweetness. The thing was, he thought, if Ian had been the 'flexible' type they might have offered him a share in the business in a year or so. But no, Ian was a whistleblower. He tutted; just how ungrateful could people be?

Earlier, before circumstances had forced him to give Ian that 'exceptional liqueur', he had considered offering him a bonus. After all, bonuses were all the rage these days and they were excellent at persuading people to keep quiet when, if they were ethical, they should speak up.

In spite of his anger, Dr Harrison chuckled loudly at the thought. Who in this day and age was ethical? Ian White is, came the reply, and he smiled again. He shot a quick glance at his watch. His special liqueur should have had its effect on Ian by now. He rapped a cheerful tattoo on the steering wheel. With any luck that problem would be solved permanently. There still remained the evidence, though. As he thought about this his grip on the steering wheel tightened and he watched as the speedometer crept up over eighty. Come what may, he would have to remove all traces.

He turned the car into the country lane, easing off the accelerator as he approached the nursing home. His headlights picked out the ornate glass door of the reception area and he thought about how he would go about destroying the files. Switching off the ignition, he felt on the key ring for the touch of the small filing cabinet key, and smiled reassured as he found it. All was not lost; in another few minutes those files would be gone. He got out of the car and hurried into the reception area.

He looked around him as he entered; no one about. It seemed that the boss had not yet arrived. He hesitated, and felt impatient and uneasy at this further delay. Time was of the essence now, in case Ian had decided to tell his friends about what he'd found out. Not that they could do anything if they had no proof.

He was about to go through the inner doors to the corridor when he noticed the flashing red light on the reception answer phone. Perhaps a new patient was due to arrive, or perhaps the boss had left an urgent message? Better find out. He bustled over to the machine and pressed the button, then stood dumbfounded listening to Cassie's message.

Adrenalin surged through him. How could this happen? That stupid bastard was still alive! Which meant that either Dr Ian White had the constitution of an ox, or that he had seriously miscalculated on the diamorphine dosage? Logic told him that whichever it was, there was no time to waste. Hastily he scribbled a note on a Post-it pad and stuck it on the answer machine, then he hurried through the doors, along the passage and up the stairs. He shot a quick glance at the lift as he passed it, but decided against using it in case he ran into a member of the night staff; that would mean more explanations.

THIRTY-FOUR

ROSA SNIFFED THE AIR. 'Must be close to supper time,' she said, 'I can even smell the Ovaltine.'

'I could do with something to eat myself,' Anna said. She peered along the side ward, 'You don't happen to have any biscuits in your pockets?' She looked hopefully at the trolley that someone had left in the middle of the ward. 'There might be some spare ones on there.'

Rosa nudged her sister back towards the corridor again, 'No, I don't,' she said angrily. 'The only thing in my pockets is mud, thanks to you. And don't you even think about nicking the patients' food. How can you be hungry at a time like this?' She tugged at her sister's sleeve. 'Go on keep moving.' She shot a wary glance back into the ward. 'We're getting some funny looks already; the patients know its past visiting time.'

'Agreed,' said Anna, she peered along the passage. 'What we need is some camouflage. Let's see if we can find anything.'

'What we need is the linen room,' said Rosa, looking about her. 'In most hospitals there's one on each floor.' They hurried along until they came to the consulting rooms and here they stopped to whisper and then listen carefully at each door, but there was only silence.

Rosa felt disappointed. 'I'd thought that we might find him here.' She leaned against the wall dejectedly.

'Cheer up,' Anna said. 'We're only on the first floor, and I'm sure that I heard Ben's voice when we were

higher up.' She walked past her sister and pressed on the
handle of a smaller door at the end of the corridor. That
too was locked, but on closer inspection she saw that the
lock was a standard one. Quickly she got out her nail file
and within seconds the door swung open to reveal a linen
store. Anna turned to grin at Rosa. 'Eureka.'

Rosa tutted, 'You're a born crook, you are.' Nevertheless, she went straight into the room and selected two
large white overalls. 'These should go over our coats,
but we need something else as well.' She thought for a
moment. 'Now if I remember rightly we passed an empty
side ward earlier on.' She tiptoed back along the corridor,
returning shortly with two clipboards. She smiled smugly
at Anna. 'They often keep these at the end of the vacant
beds,' she explained. 'This way, we'll not make anyone
suspicious and it's always best to look the part.'

Anna donned the overall and took a clipboard from
her sister, 'Dear Rosa, you're ever the one for detail.' She
went towards the stairs that led to the next floor and took
a deep breath. 'Come on, let's find your Ben.' And she
set off up the steps.

Dr Bob Harrison panted breathlessly as he clambered
up the stairs. First task was to get to those files; the next,
to dispose of them. He could use the shredder, he thought,
as he unlocked the door and went to the filing cabinet.
Eagerly he inserted the small key in the lock and jiggled
it impatiently, 'Come on, come on,' he growled, 'let's get
this over with.' The lock turned, he pulled the drawer
open and hauled out the incriminating files. 'Make sure
you've got them all,' he told himself. 'You can't afford to
be careless.' He worked quickly. 'That's all of the hard
copies,' he muttered as he placed them on the desk, 'now

for the rest.' He sat down, switched the computer on and drummed his fingers impatiently whilst he waited for it to boot up. As the appropriate files came on screen he deleted them, then with a grunt of satisfaction he removed the back-up stick. 'That takes care of that.' He looked at the computer thoughtfully; he knew that the law would need absolute proof before they could remove the hard drive. Tonight he had done his damnedest to make sure they didn't get it.

'Now to put the shredder to work.' Picking up the files, he hurried across the room towards it, then looked down doubtfully at the documents that he was holding. He remembered having read about a machine that could reconstruct shredded material if it was important. What if someone were to reconstruct these? That would never do. Another thought crept into his mind; what if young Ian White were ever to get hold of him? With a shudder he went over to the medicine cupboard and unlocked it. Best take out a bit of insurance, just in case. Having done this he relocked the filing cabinet, picked up the files and went out of the office, locking the door behind him.

He hurried along the corridor and headed down the stairs. He wasn't going to take any risks; the only safe thing would be to burn these files. He smiled grimly as he thought about this. Cremation, as he well knew, destroyed most evidence. But where could he burn them? He couldn't use the boiler room, as old George, the caretaker, was prone to wander in and out of there at all hours and too many questions would be asked. 'Use logic, man!' he muttered, 'hide them in your car, then you can have a bonfire at home when no one's about.' Clutching the files to his chest he bustled through reception, out of the main door and down the driveway to his car.

ANNA STOOD AT the top of the stairs and waited patiently for her sister to catch up. 'Get a move on, will you,' she hissed.

'Just thought I heard a door being locked earlier,' said Rosa and she turned to look back down the stairs. 'You don't think it could be—'

'It's not Ben. We checked, remember? It's probably a nurse or an orderly. Now hurry up. We've got to keep moving.'

'This is the second or the third floor then?' Rosa gasped as she looked about her and tried to regain her breath. 'How many more floors are there in this place?'

'Now there's a question,' Anna said. 'I can't even remember which floor we came in on.'

Rosa sniffed. 'And you a former policewoman?'

'Don't start that again, else you're on your own. Now let's get on with checking these doors.' She looked around uneasily, 'Sure is quiet up here. It feels as if it's deserted somehow.'

'Fair gives me the shivers,' muttered Rosa as she peered into an empty side ward.

'Let's try these doors along here,' Anna whispered and they set off along the corridor. As they reached the first of the consulting room doors, Anna tapped gently on it then tried the door. It was locked. She listened for a few seconds and was about to move on when she heard a voice.

'Who's that?'

'That's my Ben!' Rosa clutched Anna's arm excitedly, 'I'd know his voice anywhere.'

'Rosa?' came Ben's voice again, 'is that you?'

'You all right, love? We've been ages looking for you.'

'Don't talk so loudly,' Anna warned, she looked around warily. 'You never know who might be about.'

'Now don't you worry, Ben,' Rosa said. 'Anna's going to open this door for us. You know how good she is at things like this.'

Anna looked worried as she stared at the lock, 'I wouldn't be too sure about that.' She started to fish in her shoulder bag but Rosa grabbed her arm. 'I can hear the lift,' she whispered.

Anna froze, listening, 'So can I.'

'It's getting nearer. Will that be the security man coming looking for us?' Rosa looked at her sister anxiously.

'We don't even know if the lift's going to stop on this floor yet,' Anna said. She saw Rosa's strained expression and tried to reassure her, 'And even if it does, it might not be him; it could well be a nurse....'

'Sounds like it's stopping now.'

The two women shrank back against the wall.'

'Ben,' Rosa leaned forward and whispered through the door, 'we think someone's coming. Best stay quiet.'

'We'll be back once they've gone,' Anna added.

They heard the sound of the lift door opening. 'Someone's coming this way,' said Anna as she heard the echo of footsteps. 'Quick, nip in here.' They scurried into a side ward and seconds later Anna peered round the corner into the corridor. 'It's the security man...and a woman,' she told Rosa. She looked again. 'They seem to be coming towards us.'

Rosa peered round Anna's shoulder. 'You know what,' she whispered, 'I think that woman looks like Ben's Miss McGuire. The poor old dear,' she added, 'how could that security man take an old lady like that prisoner?'

'Perhaps he's going to put her in with Ben? It sure looks like it.'

'What are you waiting for?' Rosa urged. 'Go on, have

a go at him. Use some of your judo stuff, and I'll look after the old lady.'

Anna clicked her tongue and said impatiently, 'It's no good me tackling him. He might grab the old woman. Besides, don't forget your Ben's still locked in there. Let's just wait a minute until they get the door open.'

Hardly daring to breathe, Anna and Rosa crouched against the wall, listening.

After a few seconds it came; the metallic click of a key turning in a lock and the fainter sound of a door opening.

'There we are,' whispered Anna. 'They're going in.'

'Let's go get 'em,' said Rosa eagerly. 'You help Ben with the feller, and I'll get the old lady out of the way.'

'Hold it,' said Anna as she looked along the passage. 'They're coming out again.' She watched as Ben, the security guard and the old lady came out of the door and walked towards the lift, then she pushed Rosa back into the side ward, restraining her.

'Stop shoving me,' Rosa said angrily. 'Let's get after them. What are you waiting for?'

'We're on the third floor, remember,' Anna hissed.

'Why not grab them now?' argued Rosa.

'What, and struggle with that security man until we get down to the ground floor? Even with Ben's help it would be tricky.'

'Where's he taking them then?'

Anna stared at the retreating figures then tiptoed into the corridor. 'There's only one way to find out.'

THIRTY-FIVE

CASSIE PARKED THE car near the gates of the nursing home, got out and stood with her arms akimbo, eyeing the distant entrance. Should she drive straight up to the door and confront Jeff, she thought angrily; she was in the mood to give him a right telling off. Her gaze moved further along the drive to the distant greenhouses and the shrubbery that surrounded them. She felt sure that by now Rosa and Anna would have managed to get through the woods without any trouble and that they'd found a way into the nursing home. More than likely their problem would be finding Rosa's husband and getting the hell out of there.

She noticed the two cars parked near reception. She couldn't see what type they were, nor could she make out the number plates. She chewed on her lip worriedly. One of them could well belong to Dr Harrison.

At this thought she turned and looked back along the road, hoping to see the headlights of a police car approaching, but there was only darkness. Cassie sighed; fifteen minutes earlier, just to be sure, she'd driven to the police station and again reported what Dave had told her. To her surprise they were not at all sceptical; they'd listened carefully and remarked that they'd already had another call earlier concerning the nursing home. The police sergeant had then said that they would send someone up there as soon as possible, but as there'd been a major accident over on the A1 they had to give that priority.

'Just how long is it going to be before the police get here?' Cassie muttered as she looked around, and what the hell did 'as soon as possible' mean? Her impatience grew; she could be standing here all night. She'd have to do something. She locked the car and tossed the keys into her handbag. As she did so she heard the clink of the keys against metal and it reminded her that she still had Dr White's keys and glasses in her bag. She felt irritated as she could hardly give them to Dr Harrison now. She would have to find some other way of getting them to Dr White, but she'd deal with that later. There were other more important things to do. She took a deep breath and set off along the driveway to the nursing home.

ROSA AND ANNA had just reached the last flight of stairs leading to the ground floor when they heard the lift doors open on the floor below them. There came a pause, the sound of footsteps walking away, then once again the lift doors closing.

'That'll be them,' said Rosa, as she tried to stop herself slithering on the steps in her stockinged feet.

Anna looked back up the stairs and watched her with concern. 'You be careful,' she whispered. 'You don't want to have an accident in here of all places.'

'Never mind about me,' Rosa said impatiently. 'You just look where he's taking my Ben. We don't want to lose him after all this.'

'All right, all right. Calm down a bit, will you, and be quiet for once.' Although she felt irritated at Rosa's bossiness, Anna crept into the corridor and listened. She could hear the footsteps echoing in the distance; she tiptoed along following these sounds until she heard the click of a door being unlocked. Racing silently to the corner of the corridor she peered round it in time to see the security man herding the old lady and Ben into his office. As the door closed behind the trio, Anna leaned against the wall and waited for her sister to catch up.

'Where are they?' Rosa mouthed as she approached Anna.

Anna gestured towards the security office.

Rosa peered round the corner. 'In there?' she whispered.

Anna nodded, 'Now what?' she asked softly. 'Are you ready to go for it?'

Rosa didn't reply, she crept past Anna and putting her ear to the office door, listened. After a moment she turned to Anna and beckoned. 'Hold on a mo,' she whispered, 'that old lady's talking. Let's hear what she's got to say.'

THIRTY-SIX

Confrontation

BEN LOOKED AROUND HIM as he was ushered into the security office. He felt confused. Just what the devil was going on? Nothing was making sense. He had so many questions that needed answers, but his brain couldn't seem to line them up in a logical order. He stopped and turned towards Miss McGuire who had followed him into the room; he wanted to speak but didn't know where to begin.

'Sit, Benjamin,' she snapped.

He grabbed a chair and obeyed automatically, then looked up at her. Old school habits die hard. 'You know my name?' he said. 'You remember me?'

'As if I could forget,' she gave a cynical laugh. 'Did you think that because I'm old, I'm senile? Just why did you keep on and on, looking for me? You must have realized that I didn't wish to speak to you.'

'I thought you were in trouble,' Ben ordered his thoughts. 'When I first saw you, I just wanted to say hello and chat about old times but you avoided me. So then I thought that something was wrong and I—'

'Came charging to the rescue, eh?' She looked across the room at the security man. 'What do you think of that, Jeffrey? I've found myself a Don Quixote!'

Jeff seemed puzzled at Miss McGuire's remark. 'If you say so, Boss,' he answered.

'Boss?' Ben stared up at her.

Miss McGuire pressed her thin lips together and smiled down at him. She seemed to be enjoying some private joke.

Ben felt his anger growing, 'I want answers,' he shouted, 'if you're the boss why are you keeping me here?'

Again the cynical smile as she looked at him, 'The short answer to that question is...you know too much.'

'I know nothing! Why am I being kept here? Why are these old folk disappearing? What is going on in this place? And,' he stared at her, 'above all else, how are you connected?'

Miss McGuire sniffed. 'I see no need to explain to such as you, but,' she gave a tight smile, 'since I will enjoy telling you, I will do so. I take it you recall my former circumstances?'

Ben nodded and thought back over the years, 'I know that you had a difficult life with your invalid mother.'

For a second Miss McGuire's eyes blazed, 'A perfect bitch of a mother,' she spat. 'She took too long to die.'

Ben gasped and recoiled instinctively.

She stared down at him bleakly, 'Did you know that not content with being a miserable crone and the bane of my life, she also ruined my one chance of marriage?' She saw his reaction. 'You are surprised that such as I should even consider marriage?'

'No! Not at all, Miss McGuire,' Ben protested, although that was exactly what he'd thought. 'It's just that to a schoolboy all teachers seem old.'

She appeared not to hear him and continued, '*She* made him leave me. When he'd gone it was as if he had died.' She paused then said quietly, 'And all the love that I had in me died with him.' Her voice grew strident. 'All that remained was work. Work and her constant whining. All that she wanted was money. There was never enough money.'

Ben felt sick. 'Surely you could have got help, even in those days the Social Services—'

Miss McGuire laughed harshly and patted him on the shoulder. 'Benjamin, Benjamin, do you really think that my parent would allow the Social Services to intervene? Her pride would not permit it. Such help was for the working classes.' She took a step towards the window and stared out. 'And when finally she died and I thought I was free...what was I left with?' She turned and loomed over him, 'Debts and more debts. That old crone had mortgaged my inheritance to the hilt. All I had was my teacher's pension.' She straightened up. 'What do you think of that, Benjamin? Such was my reward for being a dutiful daughter.'

He said quietly, 'I sympathize. Even as a lad I remember—'

Again she overrode him. 'However, when I retired I was offered a part-time position at this nursing home, keeping the accounts, for as you may recall my particular area of expertise is in mathematics.'

Ben rubbed his forehead and muttered, 'Yes, you were quite the genius at that.'

'I had only been working here a few months when a patient died from an overdose.' She gave a thin smile. 'At first we were surprised, then we realized that the patient's great-grandson was responsible for the death.' She shook her head reprovingly. 'It was a rather clumsy execution but one had to sympathize with the young man. People should not be allowed to outlive their usefulness.'

'Allowed?' Ben blurted, 'Who gives you the right to judge such things?' She stared in amazement then gave a

She smiled. 'The young man was more than grateful for our assistance in concealing his actions.' She looked down at Ben and her smile deepened. 'Need I explain why this incentive gave me and my partner an idea?'

Without waiting for his reply she paced the room, her eyes glinting as she continued, 'We realized that we'd stumbled onto a lucrative source of income.' She stopped abruptly in front of him. 'Can you remember, Benjamin, what I taught you about business?'

He hesitated. 'That it's all a question of supply and demand?'

'Excellent! You always did have a retentive memory. So you see, we've found a niche market. The greedy relations have the "demand", and we can "supply".' She spread her arms wide. 'Here we have the perfect place to treat new clients.'

Outraged, Ben attempted to stand, but Jeff shoved him back on the chair. 'You mean you're killing off all the old people?'

'Don't be absurd, Benjamin. We don't "help" all of them, only the ones with collateral and greedy relations. Of course, business being business, the relations need to find a substantial deposit before we proceed. After that,' she shrugged, 'balance on completion.'

Ben felt stunned; he searched for words. 'This is murder! You're not going to get away with it.'

'Facts are facts, Benjamin. We have done until now.'

He said quietly, 'I think you're mad.'

She laughed and shook her head, 'No, I'm not insane, but I am rich and that gives me power. I have sufficient money to do anything that I please. I can go anywhere. I can take a life or leave it be. And you, dear boy, have created a problem for us.' She paused to stare down at him thoughtfully. 'It was unfortunate that you happened to travel on the one coach that I had singled out to check our operation, you see—' She broke off as the office door burst open and Anna and Rosa were thrust into the room. They were followed by a chubby elderly man holding a syringe.

'Look what I've found crouching outside the door,' the man said. He held up the syringe, eyed Rosa and warned. 'You do know what a shot of insulin can do to the average person, don't you?' He gave a wry smile as he saw Rosa's face turn pale. 'That's better; I don't want any more struggles.'

'Doctor Harrison, who are these women?' asked Miss McGuire.

'That's my wife and her sister,' Ben shouted. He glared at the doctor. 'I don't know who the hell you are, but don't you dare touch them.'

Dr Harrison glared back at Ben coldly then addressed Miss McGuire, 'We can assume that these ladies heard every word you said.'

'Indeed?' she said, 'That changes everything.' Briskly she strode over to the desk and unlocked the bottom drawer.

'Please,' said Rosa, 'just let us all go.'

Miss McGuire turned to face them and Ben saw with horror that she was now holding a gun. She stared at Rosa and Anna. 'I think not,' she said. She looked at Dr Harrison who nodded silently, then she added, 'It's too late for that.'

AS CASSIE HURRIED ALONG the drive she felt the crunch of gravel under her feet. She stumbled, swore softly and wished she'd remembered to put on a pair of flat shoes.

She'd nearly reached the entrance when she heard the

sound of a car coming up behind her. Feeling a great sense of relief she stopped and turned to look at the approaching headlights. At last the police were coming to sort things out. She waved at the vehicle eagerly, then felt disappointed when she saw that it wasn't a police car, but a taxi.

She watched as the tall, pale figure of Dr Ian White got out and paid off the driver. With a mixture of guilt and anxiety she hurried towards him. 'Doctor White? What are you…are you all right? Shouldn't you be—'

Ian held up his hand, 'I'm okay, Mrs Hodgson.'

'Just call me Cassie,' she said, 'everyone else does.' She looked up at him in the half-light and added, 'You do look poorly, though.'

He smiled at her. 'I'm going to be fine, Cassie.' He turned to stare grimly up at the nursing home, 'At least I will be once I've dealt with a certain situation. But first things first. I need to get Security to open my office up and then Doctor Harrison and I have several scores to settle.' He made as if to walk to the entrance.

Cassie grabbed his arm. 'Hold on a mo.' She opened her handbag. 'I've got your keys and your specs.' She fished in her bag and handed them to him.

He looked at her, clearly puzzled. 'How did—'

'I was the one who found you. I called the ambulance.'

'Well, I'm really grateful for that. I did wonder.'

'There's no time for thanks now,' Cassie interrupted, 'but before you go in, there are some things you should know. Quite a lot of things, in fact.' She looked around. 'Let's go sit on the steps a minute and I'll tell you.' Then taking a long deep breath, she told him all that she knew and suspected about Dr Harrison and the nursing home. When she'd finished she looked up at him anxiously.

'I've got to check my office and my files,' Ian said quietly, 'and then I'll help all that I can.' He got up, turned towards reception and said softly, 'Back in two minutes.'

Cassie watched him go through the doors. She stood up and fought back her feeling of impatience. She peered again down the driveway. Where the hell were the police? Were they going to take forever to get here?

IAN CLOSED HIS OFFICE DOOR, locked it and for a moment leaned against it trying to control his rage. Bob Harrison must have got here before him. The files had disappeared.

As soon as he'd realized this he'd checked the computer and had seen that the files had been deleted. The police could probably recover them, but they would need convincing that it was necessary. He had to find the hard copies! Surely old Harrison wouldn't have had the time to destroy them yet? He raced down the stairs, taking them two at a time.

As he rushed past the security office he heard voices. He stopped, backtracked and listened at the door, recognizing one hated voice. Forcing down his impulse to confront Bob Harrison, he raced silently along the corridor and out of reception to where Cassie was waiting.

'I couldn't find what I needed but I know where Doctor Harrison is,' he said, as he ran up to her, 'and I think your friends may be in there with him.'

Cassie started forward. 'Let's go then.'

Ian held her back. 'It would be best if you were to stay here and tell the police to come to the security office.' He saw her hesitation. 'It wouldn't do, would it, if we were to disappear as well?' Without waiting for Cassie to reply he hurried through the doors, crept silently towards the office and listened.

'No! It's not too late!' a man shouted. He sounded desperate. 'You could let the women go and keep me—'

'Don't be stupid,' a woman replied. Ian thought her voice sounded vaguely familiar. 'They would not keep quiet.'

'They would if you kept me as hostage,' the man pleaded. 'It would buy you time to set up in business elsewhere…overseas perhaps. After all, you've got enough money.'

Ian heard Bob Harrison laugh loudly. 'Must you keep on making absurd suggestions? Surely you know the simplest solution is always the—'

Ian wrenched open the door and burst into the room. Bob Harrison turned towards him, syringe in hand. Ian wrestled it from him and forced the older man into an arm lock. 'Surprised, eh? Well, as you can see, I'm not dead,' he panted.

'Not yet,' a woman said.

Startled, Ian turned to look at her, recognizing her as Miss McGuire, the elderly part-timer who did the accounts. She was holding a gun. Ian pulled Bob Harrison in front of him as a shield and his grip on the doctor tightened.

'Careful with that thing!' Dr Harrison whimpered.

Miss McGuire smiled, grasped the heavy weapon with both hands and moved it in a slow arc. 'Who should go first, I wonder?'

Ian froze; cautiously he glanced around the room. A middle-aged man was seated on a chair and Ian guessed that he must be Ben. Jeff of security stood close to him and Ian saw that he was sweating. Two other women were standing near to Jeff. They seemed calm. Ian relaxed slightly; that was good.

'No volunteers then?' Miss McGuire asked archly.

'Do you think that by shooting us all you've solved the problem?' Ian challenged.

Miss McGuire looked straight at him, 'I need only shoot one, in the first instance,' she replied. She pointed the gun in his direction.

Ian crouched down, making sure that Bob Harrison's body shielded him.

'No, no,' whimpered Dr Harrison.

'Boss!' Jeff blurted suddenly. 'You can't do this! I never knew…killing folk's not—'

'Be silent!' Furious, Miss McGuire took a step towards Jeff. As she moved, Ben stuck out his foot and tripped her, and she stumbled and fell. The boom of the gun reverberated around the room. Jeff fell backwards clutching his shoulder as Ben grabbed the gun and wrenched it from Miss McGuire's grasp.

Ian let out a sigh of relief. He watched as Ben held on to Miss McGuire and the tall woman strode across the room to help him haul the woman to her feet. The smaller lady rushed to help Jeff, who was bleeding profusely. Ian could hear the police sirens approaching and felt glad that help was almost here. He began to shake and knew that his adrenalin rush was wearing off.

'Surely we can be civilized about this incident, dear boy?' Bob Harrison wheedled as he turned to look up at him.

'To hell with that!' Ian snapped and, summoning up the last of his strength, he punched Harrison straight in the face.

THIRTY-SEVEN

One year later

BEN FOLDED HIS NEWSPAPER, took a last gulp from his mug of tea and called out to Rosa, 'It says in here that old Doctor Harrison's gone and bought it.' Rosa's head appeared round the kitchen door and Ben waved the newspaper at her. 'Seems like he had a stroke three weeks before he was due to go on trial.'

Rosa nodded. 'Then there is justice after all.' She looked at the paper that he held. 'Is there anything about your Miss McGuire?'

Ben pulled a face and said, 'They reckon that she's unfit to plead and that she'll never come out of that secure mental home.'

'I'm not surprised,' said Rosa. She strolled over to him with her hands behind her back. 'Mad as a hatter, she was.' She looked down at the newspaper. 'You finished with that yet, love?'

'Well, I was going to tell you about Jeff, the security man. He's got a suspended sentence and six months community service. I'm pleased about that really; he wasn't all that bad.'

'That's true. If he hadn't protested when he did, I shudder to think what would have happened. As he said, he was only doing his job.'

'That's what the Gestapo claimed in 1945,' Ben snorted.

'Now, Ben,' Rosa waved a finger at him, 'don't you start bringing your blood pressure up to the boil again. It's over and done with now.'

'At least things have got sorted and folk have moved on,' Ben said.

'And I'm glad that nice young doctor got a good job at another hospital,' said Rosa.

Ben smiled in reminiscence and leaned back in his chair. 'Thinking back, it was kind of exciting, though. I mean, who would have thought that a simple day out on a coach trip—'

'I wasn't excited,' protested Rosa, 'I was a ruddy nervous wreck wondering where you had disappeared to. I'll have you know I had chronic indigestion for weeks afterwards.' She hesitated, then said, 'Now all I want is a little bit of peace and tranquillity…someplace nice and calm and relaxing.'

Ben looked closely at his wife and saw that there was a twinkle in her eyes; suspicion dawned. 'What are you up to?'

'I thought you might fancy a day out visiting Cassie and Dave. She rang me yesterday. They've got a new pub, it's still in the Yorkshire dales, and they love it. She's invited us to drop in there any time.'

Ben shifted uneasily in his chair and hedged, 'Not the Yorkshire dales, love, if you don't mind. I've still got a thing about visiting pubs in the middle of nowhere. It would bring back me nightmares.'

Rosa grinned. 'I had thought that as well, but we can always go see them once you feel up to it.' She moved up close to him and held out the brochure she'd been hiding behind her back. 'But I did wonder whether you'd like to go on another holiday, somewhere different...on a nice relaxing cruise, perhaps?' She waved the booklet under his nose.

'What?' Ben shrank back, 'You want me to be locked up in some ship's cabin after all I went through in that bloody nursing home?'

'Ben,' Rosa said swiftly, 'this is not the same thing at all. There are state rooms on board these ships and they are fitted with every luxury and convenience.'

Ben eyed his wife and said cautiously, 'I wouldn't mind another holiday. Tenerife was nice at Easter...it would have been nicer still if your Anna hadn't decided to tag along.'

'Now, Ben, don't start.'

'These cruises,' said Ben hurriedly, 'the state rooms, as you call them. They are just for two people, aren't they?'

'Of course they are,' said Rosa. 'As for the ship, well they're really like a city afloat. They carry more than two thousand passengers, y'know. The new ships have got at least eleven restaurants on board, loads of shops and swimming pools, and heaven knows how many bars.'

'Eleven restaurants, did you say?' said Ben with a hint of awe in his voice.

'At the very least. There's cafés as well, you can eat twenty-four hours a day if you like. It's all included.'

Ben started to smile.

'Just have a look at the brochure,' she said. 'I quite fancy the trip to New York, then on to the Bahamas. It would be a once in a lifetime holiday.'

He looked up at her. 'Before I agree, there's a question. Have you mentioned this to your sister?'

Rosa's eyes widened. 'I've not said a word, honestly.'

Ben grunted, looked closely at the price lists in the

brochure, then said, 'All right then, let's give it a go.' He watched as Rosa darted to the phone and made the booking.

'It'll be an adventure, love,' Rosa said as she came back to him and hugged him to her excitedly. 'We'll be out there on the Atlantic with no one to pester us.'

'Thought you said you didn't like adventures,' said Ben, his voice now muffled.

'I meant I didn't like excitement, least not the kind you put me through.' She pulled away as she heard a knock on the back door.

'It's only me,' called Anna as she came in through the kitchen. 'I've just come to tell you I found your brochure and your note,' Anna laughed excitedly, 'and I've made the booking. I'm on deck B.'

'We're on that as well,' said Rosa.

Ben stifled a groan.

'There are over two thousand passengers on this ship, Ben. We'll hardly ever see her,' Rosa hissed.

He glared at Rosa. 'You swore to me you'd not said a word.'

'I didn't,' Rosa said softly, 'but Anna can read. We're still going then, are we?' Rosa asked.

'Yes, I suppose so, but I want you to think about what happened last October when I went on a trip with you two.'

'This is different, Ben. I mean, whatever could go wrong on a cruise ship?'

Ben shook his head. 'Knowing my luck, I'll probably end up overboard.'

* * * * *